A Texas Christmas Miracle

A Texas Christmas Miracle

A Raffertys of Last Stand Romance

Justine Davis

TULE
PUBLISHING

Dedication

To all the brave, loyal dogs who never came home.

Chapter One

ANYONE WHO KNEW him would find it beyond odd that Chance Rafferty was talking so much. He found it odd himself, even though he was only talking to the dog huddled in the corner of his small living room. The dog watching him with the wariness of a well-trained animal who sensed a threat.

But Chance knew everything and everyone seemed a threat to the creature just now. And so far, nothing he'd done seemed to overcome the trauma the animal had suffered on that last deployment. Losing his left foreleg was only part of the damage done.

Chance had put everything else on hold, including taking on other dogs, for this last-ditch effort with the jumpy animal, because he needed full attention. It all had to be confusing to the sleek, lean Belgian Malinois, but he never gave up. Even with only three legs he was still agile, if a bit awkward. Hence the nearly wall-to-wall throw rugs covering the slick wood that had sometimes made the dog slip.

"Tri ol' boy," he said aloud, "if I hear one more Christmas carol, see one more Christmas decoration, or one more truck with a silly wreath hanging on the grille, we may just hole up here until New Year's. I hate this time of year."

The dog's big, dark ears twitched. He clearly responded to his relatively new name; they'd come that far at least. Lucas, the orphaned kid his brother Keller had taken in—and hadn't that led to some upheaval?—had picked the name, not just because it was short for tripod, but because it also sounded like try, which the dog never stopped doing.

He felt a jab of…something as he thought of his older brother. It wasn't that he begrudged him his newfound happiness, it just made Chance feel even more apart. Separate. Because what Keller had found with his now fiancée, Lucas's cousin Sydney, was something Chance would never have. He'd long ago accepted that, so he didn't understand why seeing them together made him feel a bit tangled.

Maybe it was because it reminded him too strongly of his mother and father. He'd had sixteen years to observe them together, minus Dad's deployments, before he'd been killed. And if there was one thing he'd never doubted in his life, it was that they loved each other. He even remembered the day he'd added "passionately" to that understanding in his mind. When he first began to realize what passion was. When he began to feel a little bit embarrassed by how obvious it had always been, but he'd been too young comprehend it.

Sometimes he'd even envied his friends who had more staid parents. But more often he'd wondered what it would be like, to feel that way about someone. He'd thought, with

Liz, that he'd found it. But her supposed love hadn't lasted past his second deployment, when she'd handed his ring back to him literally as he was leaving to get on the plane, saying she wasn't cut out to be a military wife. It had seemed devastating then. Later he'd known it was a lucky escape.

He heard the low rumble of a suppressed growl. When he looked over, he saw the dog's head up and turned toward the east side of the house. Guardianship had been bred into the breed, which was why the Malinois was so often used as a working dog. The military then honed that instinct to a razor edge, creating the weapon known as a military working dog, or MWD, with the payoff being countless lives saved.

But not every life. No dog, and no tactic could keep what they did completely safe. And it wasn't safe for the dogs, either.

His mind skittered away from the old pain, knowing it was pointless. His own four-legged partner had been taken out by a terrorist's bullet on his first mission with his new handler. It could have happened anytime, could have happened with him, but it hadn't, and sometimes he had to fight not to blame the new guy. Chance would have given anything to have been able to bring Hondo home with him, but the dog had a few more years to serve. He'd put in the request to adopt him the moment he was done, but instead had gotten the phone call he'd dreaded, three years ago next week.

Merry freaking Christmas.

Tri growled again, still focused on the east side of the house. His family knew well enough to announce themselves, so it wasn't hard to guess it was a four-legged creature rather than two.

"Probably a white-tail," he told the dog reassuringly, although so far reassurance hadn't registered much with the wary animal. But he kept talking anyway. Even though it was against his nature.

He'd not taken on any new animals since he'd acquired Tri, even though he was set up to deal with more. He'd sensed from the first moment he'd met the traumatized creature that this one was going to need all his focus. And he deserved it, given Chance's part in what had happened to him.

But it had been nearly seven months and he sometimes felt as if they'd made no progress. Yet he kept resisting the idea that the dog would be one of those who was permanently lost. It happened—he'd had a couple of them here, little tamer than the coyotes who roamed the Hill Country. But at least here they got to live out their lives. And with more freedom than they would have had in most other places, thanks to Sydney Brock.

The woman who had so brightened his older brother's life had also helped him; her company's sizeable donation had not only provided operational funds for the next year but enabled him to finish the fence he'd been building bit by bit, and now the dogs had several acres to run free on. And she'd made that donation before she and Keller were a thing, simply because she liked what he was doing, and thought it worthwhile.

Who'd've ever figured Keller'd end up with a globe-trotting businesswoman?

Although she'd called a complete halt to the globe-trotting that had built her business, leaving it to others while she and Keller built a family with Lucas.

Another growl, and he searched for something, anything to say. It was difficult. He'd never been a chatterer by nature, and that tendency had influenced his decision to live his life out here on this remote corner of the ranch. That it was the ranch where he'd grown up let him keep that tenuous grip on being part, albeit barely, of the Rafferty family. He owed his father that much tribute, no matter how difficult it was, no matter how much he'd like to be somewhere where no one knew him or expected anything from him. Anything like human contact. So he was secretly relieved that the nature of his work with the dogs required some separation.

He resorted to explaining the presence of what he was fairly sure had the dog's attention.

"Food gets a little scarce out there this time of year. But some plants have this antifreeze kind of stuff in the sap, so they keep their leaves. The deer have to hunt those plants down, though. So, they come closer than they usually would."

It half-worked. The growl stopped, but the dog's head

never turned away from the sound outside.

"With some plants it's not worth the effort even for the high energy value. I mean, chomping down on a prickly pear?" he went on, noting how raspy his voice sounded. He hadn't talked this much at once in…well, a very long time. Even when he'd gone to pick up Tri—then called Atlas— and had run into a couple of guys he knew, he hadn't talked this much.

"If it didn't mean they were desperate, I'd like to see them clear out all that damned Christmas cactus. I'm sick of hearing the name. And let's not even start on mistletoe. Stuff ought to be banned. Or the people who decided it meant you have to kiss whoever's standing under it."

And finally he had the dog's attention. Problem was, he didn't know if it was because he'd gained it himself, or the critter outside had moved beyond whatever mental perimeter the dog had set himself. Either way, Tri was looking at him now. Still wary. Less wary than when he'd arrived? Maybe. Or maybe that was wishful thinking. Not that he indulged in that much, if ever. He knew how futile it was.

He stifled a yawn. He didn't sleep a lot anyway, but since he'd brought Tri into the house it had been even less. Partly out of caution—it wouldn't do to be neck-deep in nightma- reland if the dog took a notion to lose what grip he had on civilization in close quarters with a human. And every time he dozed off, when he snapped awake it was to see those near-feral eyes on him. He didn't know if the dog ever slept at all.

Still, Tri didn't growl at him like everyone else, and he'd accepted a small level of command from him, so Chance guessed that his scent must be somewhere in the dog's jangled memory. He and Tri's handler had been in the same unit for a while and had become friendly. Chance had seen him and Atlas on his own last deployment, before he'd mustered out and come home. But they had had another deployment to go.

One deployment too many.

He gave a shake of his head before he spiraled down into fruitless wondering. Wondering why he hadn't been able to convince the brass about the folly of that mission. Why they'd decided he wasn't worth listening to. Why he'd been the one spared when the man with a loving wife he adored had gone home in a damned box. Chance had a family too, but he knew that while they'd no doubt have grieved, his absence wouldn't have caused much of a ripple in their lives, because he was barely in their lives on a day-to-day basis. And now that he was home that hadn't changed much, even after nearly four years.

He doubted it ever would.

Chapter Two

ARIEL LARSON READ the mileage sign with satisfaction; seeing the distance to Last Stand in less than three digits felt like an accomplishment. The flight to Dallas from San Diego had only been three hours, but with the time difference it had cost her five, and she'd had another five in front of her on the road. More in fact because she stopped to eat something. That had been a lesson hard-learned, that without fuel, her body—and brain—gave out eventually.

She'd had to weigh the familiarity of the interstate—and the unfamiliarity of her rental car—versus the smaller state roads her map program said would be faster. She'd gone with the route that required less thinking. She only realized later that she probably would have been wiser to have made the other selection; she could have used the distraction of having to concentrate on where she was going in this unfamiliar territory.

She always needed distraction. Otherwise she ended up mired in thoughts that just dragged her down. Again.

But now she had a goal that meant more to her than any-thing had since what she termed in her mind "That Day."

She knew she was probably building this up too much, thinking that doing this would allow her to let go of some of the huge, crushing load, but it was the only hope she'd been able to find. The connection was tenuous, but it was there, and it was all she had.

She'd never been to Texas. She mostly equated it with "big" in her mind, with a dash of admiration for how they tended to go their own way. And big was definitely an appropriate word for it; the lady next to her on the flight had pointed out that from the westernmost point in Texas, you could get to California sooner than you could get to Dallas.

"You're headed to Last Stand?" she'd asked when Ariel had answered her inquiry. At her nod, she smiled widely. "I've been there. Great little Hill Country town, especially this time of year."

"This time of year?"

"Yes. They really do up Christmas right."

Christmas.

She'd actually managed to put it out of her mind, for a while anyway. It was an effort anytime after Halloween these days, let alone today, December first. When she'd walked into a store the day after Halloween this year and heard the Christmas music, she'd turned around and walked back out again. She'd taken to making sure she had her earbuds always with her, so she could listen to something else when she had to be places that had succumbed to the two-month-long endless loop.

She'd managed to smile at the kind woman but had excused herself and turned her attention to her phone, and the research she'd done before she'd set out on this journey.

She remembered that research and how impressed she'd been with the website for *They Also Serve*. It was sharp, slick and efficient, with beautiful photos of the dogs that had been helped and placed, their histories, and their happy endings. And more photos of dogs that still needed help, their heart-tugging stories, and an easily accessible donation method.

What was curious was how very, very little there was about the man who had started and still ran the place. Not even a picture. In fact, after scouring the site, all she knew was that Chance Rafferty was Texas born, had been a K-9 handler in the military, and ran *They Also Serve* from his family's ranch just outside of Last Stand. She admired that, that the focus was on the animals, but it also made her nervous. She liked to know everything she could before approaching a project, and she felt as if there was a gaping hole in this one.

The moment she made the turn onto the ubiquitous Main Street, she groaned aloud. It was as if she'd driven onto the set of some sappy Christmas movie. Every pole was wrapped with garlands, ribbons and lights. Huge, tinsel-clad structures holding more lights and decorations spanned the street every block. Everything that could possibly be festooned was. It was the kind of thing that would have made her ooh and aah as a kid. It was the kind of thing she hated with what limited passion she had now.

Which was why she'd decided to do this the moment she'd learned the truth, despite the season. And her father's concern.

Honey, I understand, but this is a bit…impulsive.

I know.

Will they even let you—

That's why I'm going in person. It's harder to say no face-to-face.

She sighed inwardly. Her father had left it there, bless him. He understood she felt she had to do this, and that was all it took for him to support her. His love was unwavering, and she knew perfectly well she might not have made it without him. Without him and Walt Larson, Dean's father, who had made a great, loving effort to keep in touch with his son's wife even after that son was gone. She'd been blessed with three amazing men in her life, which was more than many got.

She drove down the colorful street, amid what traffic there was at 5:30 p.m. She noticed a big, solid structure on her left that looked as if it were built out of more of the light-colored stone she'd seen elsewhere. Limestone, maybe? It also looked as if it had stood there forever. Maybe it had; there was a big, brass plaque with some kind of explanation attached near the front door. When she noticed the sign indicating it was the Last Stand Saloon, she found herself smiling despite the annoyance at the overabundance of Christmas cheer. She might have to stop and look at that, if she was here long enough.

She had to admit being away from home, and all the reminders, was a relief. As if she'd put down a part of a heavy burden. Temporarily, it was true, but still noticeable. And surprising. She'd expected she would simply carry this load until the day she died, and it would never change. No matter what they—the "they" who supposedly knew—told her.

She passed what looked like a full block of city buildings, a courthouse with a sign indicating city hall was just behind it, and then a large, rather grand-looking library built out of a slightly darker stone. She was just thinking she liked the solidity of it, the sense of time survived, when she noticed the statue on the corner. A tall, bronze figure with another plaque at his feet, atop a pedestal that held—of course—a Christmas wreath, and appeared to have taken a hit of some kind, judging by the chunk missing from the base. There was another, smaller plaque there, and she wondered what had been so momentous they'd decided to commemorate it rather than just repair the pedestal. She might have to take a look at that, too.

Odd, she hadn't expected this interest in a small town she'd never see again, once her task here was done. Hadn't expected to be curious about it. Of course, she hadn't been curious about much of anything for so long...

She'd been so focused on the statue in front of the library—Asa Fuhrmann, she'd been able to read in bigger letters at the top of the plaque—she almost missed the turn she needed to make at that very corner. But the map program on her phone reminded her just in time, and soon she was headed out of town on Hickory Street. According to the map it would connect with the Hickory Creek Spur, and on that road was her goal, the bed-and-breakfast where she'd booked a room. It had looked comfortable and peaceful online, but what had decided her was an article she found about it, in something local called *The Defender*.

The writer had interviewed the couple who ran it, Frank Buckley—of all things a former Texas Ranger—and his wife Karina. The man's simple words, that his wife had endured two decades as the wife of a Ranger and so now it was her turn, and turning the family ranch into a B&B had ever been her dream, had sold her.

When she made the turn at the carved wooden sign that said "Hickory Creek Inn" she had the oddest sensation of…relief. Natural at the end of a long day of travel, but this felt like more than that. Then the long drive curved, and she got her first look at the inn itself. It was a large, pristine white building, square with a huge, covered front porch, a rounded gazebo on the side, and in the center, rising above the second story an observation tower that must give an expansive view in all directions. She'd have to check that out, too.

Weird—all of a sudden she had a list of things to do other than what she'd come here for. She pondered that oddity as she continued slowly down the long, curving drive. The building grew more impressive the closer she got. Even the Christmas decorations didn't seem quite so overwhelming; the garlands wrapped around the porch posts and railing, complete with lights and ribbons, seemed more…welcoming. The American and Lone Star Texas flags on each side of the main steps to the front doors hung unmoving; there was no breeze on this first day of December, and the thermometer in the car's dash indicated it was an even sixty degrees outside. With a jacket, tolerable even for her California blood.

She found a spot at the side of the building labeled "Check-In" and parked there. She turned off the car and sat for a moment, glad to have arrived at last. Then something nudged its way into her consciousness and she let out a heavy sigh. Christmas music again. And piped outside. That was a bit much.

She gritted her teeth as she grabbed her bag and opened the car door, hoping her room would be well soundproofed. Although as Christmas music went, this was fairly inoffensive. In fact, she'd never heard anything quite like it. A cappella for one thing, a resonant, beautiful male voice hitting every note with just the right amount of softness or power, to get the most out of the song. He didn't need the instrumental help, obviously. She didn't recognize the voice, although he had to be famous. The song was a familiar one, a carol she knew began quietly but soared to an amazing height, which the artist hit at the moment she thought it.

She marveled at the steady strength of the note he held for what seemed like forever—

"Ouch!"

The song stopped abruptly at the sharp exclamation. She blinked. Wait, that had been...live? Someone here had just been singing?

A man walked around the corner of the building, his right hand up to his mouth and a pair of hefty garden clippers in his left hand. He moved his hand back and looked at it, and she guessed that had been the reason for the yelp of pain. But then he looked up, and she found herself gaping at a man who looked too beautiful to be real.

"Hi," he said with a smile that would have sent any woman's pulse racing, even hers. If she still had a heart, that is. "You must be our new guest."

Our? "You're not Mr. Buckley?" The guy was far from old enough to be retired.

He laughed. "No. Believe me, you'll know him when you meet him. I'm just the handyman. Name's Kane. Welcome to Hickory Creek."

A singing handyman. What would be next in this place? She felt as if she should say something about his voice, but it seemed her father was right about that, she'd lost the knack for small talk with strangers. She tried to divert her thoughts, but all she could land on was that he didn't have as much of an accent as some she'd encountered since landing in Dallas.

"Can I get that bag inside for you?" he offered.

She declined politely and headed inside. The lobby was spacious, with various seating spaces both small and large, one comfortable-looking one arranged around a large fireplace at the other end of the room. There were what looked like banquet tables on the far side, no doubt for the breakfast part of the equation. Beyond those was more seating, smaller tables next to the big windows that looked out over the creek she could now see glinting in the near-winter sun, and three sets of French doors that opened out onto a deck beside the flowing water. Despite its size the whole space had a homey, welcoming feel.

And the Christmas décor was definite, but restrained. Thankfully.

The woman behind the counter, recognizable as Karina Buckley from the photo on the website, looked up as she entered and gave her a wide smile. "Mrs. Larson? I see you made it right on time. Welcome to the Hickory Creek Inn."

"Thank you." She managed a creditable smile at the woman's warm and welcoming tone. Or perhaps it was the woman herself; she had that kind of air about her that said she was delighted to be doing what she was doing.

It's her turn now.

Ranger Buckley's words in the interview she'd read echoed in her mind. *Be glad,* she silently told the petite brunette who was briskly going about checking her in. *Be glad you're getting your turn. It's more than I got.*

And enough of the self-pity party.

"I met your singing handyman," she said hastily, before she could sink into that morass she hated for so many reasons.

"Kane?" the woman said with a smile. "Isn't he amazing? We're going to lose him, I know—he's already a musical sensation in the county, and I'm amazed he's content to stay and putter around here. But he promised us a year, and he's a Highwater, so he'll keep that promise."

"Highwater?" She'd read something else in her research about the town, about a foiled terrorist attack some time ago. The article had credited a man with that name with saving hundreds, if not thousands of lives. "Any relation to the police chief?"

"His youngest brother," the woman said with an even wider smile. "The Highwaters are one of the founding families of Last Stand. Plus the Herdmanns, the Corbyns, the Valencias, the Raffertys—"

"The Raffertys?" she interrupted.

"Yes. You know them?"

The woman was obviously well versed on the locals. "Do they live far from here?"

"Their ranch is a couple of miles outside of town."

The curiosity was evident, and she decided she should offer a little more. "I'm here about…the dogs."

The woman's expression changed then, to one Ariel couldn't quite put a name to. Understanding? Acknowledgment, of good work done perhaps? But it was all overlaid with something like sadness that Ariel recognized all too easily.

"Is there…a problem?" Ariel asked.

"No, not at all." The small smile she gave was tinged with that same sadness. "We just don't see Chance much anymore. He was such a livewire as a boy, but…" The smile got better. "He's doing good work out there, though."

And bitter, self-pitying soul that she was, all she could think as she made her way to her room was, at least Chance Rafferty had come home alive.

Chapter Three

T RI BARELY REACTED at all to the little drone.
Chance watched the dog watch Cody's device hover, then set down neatly. He knew it would be a familiar sight for the animal, as it was these days to any military dog; drones were a frequent tool.

Here, the drone had become the easiest way to reach Chance, due to the iffy cell signal out in this quarter of the ranch, and because he was usually outside, away from the landline his mother had insisted on despite the cost of running the line this far out. Being his mother, and incredibly wise, she hadn't couched it in terms of her worry over him, but in terms of the dogs; what if one of them got hurt, or if he needed help with one of them? Not to mention if he was going to be set up as a functioning entity, people needed to be able to reach him.

That he didn't want to be reached seemed a petty reason to say no, given what he was trying to do here.

He walked over to the drone. Tri sat on command as he bent to pick it up. This smallest of Cody's fleet was the main messaging device, as Cody called it, a more traditional type without the fancier additions his clever brother had made in his drive to create the perfect drone, with the range of a motor-driven version, but the tactical silence of an electric-powered one.

He knew why this was his brother's obsession. It had, in a way, been his fault. He was the one who, in their darkest days, had said if that damned drone hadn't given them away, their father's platoon might not have been wiped out. And a driven, perhaps impossible quest had been born.

He took the little flyer back to the house, Tri at his side. He had to track down his rarely used cell phone, which had a Cody-designed app that would communicate directly with the drone to download the message. His brother had jokingly named the app *Chance It*, and asked him how it felt to have an app no one else in the world had. He'd thought a better question was how it felt to have a brother who could even dream up such a thing, let alone create it and make it work.

He found the phone in a drawer in his small kitchen, with barely enough charge left to carry out the function. Making a mental note to put it on the charger, he started the app. In moments it had downloaded the message.

On my way in ten with someone about the dogs. Brace yourself.

Brace yourself? He stared at the words, his brow furrowed. Not that it was unlike Cody to jab at him about his aversion to visitors, but somehow without seeing that crooked grin of his it seemed…more pointed.

It would be easier, give him ammo for return fire, if his little brother was the stereotypical tech nerd, awkward and introverted, but he was not. Instead he was the opposite—outgoing, friendly…well, he always had been until Sydney had arrived on the scene. Cody had somehow known from the moment he'd seen her and Keller together that everything was going to change, and he hadn't been happy about that.

Chance shook his head sharply, focusing on the important part of the message, that someone was coming with his brother. That in itself was unusual; most times Cody would make him come get the person, joking that was the only time they got to see his ugly face. Some of the donors wanted to see things in person, and he understood that. He didn't like having to play the supplicant—and, in fact, sucked at it—but he understood.

And when it came down to it, he'd do worse than beg for the dogs.

He entered simply, *Copy*, then took the drone back out, set it down and hit the button that would have it reversing course and heading back to the main house. The system they'd come up with worked well, since you had to pass the main house to get to his place. As long as somebody was home, he got a warning.

At least his place wasn't a mess. He didn't generally own enough stuff to make a mess, except books. So that wasn't an issue. With luck, and if he met them outside, whoever it was wouldn't want to come inside at all. He was in no mood to play host today, but then, he never was.

With a grimace he went back in and put on a fresh pot of coffee to brew, which was about as far as his host capacity went. His phone had died in the interim, and he dug out the charger and plugged it in. Then he went back outside and walked over to the corral, where his horse Dorado was watching curiously.

The corral had been here as long as the house, and Chance had built a small, two-stall outbuilding when he'd first moved in. Only Dorado had ever lived in it; the second stall was mostly full of horse feed, hay, and dog supplies. The kennels and runs had been a bigger project, but he'd had help on those; once they'd heard what he was doing, several retired and active K-9 handlers and others had turned up to help, including all the Highwater boys. He'd never found out exactly how they'd all heard about it, but he suspected his mother had had a hand in it. No one in Last Stand would dare turn down Maggie Rafferty.

He walked over to the fence, and Dorado stuck his head over for a pat. He slapped the horse's neck as the animal whickered softly. He took some teasing over the palomino's flashy, blond looks, but he'd stack the animal's temperament and work ethic up against any horse on the ranch. He was calmer than Keller's Blue, more spirited than Cody's docile—with good reason, given his little brother didn't ride nearly as much as the rest of them did—Trey. His brother

Rylan's Flyer was the best visual contrast for Dorado, and together the two horses made a striking picture, one gold with flaxen mane and tail, Flyer a gleaming black like Ry's hair.

Of course the most favored of them all was Bonnie, a spirited buckskin mare, granddaughter of their father's beloved Buckshot, who had died a couple of years ago at the ripe old age of twenty-eight. The mare had foaled her first just shy of six months ago, and the gangly colt showed every sign of becoming the spitting image of his great-grandsire.

Chance half turned as he heard a distinct growl from inside the house. Tri, low, fierce, and full of warning. He wondered if the dog would scare off the incoming visitor. That might solve his hospitality problem. But scaring off donors was not a good way to run a nonprofit, even he knew that. He'd better get him into his run just in case they did end up in the house for that coffee.

The dog was on hyper alert, but he generally was when anybody approached, let alone a stranger. He'd been a little bit better with Lucas, probably because he was just a kid. He accepted the boy now, as much as he accepted anyone, which at this point only meant a different tone in the growl, and an eventual calm.

Once in the run, where he felt safer, the dog settled into a lower, quieter grumble, which likely wouldn't be audible from more than fifteen feet away. Dorado gave a snorting shake of his head, clearly aware of the dog's unhappiness.

Chance walked over and soothed the golden animal's nerves; the horse, at least, trusted him completely and calmed under his touch.

But moments later Tri erupted into a cacophony of barks, telling Chance the threat was nearing. The ranch truck crested the hill and headed down toward them. When it came to a halt just a few feet away, Cody slid out of the driver's seat. Chance froze before he took the first step toward the truck, because his youngest brother was wearing a rather suspicious smile, the one Chance had seen too often as the kid was growing up, the one that usually meant trouble.

Wariness stirred in him. Then spiked as Cody hurried around to the passenger side and opened the door.

Finally he looked at the other person in the truck.

Female.

Very female.

Redhead.

Tall, judging by her height in the seat.

Yes, tall, he thought as she slid out to the ground. But delicate. Not just slender, thin. Fragile? She was wearing jeans and a blue sweater beneath a darker blue jacket. Sturdy, not flashy, low-heeled boots on her feet; no out-of-place stilettos here.

Oddly, Tri quieted. Did the dog somehow sense she wasn't a threat? That made no sense; right now every stranger was a threat to the dog's jangled mind. He had an instant to register the animal's next sound, a quiet, almost longing sort of whine that he'd never heard from him before.

The woman closed the truck door and lifted her head. She looked at Chance. For a long moment he went still, as nothing registered except the color of her eyes—a light, dawn-sky blue—and the haunted expression in them. An expression that was all too familiar, since he'd faced it in the mirror far too many times.

On some level he realized he hadn't taken a breath and he sucked in some air. As if his brain had been starved for the oxygen it kicked back in again, and he started to notice other things. The red hair, bright but not garish, a rich, fall-leaves color, long enough to be tied back at her nape, with bangs falling over her forehead. She was indeed tall, maybe only three or so inches shorter than him. And yes, thin, too thin.

Coupled with that look in her eyes he guessed it was not intentional; he remembered too well what it had been like—sometimes was still like—to have to force himself to eat. Sometimes only the knowledge that he needed to have the energy to deal with the dogs got him to do it.

He realized he still hadn't spoken. She was just…looking at him. Oddly.

And his brother was studying him, not smiling now. Not upset, but curious. And a curious Cody was something to be wary of.

Chance took a steadying breath and closed the short distance between them in two strides. He tried for words, something generic, expected, but was distracted by the faint whiff of something that reminded him of a spring morning. Perfume? He didn't know. It didn't matter. What the hell was wrong with him? He didn't react this way to…anyone.

Somewhat desperately he reached for the manners he'd had drilled into him all his life. Manners Cody seemed to have forgotten, or was intentionally ignoring, given his lack of a simple introduction.

Good manners can be a way to open a door, or keep it closed. Let people in or keep them at arm's length. So they're a good skill to have.

His father's words echoed in his head. He wasn't sure which goal he was going for in this case, but he knew the wise advice held. Still, when he finally spoke, it came out a little ragged.

"I'm Chance Rafferty. What can I help you with?"

And then she blasted what little composure he'd managed to construct since he'd looked into those eyes.

"I'm here about Atlas."

Chapter Four

H E WAS NOT what she'd expected.

As they'd driven up, she'd been looking at the small house, which seemed more like a cabin, and liking the solid, cozy look of it. Then she noticed the man standing by the corral, patting the neck of the unexpectedly pretty horse. A palomino who looked like he'd be at home prancing down the street in some holiday parade. The horse tossed its head. and the flaxen mane went flying.

Just as she was wondering if that was the man she was here to see, Cody murmured, "Good. He didn't run."

"Run?" Why would he run?

Cody glanced at her. "My brother's a little…" He grimaced. "He doesn't care about much, except the dogs. We've been trying since he came home to—Never mind. Let's just say he doesn't talk much. Don't take it personally."

"I'll try not to." She understood, in fact. Her own withdrawal had nothing to do with whether she liked someone or not, it was all within her.

Cody got out of the truck the moment they'd stopped, heading around to politely open her door. She took that moment to try for the practiced smile she glued on when meeting new people. The one that freed them from having to search for some saccharine platitude that would only make her angry. The one that allowed them to ignore the wreck her life had become.

She gave Cody a quiet thank you as she slid out of the truck.

The man by the corral had turned around, but then stopped dead, staring at her. She had barely noticed because she was staring back, in a frozen moment unlike anything she'd felt before. Everything seemed to have stopped, the sound around her, her breath, even her heart for an instant. It was as if the connection of their gazes had, for that instant, stopped the world.

On the periphery she was aware of other things; he was wearing the camo pants that were familiar to her, a matching baseball cap, a plain T-shirt and a lightweight tan jacket. He was tall, looked fit, tanned, hair dark but touched at the temples with a tiny bit of gray that seemed out of place with his young-seeming face—until you saw his eyes. Eyes different in color than her own but with the same weary, battered look that she saw in the mirror every day. Overall he had that look she knew so well, that of a warrior. Those eyes she couldn't seem to look away from were a bluish gray, but the color was secondary to the pain in them, the memory of things seen and never forgotten.

A moment later she was certain she'd imagined that frozen moment, because he merely came close enough to speak, told her his name—he was indeed Chance Rafferty—and asked her, in a rather rough voice yet politely, what he could help her with. And her goal, the reason she was here at all, came flooding back.

The moment she had told him she was here about Atlas, he looked as if she'd said something stunning.

"Mr. Rafferty?" she repeated now in a questioning tone at his shocked expression.

Then she heard a low, canine whine. His head snapped around, his brow furrowing simultaneously. She looked in the same direction, but from where she stood the corner of the house blocked her view of the kennels and runs she'd noticed when they'd driven up.

"Is he—" she nodded toward the sound "—all right?"

"I...don't know." His expression became a frown now. "He's never sounded like that before."

"Maybe he's finally bonded?" Cody suggested, the first words he'd said since getting out of the truck. A bit at a loss about the sudden tension, all she could think was that Cody should be the one with the pretty horse, pretty blond that he was. They'd be quite the sight. The kind that she'd register and move on, because it meant nothing to her. Very little did anymore.

Except the reason she was here.

It had been the only thing that had kept her going for the weeks she'd spent tracking, tracing, calling, demanding.

It had driven her halfway across the country, to this man's doorstep. And now that she was here, she was feeling a bit impatient. Which in itself was odd, because that was a fairly strong emotion, and she didn't feel those anymore.

"Mr. Rafferty, I came here to—"

In the same instant he, still staring behind them, threw up a hand to stop her words, she heard an odd, clanking sort of sound, like something rattling metal. She couldn't see what he saw, but he snapped out a harsh command that sounded like "Try, hold!"

And then, suddenly, the man was in front of her. Bigger even than she'd realized, broader in the shoulder, yet quick, so very quick. He was close in front of her, but with his back to her. She could barely see over his shoulder as he broadened his stance.

Putting himself between her and whatever it was.

Facing the threat.

Protecting.

God, these men, they always—

"Holy crap," Cody yelped. "How did he—"

She saw the movement then, past his shoulder. A dog, heading toward them in an odd, hopping sort of run that still seemed fast. And intent. Very, very intent.

In the moment she realized why the strange gait, she knew. Her heart gave a little leap; she'd reached her goal at last. She'd found him, this amazing animal who had lost so much, sacrificed so much. Only her knowledge of how these war dogs were trained—and the reaction of this man who knew this dog best right now—held her back from running to him. *You're a stranger to him. He doesn't know who you are.*

"Down," the man in front of her snapped out. "Now."

The dog skidded to a halt. Clearly reluctant, he dropped down. Another of those whines, soft and aching, came from him again. And he stretched out his neck, nose working madly. But not toward the man who had saved his life by pulling him out of that deadly place, not toward the man who had been working with him all this time.

Toward her.

"I can't believe it," Cody was saying, his tone incredulous. "I know, you always said he could if he really wanted to, but dang, how'd he get over that fence with only three legs?"

"Sheer, fearless determination," his brother said, crouching now to both stroke the dog's head and grab his heavy, nylon collar.

The dog seemed to calm a little, but he was still looking at her, not the man beside him. She wanted to go to him, to pour out everything she was feeling, but she knew he was a trained, fierce creature who was here because he couldn't adapt back to civilian life. And she was full of such tangled emotions she didn't know what to do or say. She wasn't used to this, she'd battered everything down into numbness for so long, but standing here now, looking at this dog, this wounded animal, and knowing…

She gulped in some air, trying to steady herself.

"Amazing," the man soothing the dog said, "what you can do when you don't care about anything else." On those words he looked over his shoulder and up at her. "Who are you?"

It was blunt, demanding, and oddly, this calmed her. This she could deal with. So much better than the usual walk-on-eggshells demeanor she encountered so often. She wondered, in the moment before she spoke, if the answer, if her name would mean anything to him.

"My name is Ariel Larson."

He went very still. Even the hand stroking the dog went still. "Larson," he said.

Slowly, very slowly, he stood. The dog beside him also got up, balancing with seeming ease on his three feet. Still staring at her. The command of the man beside him was still holding him, but the animal was practically trembling with the effort of staying still.

The man stared at her for a long moment. She saw his eyes, those gray-blue, seen-too-much eyes, flick to her hair, then back to her face.

"Red," he said, and it was a whisper. "You're Red."

The sound of the nickname she hadn't heard in so long nearly broke her. It took everything she had to hold his gaze evenly.

"I am. And I'm here for the dog who nearly died trying to save my husband's life."

Chapter Five

YOU GOING TO drool on that email?

My Red, she's the best thing that ever happened to me. I'm the luckiest man in the world to have her love me.

The image that flashed into Chance's mind was vivid and heartbreaking. He'd stopped to rag on Dean when he'd seen him reading the same page over and over. And there had been no doubting the utter sincerity of what he'd said. Chance had only seen that kind of expression on a man's face once before. And that had been his father, looking at his mother.

And less than a year later, Dean was dead, and his partner in arms maimed. While he had survived to come home, to his family and a safe, quiet life. Too quiet, his mother said, so quiet it was almost empty. He didn't know how to explain to her that the emptiness wasn't in what surrounded him, but inside him.

But he'd filled that empty place he brought back with him with this work, the work that meant more to him than anything else. Or maybe it was the only thing that meant anything. He wasn't sure anymore if there was much difference.

A low whine jogged him out of the memory. And snapped him back to the incredible thing that had happened here. Tri, battered, scarred, scared and fierce, had not only cleared the kennel fence despite his missing foreleg, but he was also utterly fixated on this woman. Not as if she were some new and fascinating being he'd never seen before. Or as if she held the answers to his upended life.

He looked at her as if he knew her.

It was crazy. He could have sworn Dean had said…

Chance had to swallow to clear his throat. Cody, for once, kept quiet, as if he sensed there was something going on here under the surface.

"How long has it been since you've seen him?" he asked, gesturing at Tri. "Or he's seen you?"

Her eyes, those morning sky eyes, flicked to the dog, then back to him. "Never in person. I've only ever seen pictures. Videos."

He stared at her. He'd remembered right—that Dean had said the timing had never worked out for them to meet. Yet Tri, once Atlas, who was so leery of everyone, was practically trembling with eagerness to get to her. To get to this woman he'd never met.

It was crazy. Impossible. Yet here it was.

Tri let out that low whine again, that pleading sound he'd never, ever heard from the dog before.

He'd have to figure it out later. Right now what mattered

was Tri, and the astonishing change in him.

"Stay there," he said to the woman, his voice a bit sharper than he'd meant it to be. But it was crucial this stay under control, for Tri's sake. "Cody, back off to the truck."

His little brother recognized it was an order, and in this realm, he was the one who gave them. Cody backed off. The woman—Dean's wife—frowned, but she didn't move. Instead, quietly, she asked, "How bad is he?"

Her voice was a low, husky, tingle-creating thing. It was also distracting, which was the last thing he needed right now. But at least she seemed to understand something of what they were dealing with.

Her husband came home in a box. Of course she understands.

"Worst I've had come through here," he said honestly. Then, feeling compelled, he added, "At least he was until this moment."

"What do I do? Or perhaps a better question, what do I not do?"

"Nothing quick. Just...stay there." She nodded, a very slight motion.

Chance studied Tri, assessing. He was still practically vibrating with the longing to move. Yet he held. Dean had trained him well.

"Talk to him," he said to her, before he remembered the weird affect her voice had on him.

She nodded again. And seemed to find nothing odd

about the order. In the same quiet voice she began, "Hello, Atl—"

He cut her off as the dog tensed. Chance grabbed his collar, just in case. "He's Tri now. I've found changing their name helps."

Again she didn't take offense. Kept her eyes on the dog. "That makes sense. Try?"

The dog's ears swiveled again.

"Spelled t-r-i," he said. "Dual meaning."

"The obvious, tripod, and…?"

"He never stops trying." He half-shrugged. "Kid named him."

To his surprise, she glanced at Cody, who was too far away to hear the quiet conversation. Most women didn't put him in the kid category anymore. Most women took one look at his blond, green-eyed good looks and put him in another category altogether.

But then, most women hadn't been through what she'd been through.

"Our…foster kid. My brother's anyway. Lucas. Soon to be our—" He broke off, wondering when on earth he'd become a motormouth. "Never mind. Doesn't matter."

"Not this minute, no," she agreed. She'd kept her voice to that same quiet, soft, tingling pitch. She seemed to understand the idea was to get the dog used to her voice. "Nor does the why of this."

So she realized this was unexpected. And she was right;

time enough to figure out why it was happening later.

"Go ahead," he said.

She began again. Soft, lulling. "Hello, Tri. We've never met, but I know you. I know what you did, how many you saved, what a hero you are." The dog was vibrating again and gave Chance a begging sort of look. He kept his grip on the collar. She went on, and he had the crazy thought the grip was as much for him as the dog. "And I know how hard it is, for your life to be turned upside down in an instant. I admire how you've adapted, getting over that fence like that. Maybe you could teach me, huh?"

Tri gave a little whine at the question, or the uptilt of her voice at the end. Then Red—no, Mrs. Larson, better to think of her that way—went on. He let it go, let her pour that soothing, soft voice over them both for as long as he could stand it. Then he put up a hand and she stopped.

"Don't move," he cautioned. "I'll let him start toward you but keep hold of him."

She nodded. He frowned suddenly as he realized she'd never questioned this, any of this. Being used as a test case for a dog he'd considered, up to now, probably unreachable. And potentially dangerous. He should stop this, make sure she knew what she was doing. But then her eyes met his again, and the resolve he saw there was fierce, unwavering. She knew what she was doing, all right. And she was utterly determined to do it.

The moment he allowed Tri to start toward her, the lean,

rangy dog's tail began to wag. Only slightly, and just the tip, uncertainly, but it was there. The only tail signals he'd ever gotten from the animal until now were warnings of one kind or another.

"Can you get down to his level?" he asked her.

"Of course." She kept the same soft tone in her voice.

"Slowly."

"Of course," she repeated.

She did it as he'd asked, slowly, sinking down to her knees, apparently uncaring about dirt or dust. She did it gracefully as well, and he got the feeling almost everything she did would have that air of grace.

"If anything happens, or if I say 'Now,' roll up into a ball and put your back to him."

That got her attention. He saw her swallow, but the determination never wavered. She only nodded again. And as they came nearer, she began to talk again, focused on the dog, not quite cooing but close.

"It's all right, my beautiful, brave boy. There's nothing but good for you here, I promise. I've waited so long, searched so long for you, so it will be very hard for me not to throw my arms around you, but I know you're not sure of me, probably not sure of anything, so I won't, yet."

It was a lovely, sweet singsong kind of thing, and the dog was responding. The wag became more certain, less tentative, although still not the wild greeting wag of dog to loved one. Chance could feel Tri wanted to move faster but he held on to the collar.

When they got within reach, he made sure he had a strong grip. At the same moment, she said, in that same tone, "I presume I should stay still?"

"Yes."

He stopped, close enough that the dog could reach, but not so close that he could strike before Chance could stop him. Tri glanced up at him, but he gave him no command. The dog stretched forward again, his nose working fast. And she kept talking in that voice that would probably soothe any scared creature on the planet.

Including you?

Well, that was the craziest thought he'd had in a very long time. He was a lot of things, no doubt including messed up, but scared?

He shook it off, knowing he needed to focus. Tri got within reach. Chance braced himself, ready to yank the dog back at the first sign of aggression. But instead, a small miracle happened.

The scarred, stressed, traumatized dog licked her cheek.

Chapter Six

ARIEL COULD SEE by Chance Rafferty's expression that he was stunned. But that was all she took time to notice before she focused completely on the dog. She kept talking, not even sure what she was saying, just keeping that same tone and inflection he seemed to be responding to. And the dog leaned in, swiping her cheek with his tongue again. He tried to put his remaining front paw up as if to touch her, an instinct he apparently hadn't gotten over. She looked into the animal's eyes, told herself she was anthropomorphizing to see both anxiety and hope there.

Worst I've had come through here.

His words rang in her mind. And pain wracked her for a moment, as she thought of how that had happened. But after two years of practice, when she had something else she simply had to focus on, she'd learned to set it aside for the moment. She did so now.

"Thank you, sweet boy. I'm sure no one's called you that in a while, have they? Now, if the man in charge okays it—" she kept the same tone and didn't look at that man "—I'd really like to pet you. Would that be all right? I'm willing to risk it if you are."

She paused, waiting. Heard a sound as if the man beside them, the man towering over them, was clearing his throat. Then, almost gruffly, he said, "Slowly. Hold out a hand first."

"Of course." She said it again, but not upset; he was just being careful. It was clear this mattered to him, a great deal. The dogs mattered to him, or he wouldn't be doing this. And the officer she'd talked to who had given her the information on Atlas—Tri, she reminded herself—had clearly been admiring.

He takes on the ones we can't deal with any longer. The ones who hit The List.

He'd said the last two words as if they were capitalized, and she knew what list he meant. The lost causes, scheduled for that final injection. She supposed it was more merciful than a bullet in the head. Maybe.

Rafferty's a good guy. He's not getting rich doing what he does, because he takes nothing for himself. The dogs are all that matter.

She wondered fleetingly if *They Also Serve* would even exist if it wasn't here on his family's ranch. If he'd be able to do it financially. But again she pushed that aside.

Slowly, very slowly, she lifted her left hand; if the dog was going to bite, better her non-dominant hand. Tri leaned in, his nose working hard again as he sniffed her. She held still and held her breath. And then, with another of those low whines, the dog shifted his nose to underneath her hand

and nudged upward, clearly wanting the touch. She made herself go slowly, lightly, barely stroking the soft, short fur. When he tilted his head slightly, opening his mouth, her breath jammed up in her throat. She sensed rather than saw the man beside them tense.

But Tri only licked her wrist.

She increased the pressure of her fingers, rubbing now, gently but firmly. The dog sighed and leaned in even more.

Ariel risked a glance upward. Saw the gruff man staring down at them, lips parted just slightly, blinking just a bit rapidly.

"Mr. Rafferty?"

"Chance," he corrected, and she felt oddly as if she'd just been given an award. And noticed that his voice was different, less gruff now. "Eight months," he said, almost under his breath.

"What?" she said, still stroking the clearly willing dog's head.

"I've had him nearly eight months, and this is the first time I've…had hope for him."

That was not the voice of a harsh, uncaring man. She remembered what his brother had said—that he only cared about the dogs. She supposed that was what had won her the right to his first name, that Atl—Tri was responding to her. Had the dog really been so bad? He must have been, or she wouldn't have been warned to be so careful.

The first time I've had hope for him.

But at least the dog was here, and alive, when he very nearly hadn't been.

"Thank you for saving him," she said softly, moving her hand to try a scratch behind the dog's ears. The dog leaned in even further, and when it apparently became too much for his tripod base, he plopped down with his head on her knee. She began to stroke him as she would a normal dog, and he gave a little wiggle of pleasure.

"I may have rescued him from a needle," Chance said, his voice noticeably thick, "but I think it's you who has the power to save him."

HE WAS STILL in shock. He didn't understand why what had happened, happened, but he would take it. Gladly. Even if it meant he was sitting here in his house with a beautiful redhead with sky-blue eyes, drinking the coffee he was now glad he'd put on after he'd gotten Cody's message.

Cody, who had bailed with barely a goodbye.

Yes, he would take it, because as she sat barely two feet away on the leather couch that had once graced the den of the main house, Tri was sitting at—make that on—her feet, his head resting in her lap. She continued stroking him, in fact had never stopped. And the dog who had never willingly accepted anyone's touch but his, was clearly loving it.

Watching them he felt an odd sort of tingle. The same

sort of feeling her voice had given him, only this time it wasn't just down his spine—it was more. And spreading.

Relief. That was it. It was just relief, at the sight of Tri, at the hope that maybe, just maybe, he might be rehabilitated after all.

On some other level his mind was racing. Not just about what had happened now—although the only possibility that had come to him didn't seem overly feasible—but what might happen from here on.

What if she was the only one he'd respond to? She'd said she was here for him, but that didn't necessarily mean she wanted to take on this possibly life-long responsibility of always watching for any sign the dog might be regressing. Maybe she didn't understand that that's what it would be. Maybe that wasn't why she was here at all. Maybe she'd only come here to meet the dog who had been her late husband's strong right hand, the K-9 partner she'd never met.

And that brought him back to the biggest impossibility of the day, maybe of these last eight months. He stared at Tri. Why? Why had the beyond-wary, skittish, restless, and anti-social animal reacted this way? As if he'd known her?

"Why, do you suppose? Any theories?" His gaze shot up to her face as she voiced the same question he'd been thinking. When he didn't speak for a moment, she went on. "I know it sounds crazy, but…it's almost like he knows, isn't it? That I'm…connected to Dean?"

"Maybe…" He had to swallow to go on. "Maybe he

does. He's not a scent dog, but that doesn't mean he doesn't have the capacity far beyond human to pick them up, catalog and remember them."

Her eyes widened slightly. "But how could he know my scent?"

And there they were, at his crazy thought. "The…last time I saw them, Dean had just come back from a short leave. He left Tri at the base." It was difficult to go on. He was afraid this was going to hurt her, bring on some horrible wave of sadness. "He said if he had the chance to see you, even if it was only for a day, he couldn't pass it up, since it would be the last time for a while."

Her next words explained her shocked expression. "I…you…you served with him?"

He frowned. "For a while. They didn't tell you that?"

"I…no. The man I spoke to at the base didn't mention it. Not his fault," she added, almost hastily. "I didn't ask, because it didn't occur to me." He liked that she was so quick to absolve whoever she'd talked to. "I should have realized, when…you called me Red."

"I'm sorry," he said, then floundered, not sure exactly what he was apologizing for. Because she didn't know the worst of it, that not only had he known Dean, but he'd been the one who knew the foray he'd been about to leave on was little more than a suicide mission. But he hadn't been able to convince the brass. All his talk had been useless, and so Dean was dead.

He tired to focus on the here and now. Wondered if he should even go on, given what he'd been about to say would probably sound crazy to her. Finally he just came out with it.

"I saw him after he came back. We were...ragging on him. Like always. He just grinned at us, knowing..." He stopped again.

"Go on," she said. "Knowing what?"

"That he was the luckiest one of us."

He had no name for the expression that crossed her face then. Sorrow, yes, to the point of pain, but something else, too. Something he guessed was born of the knowledge that Dean Larson had indeed felt that way.

"Anyway," he went on hastily, "at one point he joked he wasn't ever going to take a shower again."

She blinked. "What?"

"Because," he said, now without looking at her because he simply couldn't, "he didn't ever want to...lose the scent of you."

A long, silent moment passed. He'd done it now. But when he finally broke and looked, he didn't see that look of pain again, but rather thoughtfulness and dawning understanding.

"That's how Tri knew me?"

"It's the only thing I can think of that makes sense. Unless he somehow just...knew."

"It does make sense," she agreed. "More than you know."

She said that with a tiny smile, one that looked familiar

somehow. It took him a moment to place it; it was the same sort of smile his mother got when she talked about his father, and how much she missed the little things.

"You see, I…had this thing I did," she went on slowly. "Whenever he had to leave, I…put a bit of his favorite of my perfumes on his collar. And told him to remember how very much I loved him, told him to remember us, whenever he noticed it."

Chance simply stared at her then. And knew with absolute certainty that they had been right, back then.

Dean Larson really had been the luckiest of them all.

Chapter Seven

ARIEL FOCUSED ON the dog whose head was a warm, welcome weight on her knee. She wanted to hug him, but she wasn't sure he was ready for that yet. She'd done a lot of reading on the way here and knew that some dogs felt trapped when enveloped in a human hug. For all that they were trained to deal with anything, she didn't want to add to the animal's stress level.

She didn't look around at the small living area, except to register that there was—thankfully—no sign of the coming holiday. No Christmas tree, no wreaths, no sparkly lights, not even a card in sight. Just like her San Diego apartment. Which to her, after the wealth of décor at the inn and that she'd driven through in Last Stand, was a relief.

In fact, the only personal touches she'd noticed at all in here were the books—everything from history to westerns to science fiction, she saw—stacked on a small table beside the big chair next to the window. And, on the wall opposite the small flat-screen TV, a colorful oil painting that hung over the sofa on which she now sat.

She wondered what was going on in Tri's mind. She had

seen many videos on military war dogs. She hated the acronym MWDs, because it made them sound like just another weapon. Replaceable. Discardable. As they had once, cruelly, been. Abandoned once the task was done, left behind, even in places where a dog was considered vermin, or worse, food. The practice had ended, but she couldn't help wondering if it would have, if dog-lovers hadn't found out about it and raised a huge fuss.

So now there was a place for them to come home, but if they didn't or couldn't adapt to civilian life, their future was worse than iffy. And they would become just one more casualty if there weren't people willing to fight for them as they, in their way, had fought.

If men like Chance Rafferty didn't exist.

She looked up from Tri—she was making a conscious, firm effort to stop thinking of him by the name she'd always heard before—although she didn't stop stroking him, since the longer she did it, the more he seemed to relax. She found Chance watching her, rather intently. No, watching Tri, she was sure. Constant vigilance, as Dean had always joked, imitating a voice and intonation from a movie character.

"May I ask you something?" she finally said.

His mouth quirked wryly. He had, among other things, a very nice mouth. Not that she noticed such things anymore. Except she just had.

"Not sure I have any words left, but go ahead," he answered.

"Where's your dog?" The instant the words were out and she saw the way his expression changed, she had her answer. Before he found any of those words he'd mentioned, she hastened to remove the need. "I'm sorry. Were you with him?"

"No." His voice was a cold, harsh, wounded thing. She wondered if he realized how much he betrayed with that voice, that look in his eyes. "I'd come home. He was still on active duty and was redeployed. He was killed on his first mission with a new handler. Three years ago next week."

"One deployment too many." *Just like Dean.* "And another reason to hate this time of year." At her words Chance gave her an oddly sharp look she couldn't interpret. "Sorry," she muttered. "Sore spot."

"Yes," he agreed, and left it at that.

She managed an even tone when she asked, "What was he like? Your dog."

His expression was a combination of sadness and smile that she suspected she herself had worn more than once. "In looks, he was darker that Tri, overall. Personality? He was…a tactical nuke on duty. A furry guided missile. Off…he was a clown. Completely goofy." The slightest of smiles curved the corners of his mouth. "We had this really full-of-himself company commander for a while. Crazy dog stole his underwear and ran through camp with it, flying like a flag. He made everybody laugh."

The image almost made her laugh, something that hadn't

happened involuntarily in a very long time. And something about his smile reached a deep, caring place inside her that she hadn't allowed to stir for a long time. It all made her voice soft when she said, "So he saved you in more than one way."

She saw his jaw tighten, thought he wasn't going to answer. When he finally did, she was almost certain it was not because he wanted to, but because he felt that his hero dog deserved it.

"He did. More times than I can count. He's the reason this—" he gestured toward the kennels outside "—exists. The reason I'm still alive to do it." That jaw muscle jumped again, and when he went on it was clearly something he'd fought against saying. "I wanted to bring him home. I put in for him, before I left. Told them I'd come get him no matter where he was stationed when his time was up. But I got that damned phone call instead."

"And how did that make you feel?"

His gaze narrowed sharply. She supposed it was because it was kind of a therapist sort of question—she'd been through enough to know—and she guessed he wasn't the sort of guy who'd take easily to that. But to her surprise, again he answered.

"Guilty."

She drew back slightly; she hadn't expected that. But she thought she understood. "Because you think if you'd stayed, if you'd still been with him, it wouldn't have happened?"

"Might not have," he muttered. "We were a team. It was like he knew what I was thinking, and maybe…"

He trailed off, shook his head, then lowered it to rub at his forehead as if he had a headache starting. She noticed again the touch of gray at his temples, at odds with the otherwise youthful look of him. It didn't detract, in fact to her, it made him even more attractive.

Attractive?

She couldn't remember the last time she'd thought that about a man. Any man other than Dean, anyway. He was her gold standard, and no one had ever come close.

She shoved aside the errant thought and got herself back on track. Thought about his feelings of guilt about the death of his own dog. She stroked Tri steadily, this time adding a bit of scratching around his ears. Then, speaking very, very quietly, she said, "Then just imagine how you'd feel if you found out, after thinking him dead, that he was hurt but alive."

"What?" His head came up sharply. His brow was furrowed, but it cleared almost instantly. "You mean Tri. You thought he was dead."

He'd gotten there very fast. She nodded. "I didn't know he'd survived until…later."

"You mean after they showed up at your door to tell you Dean was dead?"

He said it bluntly, almost harshly. For a moment she wondered if his intent had been to hurt. It could have, if she'd let it. But upon a moment's reflection, she realized she preferred this to the platitudes people usually came up with, to dance around the reality of it.

"Yes."

"Great, isn't it? They do it to 'break it gently,' they say. But the instant you see them coming..."

He lowered his gaze again, just as a sudden thought hit her. She searched her memory, trying to recall exactly what the minimal bio on the website had said. Something about following in his father's footsteps? That had been it, no details. But still, she knew. She could hear it in his voice, see it in those eyes that looked more gray than blue at the moment.

"You've been there." It wasn't a question; she hadn't intended it to be.

"Yes."

"Your father?" she finally asked when he said no more.

"Yes."

She wondered how old he'd been. Not that it mattered, not really, not with a loss that size. And suddenly it was there, that dark, consuming place inside her, the yawning, empty chasm of grief. All the years ahead, without Dean, were in that hole, and she had no choice about whether to face it. Her eyes burned and she angrily swiped at them; they were so useless, the tears. They accomplished nothing except to make her feel worse because she couldn't stop them.

"It never stops." She wasn't even aware of having spoken

JUSTINE DAVIS

the words aloud. She hadn't meant to.

"No."

His short, flat answer was the first moment she realized she had indeed voiced the question. She looked up to see in his eyes the weary knowledge of one who had carried this burden much longer than she had. And again she appreciated the lack of false assurances.

Then, unexpectedly, his gaze softened. "It never stops," he said, still bluntly, "but it…changes. Eases a little. And you learn. To live with it."

It was choppy, in bits, but it was an answer. She remembered Cody Rafferty's words, and his warning: *…he doesn't talk much. Don't take it personally.* So clearly talking like this was not something he usually did. Maybe he didn't usually talk at all. That he was now, to her, did more to ease the sudden rush of pain than any platitude ever had.

"Thank you," she said, a shaky whisper all she could manage. "Thank you for not…"

"Not bullsh—" He broke off and shifted to, "Lying to you?"

"Yes." And somehow that polite catch, that mid-course correction made for her sake, made the gaping blackness recede a little more.

Chapter Eight

C HANCE WAS RATTLED. He could admit that much. He just wasn't sure if it was what had happened with Tri, the totally unexpected change in him that was little short of a miracle, or that he'd been talking—hell, chattering—like a guy with no guardrails practically since this woman had arrived. Well, chattering for him, anyway, which as his mother often pointed out, meant saying more than three words at a time.

So now, with a conscious effort, he shut up. He simply watched, telling himself he was looking for any sign the dog's newfound calm and peace was temporary. That in order to do that, he had to also watch the gorgeous redhead was just…what? A bonus? An annoyance?

He couldn't remember the last time he'd noticed this much about a woman. Oh, he was male and breathing, so his mind registered when he encountered an attractive woman— not that he was out among people enough for that to happen often—but that was as far as it went. And it usually had no more effect on him than noticing a beautiful sunrise, or the soaring flight of a red-tail hawk. A moment of appreciation, and then back to the numbed day-to-day of his existence.

Oddly, he fixated on her hand, stroking the dog's head. Slender, graceful, with long, elegant fingers. But no long nails or fancy manicure for her. Funny how he always noticed that, followed by thoughts of how nearly impossible it must be to do simple things without contorting your fingers and hands unnaturally. It had always seemed flashy and unnecessary to him, nails that long, until it had been pointed out to him that they could also function as a weapon.

By Dean, laughingly, he remembered suddenly.

I'm glad Red doesn't go for that. Those things could take an eye out.

She has a temper?

Goes with the hair. But she gets over it quick. And the making up is spectacular.

The memory of that grin, that satisfied male grin as he'd spoken the last words, had made Chance laugh even as he admitted to a certain amount of envy. Larson was, another platoon member had said, the most married guy ever. And now, as the woman he'd been married to sat just a few feet away, he could see why.

He felt a twinge of that old envy again. Two years gone, and she still loved him. Dean had indeed been a lucky guy.

The irony of that thought was like a slap to the side of the head. *He came home in a box.* Why was he having to remind himself of that?

"How old were you?"

He snapped out of his uncharacteristic reverie. "What?"

"Your father. How old were you?"

He didn't dare speak in the flat, cold voice an answer would have normally come out in, not when it might affect Tri at this crucial moment. He tried for a level tone, something he didn't usually, after years of practice, have to strive for. It was more of an effort than it should have been to say evenly, "Sixteen."

She studied him a moment before saying, very quietly, "What an awful age to have to confront the concept of gone forever."

"Is there a good age?" he asked, and a little snap crept into his voice. Tri's ears moved, and he clamped down hard on the biting edge that wanted to rise in him. He thought he'd blunted that long ago, permanently, and he didn't like it or understand why it was surfacing now.

"Not good. But I'd think losing him when you were, say, seventy might be better." Her expression and her tone of voice were so carefully neutral he knew it was a reaction to his snap.

Chance lowered his gaze, sucked in a long breath and let it out slowly. His mother would have chewed a piece out of his hide if she'd heard the way he'd spoken to this woman, who had done nothing but come here to help. A woman who was apparently succeeding with the creature he'd feared was lost.

And even at his age, he didn't want the woman who had

held the Raffertys together mad at him.

The problem was, he didn't know how to fight this because he didn't know what this was. Didn't know why he was so edgy, why the leash on his usually numbed temper had snapped.

"My apologies," he said. It came out rather formally, but better that than with that nasty edge.

"And mine. It's none of my business."

His gaze shot back to her face as she voiced the words he'd bitten back. He opened his mouth to speak, although he wasn't sure to say what, but something in her expression—a touch of puzzlement or surprise—stopped him.

After a moment, brow furrowed, she murmured almost too quietly for him to hear, "And I'm not sure why I asked."

I know the feeling.

He almost said it but managed not to. Right now it seemed the less he spoke, the better. Because when he did talk, he ended up saying things he never ordinarily would.

It's Tri. Hope will screw you up big-time.

He made himself focus exclusively on the dog. The fierce war dog who had given a piece of his body and nearly his life to the work humans asked him to do. The dog who had lost that part of him trying to keep his handler safe, keep him away from the explosive device set by the very people they had been tracking.

The dog who at this moment, amazingly, looked like nothing more radical than a contented house pet.

Who wouldn't be content, snuggled up to a woman like that?

The breath he sucked in then was audible. And the sound seemed to draw her gaze from Tri back to Chance's face. He tried to cover it with a cough, before she could ask if he was all right.

Because at this moment, he didn't know the answer to that question.

ARIEL TRIED TO remember the last time she'd actually been curious about someone. Things, yes—it would occur to her to wonder about new things she encountered—but people? Not for a long time. But apparently she was curious about Chance Rafferty. That it was only curiosity she was certain. She wasn't capable of anything more. She hadn't been for two years. It must be Tri. That's why it mattered to figure this man out. Because when it came down to it, the dog was the only thing that stirred the slightest bit of life in her.

She'd been told Chance was very, very protective of the animals, and had more than once turned down people he didn't think were equipped to handle a particular dog. She couldn't let him decide she wasn't equipped to handle Tri. And she'd do whatever it took to convince him otherwise.

"Tell me about Tri. Please." He looked almost relieved at the shift to the reason she was here.

"What do you want to know?"

"I already know the basics, about his training and such. And I know...the details of what happened. But I don't know anything about him, specifically. His personality, that kind of thing."

"Neither do I."

She blinked. Stared at him, nonplussed. "What?"

He shifted his gaze to the dog, and she saw his expression change yet again, become something gentler, softer. And if she had had any doubts that this man was doing this work because he truly cared about these animals, they would have vanished now.

"I don't know his true personality. It's buried somewhere underneath the fear and trauma and guilt."

"Guilt?"

"He knew his main job was to keep Dean safe. He failed. And he knows it."

She drew back slightly. "That's a bit..."

"Think I'm projecting? Imputing human responses to an animal?"

"It does sound a bit that way."

"With ordinary dogs you'd probably be right. But not these dogs. I've seen too many of them come through here that feel that way. Maybe it's just instinctual responses, or whatever researchers claim. But the end result is, their emotions exist. Different than ours, but they exist."

She had the feeling he'd explained this more than once. Wondered if that was why he suddenly seemed...not calmer, she doubted that was ever an issue for this veteran, but more back in familiar territory. He'd probably had to explain this before, often.

"But," he added, looking back at Tri now, "I think for the first time some of his true self is showing."

That made her smile, because the implication that it was because of her was clear. And for the first time since she'd latched on to this idea, since she'd begun this quest—for it was nothing less than that, for her—she was certain she would get it done.

She had to. It was the only thing left in the world she could do for the man she loved.

Chapter Nine

"SO WHAT HAPPENS now?"

Chance had been dreading the question even as he knew it was inevitable. Not because he was afraid she wouldn't want to go through with it, wouldn't be up to it, but because he was afraid she would be. He could sense the determination coming off her in waves. This was a woman with her mind set, and he'd been raised by one of those.

Which meant he was going to be spending time—a lot of time—with her. And she'd already rattled him more than anything in recent memory. In the matter of a couple of hours. When he found himself wondering if he could scare her out of it, he knew just how rattled he truly was. He couldn't even find the words for his usual cautions to someone with their heart in the right place, but without the knowledge or capacity to deal with what one of these dogs required.

"That depends," he said carefully, "on why you're here."

She frowned, just slightly. "I'm here for him—" she glanced down at the dog she'd never stopped petting "—as I said."

"Obviously you're here because of him," Chance replied, still carefully, "but what exactly do you mean by 'for' him?"

Her expression cleared. "Oh. I want to adopt him, of course. To take care of him, to give him a good, loving home."

"So do most of the people who come here."

She studied him for a moment. "Are you saying they don't do it?"

"More like can't."

Her head tilted. Those eyes fastened on him, she silently waited him out. And he wondered if she'd always had that tenacity, or if it had been forced on her two years ago. Either way, it was there, and he knew she wouldn't give up on this idea easily. He remembered suddenly how, after Dad had been killed, he'd become fixated on something, anything that would fill the black emptiness. First it had been Dad's stallion, Buckshot. Then it had been repairing every mile of fence on the ranch. Then it had been the military. Each thing received his entire focus, to the exclusion of all else. Even though he knew, deep down, that nothing could ever fill the void in his soul his father's death had left behind.

He wondered if she was on the same path, looking for something, anything that would fill the void. He reached for the words that had become a sort of anti-sales pitch.

"When I started this, I was so glad to find them homes I wasn't careful enough. Too many came back, and in worse mental shape than before. It wasn't the adopter's fault, most of the time. They had the best of intentions. They just weren't...equipped to deal with dogs like this."

"Go on," she said when he paused.

She didn't seem to be taking offense, so he continued. "This isn't like adopting a dog from a shelter, where they may have some quirks it will only take time, consistency, and kindness to overcome. These are trained warriors, and some of them can never, ever get past that. And if you manage to get one to bond with you, that comes with them being ready to defend you to the death. Against whatever they see as a threat."

He stopped again, watching her. She was still stroking the dog. She hadn't stopped since the moment it was clear he was loving her touch. What guy wouldn't?

Damn. Get a grip, Rafferty.

After a moment she said quietly, "And the problem is that to a traumatized warrior, almost everything is a threat?"

She'd gotten there quicker than most. "Yes," he said flatly. "Tri spent nearly four months in the veterinary hospital, then almost a year in the army rehab program. Now he's been here for eight months. So two years away from the battlefield, and he's not much calmer than he was when he arrived."

"Believe me," she said, her voice cool now, "I know exactly how long it's been."

Of course she did. Not like she would forget the day her world had crashed in on her. He considered, briefly, apologizing—again—but decided she probably wouldn't want to hear it. But that drove him to give credit where it was due.

"Not much calmer until now," he amended, looking at the dog who was more relaxed now than he'd ever seen him.

She took it as he'd meant it, as the regret he hadn't voiced. "Seems a good first step."

He couldn't deny that obvious truth. "Yes."

"So...I'll ask again. What next?"

This was the last thing he wanted. What he wanted was for her to change her mind, to decide this would be too hard, too much, and go back home. Because if she insisted, it meant hours—a lot of hours—spent with her, assessing, teaching. But then he looked at Tri, the dog who had been strung tight and constantly on edge for a huge portion of the months he'd been here.

Until now.

He couldn't deny Tri this chance. It was why he'd started this. Dogs like Tri were the reason.

But maybe she'd change her mind. When she realized what would be involved, what his requirements were, maybe she'd just get on a plane back home. Wherever that was.

"Some questions," he finally said, resigning himself. He would do worse than this, for Tri's sake.

"Go."

She said it like someone who expected to be cross-examined on a witness stand. Which wasn't all that far from the truth, he supposed.

"Where do you live?"

"San Diego."

"Family?"

"Not close by. My parents recently moved to Florida." She paused, then added, "I live in a one-bedroom apartment, which I am more than ready to give up so he can have a yard of his own."

One bedroom. So she hadn't acquired any kids. He struck that question off the list. "You can afford that?"

It would normally be a rude question, but she answered easily. "Yes. Dean saw to it that I'd be fine."

He got the feeling she would afford it no matter what it took, she was that determined. "What do you do?"

"I'm an event organizer."

He blinked. "That's…a thing?"

She raised a brow at him. "It is. A lucrative thing, in many cases."

"What kind of events do you organize?" It had nothing to do with Tri or why she was here, but he was curious.

"Business functions and parties. Fundraisers. Weddings and receptions. Seminars and conferences. Anything that requires the coordination of goals and large groups of people."

"Sounds like a nightmare to me," he said frankly, before he could stop himself. To his relief, she only smiled.

"It can be, logistically." Then, with a steady look, she said, "But I don't imagine it's any worse than coming up with a battle plan, or mission directives. With a lot less fallout if you make a mistake."

"Touché," he said, with a slight nod to her accurate point. Then he made himself continue. "Have you ever had a dog?"

She nodded. "Grew up with them." She gave him a crooked smile. "Real dogs, not yappy ankle biters."

He blinked. Barely stopped a smile. This was supposed to be serious. He was supposed to be hammering her with the impossibility of this, not laughing. He made himself focus.

"But you don't have one now?"

"No."

"Would you be looking for one if it wasn't for Tri?"

"Probably not yet. Although the thought has occurred a few times."

"Do you own a weapon?"

She drew back slightly, then answered a bit archly, "I own a car, does that count?"

"It wasn't a rhetorical question."

She appeared to think for a moment before speaking again. "You're saying having Tri will be like having a weapon."

"Yes. And for the foreseeable future you'd have to keep an eye on him like a grenade with the pin pulled."

He didn't dare look at Tri at the moment, when he was trying to make this sound so difficult, because the dog was trying to inch his way onto her lap. Not that he blamed him, not at all, but it was still a bit shocking, to see the wary, edgy animal turn wannabe lap dog.

"All right," she said, shifting her position slightly as she still, endlessly, stroked the dog. She'd done it to make it easier for Tri to get up with her, Chance realized. And he felt an odd tightness in his chest. Because he was so happy to see Tri's response, not because at this moment he was envying him.

"Don't blow that off, Mrs. Larson." Yes, that was good—use that name, that should settle this crazy reaction. Remember who she is. Dean's widow. And remember why she's a widow. Besides, she hadn't told him he could use her first name anyway.

"I'm not. I'm aware he would require much more vigilance than an ordinary dog. Because there's nothing ordinary about him."

"No, there's not." He sucked in another breath, then went ahead in the most businesslike tone he could muster. "There are requirements, Mrs. Larson. Markers that have to be met by anyone who wants one of these dogs."

"I assumed. I'll meet them."

He just looked at her for a moment. Tried to ignore the admittedly beautiful surface and see down to the heart and soul of her. Tried, even though he knew he couldn't.

But apparently Tri could.

"Why do you want to do this?" he asked, the businesslike

tone vanishing.

"Isn't that obvious?"

"No. Do you want to do it for the dog's sake, or yours?"

Her chin came up. "Yes."

"Mrs. Larson—"

She interrupted him rather sharply. "I want to do it not just because I owe him for the times he kept Dean alive, and owe it now to my husband's memory, because I know how much he loved him. But because we as a country owe him and all of the dogs who serve. They are living creatures willing to die for us. Not for an idea, a system, or a country, for *us*. We have no right to discard them."

He stared at her. He had no words to answer with, because he had just heard his own words, almost identical in phrasing, thrown back at him with the same fierceness with which he'd once said them in his pitch to be allowed to take the dogs they'd written off as lost. A fierceness that stirred something deep inside him, long dormant.

And he knew this could well be the biggest mistake of his life.

But he was going to do it anyway.

Chapter Ten

SOMETHING HAD CHANGED again. Ariel could sense it, could hear it in the undertone that had come into his voice. She didn't know what had caused it. She thought it might be wise to give up trying to figure that out. This man was many things, she was certain, but an open book was not one of them.

"What are your requirements, Mr. Rafferty?"

It was a moment before he said, quietly, "I thought we agreed on Chance?"

"Yet you call me Mrs. Larson."

For an instant he looked oddly unsettled. Then he seemed to recover. "You never said otherwise," he pointed out.

"True enough. Call me Ariel. And hold the red-haired mermaid jokes, please."

A near-smile flickered for an instant, but he only nodded. "Ariel."

"So about those markers?"

"Time," he said. "You come here every day and interact with him. In this case, until we know it's not just a one-time fluke." She nodded. She thought he yet again hesitated before going on, but his tone was brisk. "Then out a bit. Into the world. In controlled conditions first, then wider. To places he's unfamiliar with."

She wondered what he meant by controlled conditions, but she'd find that out later. "And if he—we—pass those tests?"

"If you get through that, you come here and stay, to take over his daily care, and see how he reacts."

Stay here? With him? Did he mean on the ranch, or...in this house that suddenly seemed too small?

She shook off the concerns and merely nodded. "And then?"

"Same process, out into the world. But you deal with him alone. I'll be around, but at a distance."

"To make sure it's not just your command presence keeping him in line?" He blinked. Then stared at her. "What?" she asked. "You reek of it. You can't tell me you haven't been told that." He was the very essence of the term used to refer to someone whose very demeanor made people straighten up and pay attention.

"Not in a while," he muttered.

"Maybe because the dogs don't talk much?" she suggested sweetly. Even as the words came out, she wondered what she was doing. She didn't know what shocked her more, that she was joking at all, or that she was teasing the man who held Tri's future in his hands.

But she knew what reached her more. The slight twitch at the corners of his mouth again, as if he were fighting a smile, even a laugh. It shouldn't affect her at all, let alone cause a little knot in her chest.

"They talk more than you might think," he said after a moment. "You just have to know how to listen."

For some reason that tightened the knot in her chest even more. "Will you teach me?" she asked, and it came out softly, almost pleadingly because it had to fight to get past that knot. And she found herself wondering what must have shown in her face when he looked away at her soft plea.

Tri whined a little. Then, with a quick look at Chance, the dog edged his way up onto the couch beside her. Again she wanted to hug him but resisted the urge, afraid both that it would stop the dog's surprising efforts, and that the man in charge would call a halt because she'd done it without his approval. She didn't normally wait for permission from someone who wasn't her boss or a client, but her instinct was telling her than when it came to these dogs, this was the man to listen to.

"Please," she went on urgently, glancing up from the dog she'd been petting for so long, without any desire to stop. "I want this to work. I'll do whatever it takes to make it work. This is more important to me than…anything."

"Why?"

He asked it softly, and he was looking at her again, with those stormy eyes. She opened her mouth to say she'd already explained why she wanted this but stopped, thinking that wasn't exactly what he'd asked. He'd asked why it was the most important thing to her.

She had to look away from that gaze to be able to speak. "Because," she began, slowly, because this was so…revealing of her pitiful mental state, "it's the only thing I care about. Feel anything about."

"The only thing that makes you feel you're still alive?"

Her head came up sharply as his quiet words struck. Struck home hard and deep. She felt an odd combination of heat and chill in her cheeks and down her spine. And when he went on, the sensations only intensified.

"When we got word about my father, I couldn't— wouldn't believe it. I spent days in denial, days trying to make it not true, certain he'd been somewhere else, that he'd stayed behind on that mission, that they'd misidentified the ones who were killed, that in the confusion they'd gotten the names wrong."

She was staring at him now. And once more his brother's words echoed in her mind, this time with the final warning: …*he doesn't talk much.* This was not talking much? This, this baring of clearly soul-deep pain?

"My older brother, Keller, gave up all his life plans to help our mother hold this family together. Ry went to silent running. Cody was too young to really understand yet. I was the one who refused to believe it. To deal with it. Because fighting it was the only thing that made me feel alive. And I knew if I stopped, the deadness would descend."

Again Tri whined slightly, as if he'd heard the strain in Chance's voice. She could have echoed that whine, as the memories swept over her. How long had she spent screaming into the ether that it couldn't be true, Dean couldn't be dead? How many nights had she spent, terrified to sleep for fear of the dreams that might come?

"When did you believe?" she whispered.

He took in an audible breath. "Probably the same time you did."

"When you saw...his body."

"Yes." His mouth twisted bitterly. "The day after Christmas."

Her eyes widened. No wonder there was no sign of the holiday in this house. She understood that more than he could know. So she told him. "For me it was the day before."

For a long, silent moment they simply looked at each other. Everything else fell away because, for that moment, they were simply two people who shared the most painful of bonds.

"I DON'T HAVE much you'd want to eat here," Chance said, as his own empty stomach growled again. They still needed to work out details, but he, at least, also needed to eat. And he was serious; he had little food fit for anyone else on hand.

Ariel finished pouring the last of the coffee, then turned her head to look at him. "And you learned what I like to eat how?"

He grimaced. "I assumed you aren't big on MREs."

"Meals Rarely Edible? Depends. The FSRs aren't so bad. I actually like the Zapplesauce."

Chance stared at her. "And when did you eat first strike rations?"

"The first time I knew he was heading into combat. I wanted to know."

He continued to just look at her. And again felt that little twinge of envy that seemed so out of place. Thinking a dead guy was lucky was just so wrong.

"Are you saying that's all you have here now?" she asked as she put the pot back on the heated plate.

"That's my go-to, most of the time."

"What about that barbecue grill I saw outside?"

He gave a shrug. "I'll grill a steak, or chicken sometimes. But I don't cook."

"I don't either," she said. "I fix, but I don't cook."

"Fix?"

"Season it, grill or roast it, toss some frozen veggies in the microwave, done. My biggest prep job is remembering to take meat out of the freezer."

This time he couldn't stop the smile. How many times had he resorted to the MREs because he'd forgotten to do just that?

"I do bake, though. It's soothing."

He could use some soothing just now. "Bake?"

"Cakes, cookies, but muffins, mostly. Easy to grab one quick in the mornings."

"Before you head out to…organize something."

She gave him a sideways look. "You still don't quite believe that's a real job, do you?"

He shrugged to hide the odd shiver that went through him at that tilt of her head. "I…just never met anyone whose job it is before."

She looked down at Tri, who was sitting at her feet. She'd insisted on doing it herself although he'd offered to refill her mug, saying she was curious to see if Tri would follow her. He had, in his now practiced hopping gait. She started to reach toward the dog. Then she stopped, glanced up at Chance.

"Are there rules about initiating contact?"

"Usually," he said, appreciating that it had even occurred to her. "But I think you've zoomed past the first few. So right now, if I'm here, I'd say go ahead as long as he's looking at you and knows it's coming. And keep talking to him."

"I understand," she said, turning back and talking to Tri in that soothing coo of a voice. "No surprises, right m'boy? I can understand that." She reached out slowly, still talking. "I'll never sneak up on you, I promise. Slow and easy, that's the ticket."

Tri reached up toward her hand with his nose, the tip of his tail wagging in invitation. And then she was stroking his head again, and the dog was blissfully—as blissful as Chance had ever seen him, anyway—leaning into her touch. And Chance remembered to breathe again, although there seemed to be a catch in it, and the coffee mug in his hand suddenly felt too warm.

"There you are, my brave, brave boy," she crooned to the dog. "Such a good boy. I know, I'm talking silly to a tough guy like you, but you like it, don't you? I can tell."

Oh, yeah, he likes it.

A flush of heat flooded him, so long unfelt it took him a moment to recognize it.

Damn. Stop it.

He needed to focus on Tri, the most important being in this room right now. What she could become to the traumatized animal was the most crucial thing, not his own sudden, unexpected reaction to her.

He'd just left it too long. That was all. This didn't hit him often anymore—he'd become an expert at sublimating the urges when they arose. It had even been a long while since Cody had ragged on him that he needed to get laid.

He tried to remember the last time the pressure had become too much, and he'd searched out a willing partner for a one-time encounter. It had been so long he wasn't sure. So that had to be it. He'd just waited too long, so the first attractive woman—and Lord, she was that—who came along, his body woke up in a rush.

Even as he thought it, he knew that wasn't quite true. This was more than a long-denied and buried urge. He wasn't sure he'd ever felt anything quite like this, so...overwhelming.

But this was not the time, the place, or the woman for this kind of reaction. Especially not the woman, no matter how attractive she was, or how long it had been. Especially not the woman who had so loved her husband she was still deep in grief two years later.

Her husband. His brother in arms.

Red. She's Dean's beloved Red. So stop it.

Shame and disgust flooded him, and did what he'd been unable to do before, quashed the rising heat and want and need. He might be messed up, but he wasn't messed up enough to poach on that sacred territory.

Chapter Eleven

"COME ON."

He said it so abruptly and sharply she blinked. "Where?"

"The big house. They have real food." He headed toward the front door. She saw Tri leap to his feet.

"Are you sure—"

"Tri, sit." The dog obeyed, but was still clearly alert. "I'm sure. I bought it."

That hadn't been what she'd been going to ask, but the answer surprised her enough to ask, "You bought it?"

"I always do. The grocery shopping, I mean. Every dratted week." He stopped at the coatrack beside the door, took down the blue jacket she'd worn, and turned back to face her.

"You don't cook, but you grocery shop?" She tried to picture this man wandering through the produce section, selecting apples, and she couldn't.

"No," he said, "I shop because I don't cook." His mouth quirked wryly. "Mom's orders. Everybody cooks but I don't, so I have to shop. Here," he added, holding out the jacket.

Not just for her to take but holding it for her to slip it on. In a gentlemanly way. Those Southern manners weren't just a myth. They were apparently so ingrained that even whatever this man had been through couldn't erase them. But that was not what she wanted to know at the moment.

"Thank you. But you eat?" she asked as she slid the jacket on. "There, I mean, at the big house?"

"Sometimes."

The flat tone of that last word as he turned his back to grab his own light jacket told her he was done talking about this. "Actually, I wasn't going to ask about the food."

He went still. And it was a moment before he turned around, almost as if he were embarrassed that he'd jumped to a conclusion. Or that doing so had made him talk about things he normally wouldn't. Like the family structure of the Raffertys.

"What, then?" he turned and asked, evenly enough.

She went back to what would have been her original question. "Are you sure I should go? I just…will Tri think I've abandoned him, after only just meeting him?"

Again he went still. Stared at her, not in an intimidating way, but more in the way of someone who was seeing…she wasn't sure what. And then he smiled. Not the brief glimpses she'd seen before, the slight upturn at the corners of his mouth, or the fleeting actual smiles, but a real one, one that lasted more than a couple of seconds. And under its impact she almost forgot to breathe. Or how to breathe.

"It's not too warm out. He can come. I planned on it. He's good in a vehicle, and he understands being left in one doesn't mean you're not coming back."

She smiled back then. Crazy, she felt again as if she'd won some kind of award. "We don't really have to raid your family fridge," she said. "There must be someplace in town where we could eat and work out what comes next."

"No, thanks," he said, grimacing now. "I was just there two days ago."

Every week, he'd said. *Every dratted week.* "So once a week but no more?"

"Unless I have to," he said as he slipped on his jacket. It was a medium gray and made his eyes stand out, although she would have bet any amount of money that wasn't why he'd picked it. If he had. If some woman in his life who had known what it would do hadn't chosen it. "Especially," he added as he reached for the door, "this time of year."

She knew immediately what he meant. "Your town does seem to go all out for the holiday."

"That's putting it mildly. And the decorations on every square foot are only the beginning."

"There's more?"

"Just had the tree-trimming party at the Corbyn house. Most of the town shows up for that one. Tomorrow night the tree lighting, in front of the library. All of the town for that. Next the Christmas parade, complete with the fat guy in the red suit. Next weekend the Christmas market downtown. Weekend after that the Christmas dance. And that's not even mentioning the music. Everywhere."

He said it all in the same weary tone she would have. And now she knew why. Christmas brought no more joy to him than it did to her.

"For someone who hates it as much as I do, you have the schedule down."

"How else would I know how to avoid it all?" he asked dryly.

She couldn't help it, she burst out laughing. She could not remember the last time she had genuinely, honestly laughed. She'd been amused before, but had always felt slightly guilty, as if she had no right, because Dean was dead. But laugh? Hard, like this? Didn't happen.

And he was staring at her as if he was as startled as she was.

CHANCE HAD NO words for what the sound of her laughter made him feel. He worked fairly hard at not feeling any-thing, but he hadn't been prepared for this. He wasn't sure there was a way to prepare for this.

The only thing he could relate it to was, a long time after their father's death, when one of Cody's wisecracks had made their mother laugh, she'd seemed a little surprised herself—as Ariel had now—but after a while had come up with an answer. "I love you boys as much as I loved your father, although in a different way. So you have the same power to make me laugh as he did."

"As long as we don't ever make you as sad," Rylan had muttered, only loud enough for Chance, sitting next to him at the dinner table, to hear.

Now, the only thing Chance could think of to do was move. "Tri, heel," he said, and the dog leapt up. With a look at Ariel, as if to be sure she, too, was coming, the dog clung to his side as they went out and walked over to his rather weather-beaten truck. It was parked heading out, as he always did out of habit, so they reached the passenger side first. The moment he opened the door and slid the seat forward, the dog leapt into the small back seat area, seemingly unhindered by his missing leg.

"He seems to compensate very well," she said as he slid the seat back.

He glanced at her, then gestured with his thumb over his shoulder at the kennels, with their seven-foot fences. The fence Tri had somehow scaled to get to her. "Yeah, I'd say so."

She smiled, and it made her laugh echo in his head. She climbed in, instantly turned to look at Tri and started talking to the dog again. After Chance got in and shut the door she reached out and gave the dog a stroke and a scratch behind the ears. Tri stretched his neck as if asking for more. If he was a cat, he'd be purring.

I get it, dog.

Chance gave himself an inward shake and started the truck.

He'd had the vague hope that everyone would be either busy or gone, and he could sneak in and throw together a couple of sandwiches or something. Nothing fancy, but that's not why she was here. And when they stepped inside the quiet house, he thought maybe he'd gotten lucky.

And then all thought of luck vanished as she spotted the large painting on the great room wall and immediately headed toward it.

"I noticed this before. Just beautiful. It's the same artist, isn't it? As the one in your place?"

"Yes," he said stiffly.

"He or she is really good," she said as she studied the colorful vista.

"Yes."

"Is that someplace around here?"

"Yes."

"On your ranch?"

"Yes."

She glanced at him, brow furrowed, no doubt over his single-syllable answers. That was what usually set people off. But she didn't speak, only turned back and leaned in toward the painting. He guessed she was looking for an artist's signature. Knew she wouldn't find one.

She turned back to face him. "Did you paint them?" she

asked bluntly.

A laugh burst from him, but it was nothing like the amused sound that had come from her back at his place. "Not a chance, as my brothers annoyingly would say. My brother Ry got all the artistic talent in the family."

"Then he did it?"

"No. Leatherwork is his thing. And he doesn't think he's an artist anyway."

"Then—"

"Well, hello!"

The cheerful greeting came from the hallway to the back sections of the house as his mother walked toward them. She was dressed in her usual tailored shirt and jeans, with the detailed belt Ry had made for her emphasizing her slim build. Her short, blond hair was a bit tousled even for her, and he guessed she must have been doing something that had her running her hands through it. Her dog Quinta was, as always, at her heels.

"I'm Margaret Rafferty." She held out her hand to Ariel, but not before giving him a sharp glance that reminded him that it had been his job to perform the introduction. "And this is Quinta," she added, gesturing at the dog.

"Ariel Larson," she said before he could speak, then added, "Hi, Quinta." The friendly dog's tail wagged.

"I heard from Cody someone was here."

Chance finally spoke. "She's here about Tri."

His mother's expression changed, became more serious.

JUSTINE DAVIS

"Are you now," she said softly, more a turn of phrase than a question. "He's a special one."

"Yes," Ariel said, the touch of tightness in her voice telling him she hadn't missed the sudden change in his mother's voice. She glanced at him, as if she expected him to explain further. He didn't. Funny, now that he was back in the main house, he felt his usual reticence enveloping him once more. Probably because he'd talked more in the hours since Ariel had arrived than he had in weeks. Maybe months. Now he felt as if he'd exhausted his quota of words spoken for the month. Hell, maybe into next year, since it was December.

It was strange, really. After a while it hadn't seemed like such an effort at all, to talk to her. It had to be simply that for the change he'd seen in Tri, he'd do a lot more than talk.

Chapter Twelve

"**I** WAS ADMIRING the painting," Ariel said rather nervously, feeling a bit...examined by the petite blonde with the pixie cut and the mottled gray dog beside her. The woman looked nothing like she would picture a mother to four adult sons. She was trim, obviously fit by the way she moved, and energetic. And her hand was no soft, pampered thing, but the capable hand of a woman who did. There were a few lines around her eyes, but the rest of her face was smooth and looked younger than Ariel knew she must be.

And now it was clear where the youngest brother, Cody, had gotten the blond hair, although not the green eyes, since this woman's were a clear blue. If the pictures she'd seen of Texas bluebonnets were for real, then their color was living in these eyes.

"It's beautiful, isn't it?" The woman looked at the painting as she said it softly, with great warmth, but her tone was tinged with something all too familiar to Ariel. Sadness. Chance's monosyllabic answers to her questions ran through her mind. And what she supposed should have been obvious struck her at last.

"Your husband painted it?" The woman's gaze shot to Chance in surprise. "He didn't tell me. I guessed from his reaction, and yours. And the painting in his house." Mrs. Rafferty looked back at her again. Ariel smiled sadly. "I know the feelings."

"She's Tri's handler's wife," Chance said quietly, his tone of respect soothing even as the present tense registered.

Everything seemed to change then. As if that had been some secret code phrase that opened a door. She knew about that door. She'd encountered it before, that entrance to the club no one wanted to join, that club of people who understood. And this woman definitely understood. There was no pain quite like the pain of losing a life partner, the spouse you were supposed to grow old with. That even after all this time it could still be so present, so raw, was both sad and achingly sweet. A glimpse of her own future?

For a moment silence spun out, as if there were no words that could be enough to acknowledge what they all knew, what they all had lost.

"I see," Mrs. Rafferty said softly. "Welcome to the Rafferty ranch, Mrs. Larson."

"Ariel, please."

"And I think you must call me Maggie."

Ariel managed a smile. "Thank you. Maggie." Ariel heard the sound of a door opening behind them, but didn't, couldn't look away from those understanding eyes. Even the dog seemed to have sensed the change, for she relaxed and plopped down on the rug on the floor.

Maggie glanced once more at her son, then she looked back to Ariel. "You've met Tri?" Ariel nodded. "How did it go?"

Not sure what to say, she looked at Chance with a raised brow. "Ask the expert," she said.

She half-expected him to say something noncommittal, because it was so early in the process, mere hours. And yet it felt to her as if it had been much longer, as if an eon had passed since the first moment she'd looked into his eyes.

But when he met his mother's gaze he gave a wondering shake of his head and said in a tone that matched, "He was a different dog. It was as if...he knew." A wry smile tugged at his mouth. "He came over the kennel fence to get to her."

Maggie's eyes widened. "Over the fence?"

Chance nodded. "And when we went inside he...ended up in her lap."

The woman's gaze shifted back to Ariel. She looked amazed. Then another voice—deep, male—spoke from behind her and she spun around, suddenly remembering that opening door sound from moments ago.

"Are we talking about the same dog I know?" The man's tone was incredulous, and Ariel realized just how bad Tri's situation must have been, for this to be such a shock to all of them.

The man had to be another brother. This one was maybe

a fraction taller than Chance, and his eyes were pure gray without the touch of blue Chance's had. His hair was black, longer than his close-cropped brother's. A bit wild, thick and with a couple of glossy strands falling forward over his forehead. Then she realized the wildness she'd linked to his hair was actually in the man himself. Chance moved with the controlled power of a trained athlete and looked like the warrior he'd been; his brother moved like a panther and looked more like a street fighter.

"The same," Chance said to his brother. Then, quickly, as if he was leery of his mother's critical look returning, he introduced them. "Ariel Larson, my brother Rylan."

The artistic talent. That surprised her. She hadn't really tried to picture the brother Chance had said that about, but if she had it wouldn't have been this…barely controlled energy.

"The leatherworker," she said as they shook hands. No hard clasp from him, but she still noticed his hands were as toughened as she imagined any ranch worker's would be.

"The artist of the family," Maggie said cheerfully. Rylan Rafferty scowled. And again, Ariel thought that if she'd run into him on the streets of Southern California, she'd have been wary. Admiring, but wary.

"I'm not an artist," he muttered.

But his mother went blithely on, not even looking at him. "As you can see by my belt."

Ariel looked at the intricately carved leather strip, her

eyes widening a little at the incredible details. Even from here she could see the images. A field of wildflowers, a horse running free, a dog at its heels… It seemed impossible he had rendered it so perfectly in such a narrow medium, but he had. She looked back at the new arrival.

"What," she asked carefully, "would you call it?"

"I'm a craftsman," he said, in the tone of one who'd said it countless times before.

"And a person can't be both?"

His gaze narrowed. "Some can. Not me. I just have a knack."

"Enough of one that two governors, a vice president, and a few celebrities have commissioned your work," his mother said.

Ariel's eyes widened as she glanced at Maggie. Then she looked back at the non-artist. "Then I'd say you've earned the right to call yourself whatever you want."

For an instant he looked startled. Then he smiled—a bright, flashing grin—and this time when she thought of him on some big-city street it was with a string of enraptured women gaping at him. "Okay. She can stay."

"Gee, thanks," she said, but she was fighting a smile as she said it.

His grin widened. Then he looked at his mother. "You still want that desk moved out?"

"Yes," she said quickly. "My new one should arrive to-morrow."

"Come on, then, bro, as long as you're already here," Rylan said, looking at Chance.

"So's Cody."

"You drew the short straw."

"Don't I usually?" Chance said dryly.

"Only because you're usually not here to grab a long one," Rylan said cheerfully. "Come on, we'll take it out the back and load it right onto my truck."

Chance gave Ariel a hesitant look. "Go ahead," she said.

"She can help me fix some lunch for you boys," Maggie said. "I presume that's why you're here, for some real food?" she added to Chance with an arched brow.

He muttered something, then started after his brother. He'd only gone a few steps when he looked back over his shoulder at her. She thought maybe he was nervous about what she might do.

"I'll stay away from Tri until you're done," she assured him.

He blinked. "Right," he said, but as he turned to follow his brother toward the back of the house, she had the oddest feeling it wasn't Tri he'd been thinking about, but leaving her alone with his mother.

"My boys," the woman beside her said, and there was such love in her voice that for a moment Ariel couldn't speak.

"It's nice," she finally managed to say, "that you've managed to keep everyone here, together."

"That's Keller's, my eldest's, doing as much as mine. He inherited his father's sense of responsibility, and stepped into those shoes at seventeen."

"So...he's a year older than Chance?"

The older woman nodded. "And Chance, on the other hand, inherited his sense of duty to his country, and followed in his footsteps."

Even though it had cost his father his life. She wasn't sure she could fully comprehend the thought process there. Dean had had his own reasons for joining up, but if he'd lost his father to the same calling, she couldn't imagine him doing it.

"And Rylan his artistic talent. Despite his denial?"

"Exactly. And Cody, he got his knack for technical details."

Ariel studied her for a moment. "So they all got part of him."

"Yes. They each honor him in their own way."

"That must be...both incredibly sweet and horribly painful."

"It is exactly that," Maggie agreed, and Ariel thought she saw approval in her gaze.

They went into the kitchen, and Maggie began to get out the makings for sandwiches. Rather massive ones, judging by the size of the rolls she began to slice. When she mentioned it, Maggie smiled. "We girls can split one, but those boys, they'll down a whole one without even thinking about it."

"Or putting on an ounce, no doubt," Ariel said wryly.

Maggie laughed. "No, they work too hard for that. This place doesn't run itself, and they all do their part, on top of their own things."

Ariel, in need of something to do, began to open the various condiment jars Maggie had set out. "That sounds like an awful lot of work."

"It is. But this place is their father's legacy. My family has been in Last Stand since the last stand, but their father's family was here even longer. Before the saloon even."

"The last stand?" Ariel asked.

Maggie smiled as she began to spread mustard and a white sauce Ariel didn't recognize on the bread. "Chance didn't warn you not to ask? I'm a bit of a history nut, and the Last Stand battle is my favorite story."

Ariel's eyes widened. "Battle? You mean it was an actual…that kind of last stand?"

"It was. During the revolution." A smile flashed. "The Texas Revolution, of course. A contingent of Santa Anna's army passed through, trying to take over the area. Everybody who could get there, took refuge in the only stone building around, the saloon."

"The saloon?" she asked with an amused smile.

"The very one that's still in operation today."

"And they fought them?"

"Stop by next time you're in town. The story is on a plaque out front. Between that and the statue of Asa Fuhrmann in front of the library, you've got the digest version."

She was fascinated, perhaps because this was distant enough in time to not remind her of her own loss. "When was this?"

Maggie had begun to layer thick slices of roast beef on the rolls, but she stopped and looked at Ariel. "Shortly after the Alamo."

Ariel went still. "So...they knew."

"What would happen if they lost? Yes, they knew. And they held. Many died in the fight, but just as many survived. And a lot of them decided since they'd fought for this little place and won, they might as well stay."

"Wow." She gave a small shake of her head. "I've never had that kind of connection to a place."

"It grows on you," Maggie said as she finished the second huge sandwich.

"No wonder you all stay."

"Keller stays because he loves the work. Rylan because we've worked out a way he can do both. Cody the same."

"And Chance?"

Maggie set down the knife before meeting Ariel's gaze. "He stayed because we begged him. And promised him the space he needed."

"For the dogs?"

"And himself." She seemed to hesitate, then sighed. "This is a tough time of year for all of us."

"I understand. He told me, that it was the day after

Christmas that…his father's body came home." Maggie stared at her, clearly surprised. Beyond what she might have expected at the subject. "For me it was the day before," she said, hoping the admission would ease whatever offense she'd caused with her apparently thoughtless statement.

"Chance told you that?"

Her brow furrowed. "Yes. When he was telling me about how he…refused to believe his father was really gone."

Maggie Rafferty's expression was nothing less than shocked now. Ariel didn't know what to say, because apparently she'd only made it worse. But then, slowly, the other woman smiled. A wide, delighted smile.

And Ariel could have sworn she whispered, "Hallelujah."

Chapter Thirteen

"**Y**OUR LADY'S HERE."

The yawn Chance had been in the middle of after picking up the landline phone receiver early the next morning died quietly at the sound of his older brother's words. He swallowed away the uncomfortable feeling in his throat. *Your lady.* No. No way. Don't even play with this, bro.

But he didn't say it. Because he knew Keller hadn't meant it that way, that it was just his mannerly way of speaking. He'd said the same thing when it had been Mrs. Yates, the older woman who'd adopted one of his first successes, a Labrador who'd been wounded in action. A sniffer who'd saved many by finding hidden explosives with his incredibly sensitive nose, the dog had been a nervous wreck. But Mrs. Yates had worked hard with him, and spoke convincingly of her quiet, calm life working from a home with a big yard. That had been nearly a year ago, and when he checked in on them, which he did regularly on his "graduates" as Mom called them, they were both so content it was obvious.

Just the word *content* brought his unusually rambling thoughts back to his brother. Keller was so damned cheerful all the time now. He didn't begrudge him the happiness Sydney had brought him because he'd earned it, the hard way, but all those good spirits got to be a little wearing. On him, anyway. It delighted his mother. Ry had accepted it with that one-step-back way that Chance guessed was part of that artist he insisted he wasn't, the part that observed rather than participated when it came to other people.

Even Cody, who had been pretty antagonistic toward Sydney in the beginning, not liking the idea of the major change she would bring to their lives, had warmed up to acceptance after Mom had had a little chat with him, and now he and Sydney joked together easily.

"You there, man?"

Keller's voice jolted him out of the uncharacteristic morass of thoughts. "Yeah. I'll be up to get her."

The interrupted yawn overtook him the moment he'd hung up. He'd had a rough night. Not quite sleepless, but he might have been better off if it had been. And he couldn't blame it all on Tri, although the dog had been so restless—pacing as best he could with his hopping gait—Chance had finally put him out in the kennel just for the quiet. He knew what the dog's problem was. It had been obvious. Tri hadn't wanted her to leave. Whereas he'd been nearly swamped with relief when her rental car finally pulled out the ranch gate yesterday.

He hadn't realized just how tense he'd been until she was gone. It had been a strange transition, since when she'd actually been in his house, he'd felt...not comfortable, really, but not crazily wired. Not the way he'd felt from the moment Mom and then Rylan had walked in at the big house, and he'd seen them both looking...he wasn't sure what. Speculative, maybe. Whatever it was, it had ratcheted up his nerves until he watched her drive away.

But what had calmed him had sent Tri into a near frenzy. He'd spent a lot of last night listening to the dog's restlessness. When he finally had drifted into an uneasy doze, he dreamed he woke up to find the dog gone, having escaped and run off to find the woman who had so captivated him. Which had segued into a dream about her, one that he was no doubt better off not remembering in much detail.

Telling himself it was because he needed to see how Tri reacted, and not because he wanted the buffer of the dog to focus on, he decided to take him along. He yanked on his lace-up boots, thinking not for the first time he needed to make the switch back to the worn cowboy boots that sat on the floor of his closet. And yet he never did. He was sure that said something about his mental state, but he didn't want to know what. Maybe he just didn't want to remember the days in uniform when his nickname had been Boots, because the wiseass in the unit had a thing about Texas and Texans.

Or, as Dean had suggested, was jealous of cowboys.

Take it as a point of pride, man. He couldn't fill your boots, cowboy or combat.

Tri was still pacing, when he got to the kennel. He was the only dog here at the moment; after a few successful herding experiments with Dodger, Keller had agreed to move the big German shepherd up to the kennel and run at the big house. That the dog had taken to his mother, Sydney and Quinta rather quickly—what was it with females and these traumatized dogs?—made Chance think maybe the dog wouldn't be going anywhere.

He snapped the heavy leather leash on Tri's collar.

"Come on, dog. Let's go get your…lady."

His mouth twisted ruefully as he used his brother's words without thought. Just as Keller had. *It's you who read into them, idiot.*

As if he'd understood, Tri jumped eagerly into the truck. Judging by the way the dog's nose was working, some trace of her scent must have lingered in the vehicle. Hell, he thought he caught a bit of it himself, that subtle perfume he'd noticed before, which reminded him of peach blossom season here in the Hill Country.

He drove slowly, telling himself it wasn't because he was reluctant. Then he laughed inwardly at himself, admitting he'd faced combat missions with less trepidation than this. Which was so absurd it brought on that self-directed scorn all over again.

As they crested the last hill before the long sweep down to the ranch house, he spotted the rental car parked where it had been yesterday. And realized he'd never asked where she was staying. He spent the last hundred yards of the drive trying not to think about what he was going to do if they reached the next stage of this process, the stage where she moved into the spare bedroom kept clear for that purpose. Mrs. Yates had been a surprising pleasure, a woman with a ready smile and a witty sense of humor, who insisting on cooking for them all the entire ten days she'd been under his roof. He guessed that dog had probably put on some much-needed pounds by now.

There was no sign of anyone outside. What there was a sign of was the season. He grimaced when he saw the wreath hanging on the door. He didn't remember exactly when Mom had gone back to decorating the house, only that when she said it was for Cody and Rylan's sakes, since they were still young, it had shut him up about it. The first year after Dad was killed they had taken a trip to the gulf coast, so no one had to deal with seeing the decorations Dad had always helped put up when he was home. And the next year Chance was already gone, and he'd spent the holiday in boot camp, rather stubbornly refusing to come home over the short break they'd been allowed.

But now she went nearly as full bore as ever; the wreath was just the start. There would be more inside, and soon a tree with all the trimmings. And they would pretend they liked it. Or at least, he would, for her sake. He had the feeling his brothers really did like it.

Before he even had the truck parked, Tri was on his feet, making that low whining sound again. As if he knew she was here. Chance parked and told the dog to stay—not that the animal had much choice, but it was the communication that was important—then got out and went up the three steps to the porch and front door. When he pushed it open a movement drew his gaze; Keller in the kitchen on the far side of the great room, pouring a cup of coffee. Something he hadn't taken the time for, but assuredly would now. It was Friday, Ry's day to start the brew, so it would be good and strong.

But before he was two steps inside a light, feminine laugh stopped him dead. With the door still blocking his view he couldn't see, but he'd heard it often enough to recognize it was Sydney. His gaze shot to Keller, who had also looked up at the sound. He was smiling, not just his mouth but his entire expression and demeanor. It was the same look their father had worn when looking at Mom. The same look Dean had worn, while reading a letter from his Red.

Something tightened in his chest. Damn it, he was happy for Keller. He deserved this, deserved someone who could make him feel that way. That it made Chance feel a bit more lost was his problem, not his brother's.

He took the last step clear of the door, and turned purposefully to close it, putting his back to the room to buy an extra second or two. When he couldn't stall any longer without it being obvious, he turned around.

Ariel was getting to her feet, standing in that smooth, flowing way she had. She was smiling, he guessed at whatever Sydney had been laughing about.

"Good morning," she said.

Damn. Her voice really was that…that…

"Hey, Chance," Sydney said cheerfully, her unusual golden eyes practically twinkling. "Ariel was just telling me about Tri actually clearing the kennel fence. Amazing."

"Yes," he said. "He's a tough boy."

"Just like you," she retorted, her sweet tone taking any sting out of it. His gaze flicked to Ariel, but she was looking at Sydney. And before he could decide if she was purposely avoiding him, his brother's irrepressible fiancée was speaking again, now to Ariel. "You'll be here long enough to meet Lucas today, won't you? He'll be thrilled to see you and Tri together, if it's going as well as you say."

"I plan to spend the day with Tri, yes," she said, and then, at last, she looked at Chance. "At least, I assume that's the plan?"

"Yes," he answered. And if it came out a little gruffly, no one seemed to notice. But then, Cody often joked he always sounded like a bear coming out of hibernation anyway.

"Did you bring him?" she asked, almost anxiously.

"Yes." It came out better that time. And then, because of the emotion in her voice—for now, at least, she was utterly dedicated to this—he added, "He hasn't relaxed since you left." *Neither have I.*

It took him a moment to be sure he hadn't voiced that idiocy out loud. And then she smiled, her eyes lit up with obvious happiness, and he couldn't think of anything else except the crazy leap his pulse took.

She's been through hell. So of course you're glad to see her look happy. That's all it is.

Self-lecture completed, he was ready to get out of here.

She beat him to the front door, racing to the truck, where Tri had climbed into the driver's seat and was already trying to come through the window to greet her. Chance wasn't sure how he'd done it, but it had probably seemed like nothing after clawing his way over the kennel fence with only one front leg. They didn't call them Maligators for nothing.

As always, whenever the part-admiring, part-rueful, part-laughing nickname went through his mind, so did the memory of Hondo. And as always, he sent a silent salute to his beloved partner, before gently sending the memory back into the compartment where he kept it. Because all he could do for Hondo now was see to his canine brothers. And none of them deserved his efforts more than Tri.

That had to be his focus. Just because he wasn't used to having to think so hard about focusing was no excuse not to.

Okay, so the self-lecture hadn't been quite over.

Chapter Fourteen

"SYDNEY SEEMS REALLY nice," Ariel said as they got in the truck to make the drive back to Chance's house.

"She is."

"So does your brother."

"Keller is...the best."

That made her smile. "They seem very happy together."

"They are." As if it were a great effort to go on, he added in that rather gruff tone she hadn't quite figured out yet, "I think they'll make it."

Tri nosed her from the back seat again, and she turned back to the dog to pet him some more. She hoped he never got over wanting that, even when he was sure of her, because it helped her as well.

When she looked back at Chance his expression had softened, as if seeing Tri reaching out to her had had the same warming effect on him. It probably had; you didn't pour your heart and soul into this rescue work as he had if you didn't care a great deal.

He started the engine but didn't yet put it in gear. Instead he looked at her. "If you're up for it, I'd like to go into the enclosure with him."

"The enclosure?"

"Behind the house. It's about five fenced acres—" he glanced at Tri "—with an angled topper that should keep even this guy inside."

"You sure?" she asked jokingly.

"It has. And it better," he amended with a grimace. "I don't want to think about what would happen if he did get out. He's still too unreliable."

She didn't want to think about it either, what would happen if the traumatized warrior dog slipped free. What might have to be done if they lost control of him.

"He'd come to you if ordered, wouldn't he?" she asked, more than a little anxiously.

"He always has. But I've sometimes had the feeling it was…iffy." He gave her a sideways look. "But that's what I want to see, what he'll do if let off leash, with you there."

"Okay." She felt heartened by the inference that he thought—and she hoped—that something different than the usual would happen.

As they started to move, she spotted a rider—Keller, she saw—coming out of the barn, on a dark horse that oddly seemed almost bluish in the sunlight. Chance saw her notice and looked.

"Starting work?" she asked.

"More likely restarting. He's probably already done more today than most men do all day."

"Surely he can't do all the ranch work?"

"No. We've got a few hands to help, and we all pitch in when necessary, but he's the boss—under Mom, of course. She's the final say, and she works as hard as any of us."

She liked the way he said that. And now having met the livewire woman that was Maggie Rafferty, she believed it.

She was distracted again as they passed a small corral, where a dark gold horse with a black mane and tail stood with an adorable miniature version of...herself, she assumed, for it certainly looked like a momma and her baby. She exclaimed in delight as the little one romped along the fence, watching them.

"How sweet!"

He glanced over. "That's Bonnie—Texas Bluebonnet, formally—and Two."

"Two?"

"He looks exactly like his great-grandsire, Buckshot. So he's Buckshot Two."

She laughed, although she thought she heard an undertone in his voice that told her there was more to that story. Then she looked back at the horses, the romping colt. "He's having such fun."

"It won't last," Chance said. When she looked at him curiously, he said, "He's coming up on six months old. Time to be weaned."

"Oh." She made a face. "Sounds scary, for him."

"Keller believes in waiting longer than a lot of people do,

until the foal starts showing signs of independence on its own. Some start the process up to six weeks earlier."

"His way sounds kinder."

"Keller loves horses. He wants to do what's right for them, even if it means slowing things down."

"Kind of like you and this guy, huh?" she said, petting Tri again.

He blinked, gave her a sideways look. "What?"

"Sydney told me you were down to just this guy right now, because he needed all your attention."

"I had Dodger, a German shepherd, up until last week," he said. "But he's turned into quite the herding dog, and gets along with Mom's Aussie, so I think they may be keeping him."

"That's good, isn't it?"

"For him, yes. This is a good place for a dog."

"That's obvious. I'd know that just from seeing your mother's dog."

He smiled at that, and her breath caught. He might not smile often, but when he did, the impact was breath-stealing. "She's another descendent. We've had one of her line on the ranch for about twenty-five years. She's the fifth generation."

"Wow, that's—Wait. Fifth? As in…Quinta?"

"Picked up on that, huh?"

"Almost anybody who grew up in San Diego would know that much Spanish," she retorted.

"At least we name them. Some people just stick with

'dog.' Or 'the buckskin,' and think we're soft."

"I have a feeling I wouldn't like those people much."

"We do stop short of naming every cow on the ranch, though," he said, as seriously as if they were discussing historic traditions.

"That would be a lot of names," she said, making her tone just as serious.

"It would." She truly could not tell if he was joking or not.

When they pulled to a halt back at his place, she heard a whinnied greeting from the corral close to the house.

"Your horse is pretty," she said as the light golden animal bobbed its head at them.

He shrugged. "I like him anyway."

He said it with such a straight face and even tone she still wasn't sure he was joking. But then he flashed her a look, and she was certain she'd seen one corner of his mouth twitching. And it hit her suddenly that, underneath the solemn, sometimes even grim demeanor, Chance Rafferty had a sense of humor. The subtle kind that she liked. And he had been bantering with her all along. She couldn't help smiling, and then it became a grin. And it felt so strange.

As if her change in expression had been a trigger, he raised his brows and added, "Besides, I'm rescuing my baby brother from the horrible fate of having to ride a horse that's as pretty as he is."

The image of the youngest Rafferty flashed through her

mind, and she remembered how she'd thought that he and the palomino did share similar blond good looks. And she found herself laughing. And realized with a little jolt of shock that she'd probably laughed more frequently since she'd arrived here than she had in…two years. Here she was, on this intense—to her at least—mission, and she was laughing.

"I don't know," she said casually. "You're kind of pretty yourself."

She couldn't quite believe she'd said that. He looked completely disconcerted. Shocked. Even stunned. Which made no sense to her; despite everything, she still recognized a good-looking man when she saw one. And since she tended to like men who were, as her mother put it, decidedly male, this one definitely qualified.

Not that she was at all looking. No, that part of her had been buried two years ago. She'd never even been out for coffee unless it was business, and had no desire to change that. Or anything else. She wasn't sure she was even capable of genuine desire, for anything, anymore. Except Tri.

And that's what she should be focused on. Not having these crazy, unexpected thoughts about things she'd shelved long ago.

Deciding to save him from reacting to her ill-advised comment she opened the truck's door and slid out. Tri let out a low sound that was half whine, half eager yip. She wanted to let him out, but she didn't want to violate the rules Chance had set and risk him calling a halt to the process. Besides, she realized he knew what he was doing, and already had faith he would always do what was best for the dogs he was trying to help.

It had never occurred to her until now that maybe she might not be the best for Tri. She'd been so full of need to do this and wanting to lavish what love and emotion she had left in her on this brave creature who had been maimed trying to save Dean, that she hadn't thought twice about coming here. And when the dog had greeted her as he had, confidence that this would work had ballooned inside her. But Chance was being careful, very careful, and she wondered if he'd had others who had started out so well but turned sour.

She would not let that happen. She could not.

And she'd do whatever that took.

Chapter Fifteen

C HANCE HAD BEEN so startled by her comment that he was still speechless as they walked toward the gate in the enclosure fence. And when she paused to pat the horse's outstretched head—without the familiarity of someone used to horses, but also without fear—it gave him the strangest feeling.

You're kind of pretty yourself...

He'd been called many things in his life, but he didn't think pretty had ever been one of them.

Because he couldn't think of anything else to say as he watched her stroke the genial palomino's nose, he asked, "Do you ride?"

"No." She didn't look at him, and he wondered if she was sorry she'd said what she'd said. Even though it had to have been a joke. "I've always thought horses beautiful, but never had the chance to learn." She did look then, but her expression was neutral. "I half expected you to come riding up to the house this morning."

"Couldn't have brought Tri," he explained, gesturing at the dog who was sitting near her feet, looking up at her expectantly. "Can't trust yet that he wouldn't take off. And besides, then I'd have to borrow a vehicle. Or a horse, and you'd have had to ride out here."

"Well, that would probably provide your laugh for the day," she said dryly.

"I can't imagine laughing at you," he said, and instantly wished he hadn't. "With you, yes, but not at you," he amended, and it sounded lame to his ears.

"You Texas boys really are gentlemen, aren't you?"

He gave her a sideways glance. "You say that like you can't decide if it's good or bad."

"How about good but unfamiliar?"

"Sorry to hear that." *But not surprised.*

She didn't answer, just watched as he reached to unlatch the gate. Then she said, "That's a big space."

"Thanks to Sydney," he said.

She blinked. "Sydney?"

"Her company made the donation that let me finish the fence."

"Oh. Wow." She looked at the long line of fence. "That must have been a heck of a donation."

"It was." Credit where it was due; Sydney had seen the need and acted. "She did it anonymously at the time, since she and Keller were...at odds then."

"Obviously resolved since," she said.

He nodded. Then said, "Let's give this a shot."

He swung the gate open. Tri leapt to his feet. "He looks

excited," she said.

"He knows he gets to run. His gait's been hampered, but once he healed his energy level got back to normal."

"It's amazing how well he gets around."

"He never stops trying. Which is why Lucas picked his name."

"Your brother and Sydney are a good match, her with big donations and him taking in a foster child." They stepped through the gate before he looked at her.

"Lucas is also her cousin." Her eyes widened, and he shrugged. "A long story."

Once the gate was closed behind them, he bent to unfasten Tri's leash. And watched as the dog, as usual, fairly trembled waiting to be cut loose. The moment the leash was off, the dog dashed, with his characteristic off-center, hopping run. And then, abruptly, he stopped, wobbling a little as he spun back on his hind legs. He looked back at them both, then focused on Ariel.

"Move forward a few feet, then stop," Chance said, his gaze fixed on Tri.

She didn't question him, just did it. The dog turned back, and moved forward almost the exact same distance, then paused to look back at her. They repeated the pattern, three more times.

"This is…different?" she finally asked.

"Yes. It's harder for him to go slow, actually, so he usually just takes off, and I have to watch the time and reel him in. The missing leg puts all the pressure on the remaining one, and it would be easy for him to strain a muscle or develop arthritis down the road."

"It must have messed up his balance horribly."

"It took him a while to adapt. Me, too. I'd never handled a tripod before. We both had a lot to learn."

She gave him a look he couldn't interpret. Which seemed to happen a lot with her. Or maybe he was just out of practice, given how much he avoided people. At least, according to his mother he did.

"He seems to be doing well now," she finally said, back to watching the dog.

"He generally does okay outdoors, as long as he has traction. It's indoors that's the problem. With only the one front leg, if he slips, he can't catch himself."

She turned her gaze from the dog back to him. "All the rugs in your house," she said in a tone of realization. "I wondered, but they're for him, aren't they?"

He nodded. "The wood floor is too slick for him, if he moves too fast."

She stared at him for a long moment, and he had no idea what she was thinking. Then Tri gave a little yip, drawing their attention back to the matter at hand. They started to walk, and this time kept going. And the dog maintained that same distance, ahead, investigating what caught his nose's interest, but never more than those few feet away, as if he were still on a leash, albeit a longer one.

Chance knew that leash was the woman beside him.

THEY LET TRI lead the way, as he investigated everything around him, but always looking back and seemingly gauging the distance between them. Another glance at Chance told Ariel he still had that slight smile on his face as he watched the dog. He was…happy about this, it seemed. That had to be a good sign, didn't it?

She'd wondered if he was the kind of person who would take offense if the dog kept responding to her as he didn't to him. The more she'd seen of what he was doing here, how much he cared, the more she'd doubted he could be that sort. And now she was sure.

The man had put down throw rugs practically wall to wall in his house, in a ridiculous patchwork, all for the sake of this dog.

They walked on in silence, watching the dog. Blessed silence. Which she then broke. "You know what I like best about being here?" He gave her a look that seemed to say he was afraid to ask. "No Christmas music," she said.

His smile dawned slowly but sweetly, and he let out a chuckle. "I know the feeling."

"I love the inn I'm at, but between the music and the decorations…"

"I wondered where you were staying."

"I found a place that's out on a nice stream, southwest of

town."

"The Hickory Creek Inn."

"Yes. It's run by a former Texas Ranger and his wife, I gather."

"Frank and Karina Buckley. They're good people."

"And good innkeepers. There was a lovely welcome basket in the room, with some amazing cookies," she said, turning her attention back to Tri, who seemed to be maintaining that distance between them with a rather surprising exactitude.

"He's pretty precise about how far he gets ahead," Chance said, surprising her as he spoke her own thought.

"Yes. It's fascinating."

It made it…almost comfortable, to have that to concentrate on. At least her mind wasn't racing off in crazy directions as long as she was focused on the reason she was here at all. Which was the dog in front of her, not the man beside her.

The man beside her.

That sounded so wrong, even in her head, when it wasn't Dean.

That triggered another memory, one she'd managed to keep buried for a long time.

"You all right? Do you need to stop?"

The concern in his voice was both warming and irritating; did he really think she couldn't manage a fifteen-minute walk? Then she realized when that memory had hit her expression must have changed noticeably.

"I'm fine. I'd be better if I could quit remembering people I'm better off without."

"Lot of those out there," he said neutrally, and for a moment she wondered if he'd thought she'd meant him. On the off chance, she decided she'd better explain.

"I just thought of one of them. My…friend, Alexandra."

"As in former, I gather?"

"Very." She drew in a breath, then went on. "Three months after Dean was killed, she came to see me. To give me a lecture and tell me it was time to get over it, and start going out again, start dating."

He stopped in his tracks. "Three months? What did you tell her?"

She stopped as well and looked into those blue-gray eyes. "I told her," she said flatly, "to come back when her husband was dead, and then we'd talk. Needless to say, I haven't seen her since."

He gave an approving nod and said, "Good for you." Of course he understood. She'd known he would. "Get over it," he muttered, in a tone of disgust. "As if you could."

"They don't understand," she said, nodding toward Tri, who had again stopped when they had, "what it's like. As if a crucial part of you has been torn away, and your life will never, ever be the same."

"They don't know how lucky they are," he said, sounding a little hoarse now. "No wonder you were mad."

"I wasn't, really. Just sad. Hurt." She grimaced. "I seem to have lost the capacity to get mad."

He started to speak, stopped, then started again, and this time got it out. "Dean said once that he loved arguing with you. Even when he lost."

Startled, she stopped in her tracks again. And being that gentleman she'd referred to before, so did he. As did Tri, although the dog looked more puzzled than anything at why they kept stopping.

"We had some good fights." *And God, the making up...* "But now...it's like my temper died when he did," she ended in a whisper. "I don't care about anything enough to get mad anymore."

She felt the old, familiar moisture begin to pool in her eyes. She tried to fight it, blinking rapidly. She wanted to run away, to hide somewhere until she got past this. She didn't want to break down into a blubbering fool in front of this man who held in his hands the future of the only bit of her husband she had left, this wounded animal he had loved and who had tried to save him. The dog who even now had come back to her, sitting at her feet as he looked up at her almost anxiously.

But she had nowhere to go, not out here in the wild Texas hills, where even his small house was now out of sight behind a rise. It was true it happened less often now than the hourly occurrence it had once been, and she could even fight it off sometimes, at least postponing the breakdown, but she had no more control over it once it started than she ever had. And she never, ever felt more alone than in those moments.

But suddenly a warm, strong pair of arms came around her, and she was pulled gently against a broad chest. Her first thought was to pull away, this wasn't Dean...but it was someone who'd been his friend, who just wanted to comfort, and right now that was a luxury she couldn't turn away from. And so she let Chance Rafferty hold her, if for no other reason than it stopped her shaking and eased the horrible tightness in her chest.

So for that moment, she allowed herself the refuge of human contact.

Chapter Sixteen

H E HADN'T MEANT to do it. If he'd thought, he would
have discarded the idea instantly. But he hadn't. He
hadn't thought at all. He'd just been unable to simply stand
there in the face of her obvious pain and do…nothing.

He should have just turned his back. Let her have a few
moments to get herself in hand. Because she could, he had
no doubt, after two years of living with her loss. She'd shown
that by the way she'd been since she'd gotten here. But he'd
never been able to turn his back on a dog in pain, so why did
he think he could have done it with her?

He just hadn't expected the consequences. How warm
she was. How good she smelled—that sweet scent that
reminded him of peaches, and that Tri had apparently
remembered. How well she fit. How despite her slenderness
he could feel the curves of her.

How right it felt.

How could it feel right if it was so very wrong, not just
for him to be holding her like this, but liking it?

His jaw tightened as he fought down his physical response. He'd definitely left it too long if simply holding a

woman could do this to him. Especially when it was not simply an upset, teary-eyed woman, but the widow of a man he'd known, liked, and respected. A man whose maimed canine partner was even now at their feet, letting out a whimper such as Chance had never heard from him before.

Some respect, Rafferty. Getting a hard-on over Dean's Red is a lousy sign of your regard for him.

If she just wouldn't lean into him like that, it would be easier. If she didn't smell so good. If she didn't have those big, clear blue eyes. If she didn't have that sweet, pink mouth. If she didn't have that beautiful hair that looked as if it would warm his fingers if he touched it. If, if, if…

And then she moved, putting a hand flat against his chest. For a moment, just a moment, it stayed there, her fingers flexing. He stopped breathing. It didn't mean what it felt like. A caress. It couldn't.

And then he felt the pressure as she pushed against him, not pushing him away as much as leveraging herself away. He released her instantly. And when she stepped back he started to breathe again, while wondering if with her palm against his chest she'd felt the leap his heart had taken at her touch.

You are totally f'd up and out of line, Rafferty. Get a grip.

He wasn't altogether certain he could follow that mental order.

"I'm…fine now." Her rather shaky voice belied the words, but even as he thought it her chin came up and he heard her take in a steadying breath. "That was kind of you. Thank you."

Kind? She wouldn't think he was kind if she knew where his mind...well, not his mind so much as his suddenly unruly body had gone.

She saved him from having to come up with a response he didn't have when she crouched down to pet Tri. "Thank you for worrying, my boy. But I'm all right. It was just one of those moments. You probably have them too, don't you, when you remember him?"

Those words did what all his self-criticisms hadn't been able to, and he was back in control. So when she straightened again, he got back to the matter at hand almost easily.

"He never got more than fifteen feet ahead of you," he said.

"Or you," she pointed out as she straightened.

He shook his head. "It was you he came back to. When he realized you were...upset."

"I...yes." She gave him a sideways glance. "I am sorry about that, I—"

She stopped when he held up a hand, shaking his head. "Sometimes we can't control when it hits."

For a moment she just looked at him, with those sky-blue eyes that, just now, seemed to see right through him. "You're quite something, Mr. Rafferty."

"Something, anyway," he muttered.

They continued the lengthy walk, until he noticed something and called a halt. "He needs a break," he said.

She looked from the dog to him and back. "How can you tell? I mean, he's panting, but he has been for a while. What changed?"

So she'd noticed that at least. "Watch where his tongue is. Like on a clock face. Between five and seven, he's okay. Could be he's just excited or stressed, if it's not hot out. If it's heading toward four, or eight on the other side, like now, he needs a break."

She nodded, this time without looking at him, just studying Tri. "And if it goes further?"

"That tongue hits three or nine o'clock, everything stops. Never hit that with him, thankfully. You just have to remember he has to work harder at everything now. But because he'll never quit, you have to watch that for him."

She nodded again, gave the dog a smile while saying, "It must be so hard for you, my sweet boy, to not be able to do what you used to."

Chance smiled slightly. And she called him kind? "I'm not sure he thinks of it that way. He just keeps trying."

"So the name truly is appropriate."

"Yes."

They stopped near the base of a small oak. Tri plopped down almost instantly. And then Ariel dropped down beside him, clearly not caring about the dirt, or caring about the dog more. That, he thought as he watched her again start to pet the tired dog, he'd buy. He sat down as well, although on the other side of Tri, a safe distance away from her. If there was such a thing. But he pulled the small, flat canteen he always carried for the dog out of the leg pocket on his camo pants, and unsnapped the attached dish and poured some water into it. The dog lapped at it immediately, but didn't down it all, so he figured he'd called the halt in time.

"Good idea. I'll have to get one of those."

"Mmm," he said, thinking it safer to avoid actual words when possible.

She studied him for a silent moment. Long enough for him to brace himself; he was already learning to be wary when that happened. "Is it all right with you if I stay to meet Lucas? I'd like to thank him for picking such a good name."

"Not my call," he said, glad it was something neutral.

"He won't mind? Lucas, I mean?"

His mouth quirked wryly. And he spared a thought for Keller for the time, thankfully still a bit in the future, when the appearance of a visitor who looked like Ariel would make the boy do anything but mind.

"He manages to put up with me," he said before his thoughts could derail into that danger zone again.

"Put up with you?"

"They all do." He shrugged. "Family. They're kind of stuck with me."

She tilted her head slightly, in an assessing way he found a little disconcerting. "And that's why they put up with you, because they're stuck? Not because they love you?"

He stared at her. That had gone south on him in a hurry. Before he could think of a thing to say she went back to Tri. And he decided saying nothing was the best course.

When the dog seemed rested enough, they got up. About three minutes into the walk back to the house, she gave him that tilted-head look again. Grabbing at any diversion he could think of, he asked, "What did you put on hold back in San Diego?"

"Nothing, really. I pretty much cleared my calendar. I handed a couple of Christmas functions and a charity auction off to people I trust. I still have a wedding to plan, but it's not until September so we're only just beginning."

He blinked. "You're beginning now to plan a wedding that's over nine months away?"

She smiled at that, although he thought she might have rolled her eyes a little. "Big society blowout. The number for the guest list has a comma."

He drew back at that. It wasn't that he didn't realize there were people who went for that, he'd just never thought about what went in to the actual planning of such an under-taking.

"I think I'd rather plan a small invasion," he muttered.

"And I don't doubt you could," she said simply. "Per-sonally, I rather enjoy organizing good times for people."

He didn't know what made him say it, but the words were out before he could—as he would have if he'd thought—stop them. "What about good times for yourself?"

For the first time, she dodged his gaze. In a tone that was light, yet sounded a little forced, she said, "Not on the agenda."

I know the feeling.

It wasn't until she gave him another of those sideways looks and said, "I figured you would," that he realized he'd spoken the words aloud.

They kept walking, Tri staying even closer now, although Chance wasn't sure if it was because he was tired, or because of the upset the dog had sensed in Ariel.

What he was sure of was that he was going to keep his hands to himself and his damned mouth shut.

Chapter Seventeen

"WOW, HE'S ACTING different!"

Ariel looked at the boy who was petting Tri. Lucas had arrived a couple of hours after they'd come back from the long hike. He'd ridden in astride a reddish-brown horse with a black mane and tail, looking fairly at home in the saddle, although not the ease she'd seen in Keller. He had the thin, gangly look of a kid growing fast, dark hair that kicked up in a cowlick at the back, and dark brown eyes that at the moment were echoing his smile.

"That's good, isn't it?" the boy asked Chance.

"It is," Chance agreed.

Those dark eyes shifted to study her for a moment. "Keller and Sydney told me you were married to his person, before he was killed."

"I was," she answered quietly.

"Sucks," the boy said bluntly. And she appreciated the bluntness as she had from Chance; she'd had enough sugarcoated platitudes to last a lifetime. And from what Sydney had told her, the kid understood all too well about death and platitudes that didn't change anything.

"Yes. Totally."

The boy looked back at the dog, then came back to her. "It's like he knows," he said. His gaze shifted to Chance. "Do you think he does?"

She didn't miss that the kid, who had been through so much, wanted Chance's opinion. Nor had she missed the easy way he'd mentioned Keller and Sydney. And together, as if he already saw them as a unit. For all life had thrown at him, the boy had landed in a good place here. And she had the feeling he knew it. This was a family who understood the kind of grief the boy was dealing with.

And the kind you're dealing with?

She silently answered her own question. Yes, they did. The forever kind. And it relieved a little of her stress to see the life Maggie Rafferty in particular had built here. And the four sons she had also had a large part in building into the obviously solid men they were.

"I think he senses there's a connection," Chance answered the boy seriously. "He's already looking out for her."

Lucas looked back at Ariel. "Are you going to take him home with you?"

"That's the plan," she said. With a glance at the man she added, "Assuming Chance doesn't see a reason to say no."

The boy nodded, clearly accepting who had the final say. "He's fair," he assured her. "He'll do what's best for Tri."

She smiled. "That's what matters most."

Lucas smiled at her, clearly liking that answer. "I'll miss

him, but it's more important that he's happy." She didn't think she was wrong in feeling that the boy was likening the dog's situation to his own. "Chance taught me that," he added, with a glance and a smile at the man he clearly respected.

"It is the most important," she agreed.

Then he shifted his gaze back to Chance. "Your mom said to ask if you're coming tonight."

"Tonight? Wha—" Chance broke off, grimaced, apparently realizing what the boy was talking about. "No."

Lucas only shrugged. "That's what she said you'd say, but to ask anyway." The boy hesitated, but then said, "I think she keeps hoping you'll change your mind."

"So she sent you, because you're harder to say no to?"

Lucas grinned suddenly. "Am I?"

"Like you don't know that."

To her shock, Chance grinned back at the boy as he said it. And it was overpowering. It changed everything about him, even made a completely unexpected dimple flash at the right side of his mouth—that mouth—and lit up those blue-gray eyes. He'd been attractive in a very masculine, quietly confident way before, but that grin put him in an entirely different category.

"She made that chicken and egg thing for dinner. She said she'll leave some in the fridge." He glanced at Ariel again. "Enough for both of you, if you're staying," he added politely. Those Texas manners obviously started young.

After the boy had mounted up and headed back to the big house, she sat down on the front step of the house next to Tri. Then she looked up at Chance. The more somber expression was back now, but she didn't think she would ever in her life forget the moment when that grin had flashed.

She looked back to the boy riding away. "Clearly he feels like he belongs here."

"He does belong here." He sat down on the other side of Tri. "And he believes it now, thanks to Keller and Sydney."

"And you," she said. He only shrugged. Again. "He seems like a good kid."

"He is."

"What's tonight?"

His mouth twisted wryly. "The Christmas tree lighting in town. In front of the library. Big tree, big crowd, big deal." He hesitated, then added, "I'll give you directions, if you want to go."

She intentionally shuddered visibly. "Heavens no." Then, curious, she asked, "Your family, they all go?"

"Yeah. Mom really pushed it, for the younger kids, starting a couple of years after Dad was KIA. I was gone by then, so I managed to avoid it."

"And now?"

"They all still go. But I'm the Grinch of the family. Sorry."

"Don't apologize. I'm the Grinch of mine, too."

"It's for kids, mostly, anyway," he said.

Kids. She looked off to where she could just see Lucas and his horse topping the hill above the main house. And suddenly the memories were there again, vivid, swamping. "We...were going to. Start a family, I mean. We'd put it off, because he didn't want me to have to deal by myself so much of the time. But this time, when he got back...I was turning thirty, and we'd decided it was time."

Lucas had disappeared down the far side of the hill, and she snapped back to reality. And was aghast that she'd again voiced those thoughts. Chance was staring down at Tri, probably as embarrassed as she was.

"Sorry," she muttered. "Don't know why that came pouring out."

"It needed to?" he suggested.

"Maybe." She grimaced, still unable to look at him. "I can't say it to my family, because..." She stopped before she said more that she'd regret.

"Because they'd start nagging you about getting out, meeting someone, relationships, ad infinitum, ad nauseam?"

Her head snapped around then. She knew she was probably gaping at him, but he'd used her exact words, when she thought about the subject.

"Exactly. Exactly that. Down to the Latin."

"Yeah," he muttered, in a tone of too much experience with the same pressure. "Been getting that a lot, especially since Keller and Sydney connected. I'm the next up, it seems.

In my mother's view, anyway."

"My mother only brings it up a couple of times. A day. And no amount of telling her it's not happening stops her."

"Why do you think I stay away from the main house?" he said dryly.

She couldn't help the smiling little laugh that escaped her. And again thought of how often that happened around him. "I understand why with me, I'm not ready. Why is it for you?"

"No woman in her right mind would want to take me on," he said, still in that dry tone. She doubted that; he could probably have them lined up if he wanted. "Let alone all this—" he gestured at the hills around them, which made it seem they were alone in the world "—isolation."

"Some might find that an attraction," she said, thinking she might be one of them.

He gave a slow shake of his head. "I can go for days without seeing another human. Never met a woman who'd go for that. Besides, I'm not...a loving kind of guy."

She couldn't help it, she let out a snort of disbelief. He looked startled. She waved at Tri, then at the kennels beside the house. "You can't tell me you don't do this out of love."

"I...that's different. It's the dogs. They do their best for us, so they deserve the best I've got. Such as it is."

She wondered if it was simple self-deprecation, or if he really felt he had so little to give. The memory of when he'd held her, comforted her, rose up with a fierce insistence, so strong she could feel the heat of him, the power of him, the pure male strength that he'd loaned to her in her moment of need. That was not the action of a man who didn't—or couldn't—care.

She realized she'd curled up the fingers of her right hand until her nails were digging into her palm. The hand she'd let linger on his chest just that moment too long, long enough to send a little thrill of tingling sensation along her nerves.

He was so strong, so solid, and it had felt so good to have his arms around her. But it had only been meant as comfort, as any man raised as he had been would offer, especially to the widow of a friend. She was the one who'd gone haywire. She'd only meant to signal that he could let go now, that she would be all right, but somehow that brief touch had awakened something in her that had been dormant for so long she barely recognized it.

She'd hoped he hadn't realized. But she doubted that, now. Because she suddenly understood that his comment about not being a loving kind of guy could have been something besides an explanation.

It could have been a warning.

Chapter Eighteen

THE THIRD TIME his stomach growled audibly, Chance gave in and suggested they go for that meal Lucas had mentioned. "They'll be on their way by now, so the house'll be empty for Tri."

Not to mention her rental car was there, and she could head out when they were done. He'd had about as much as he could take of...whatever this tangle of feelings he'd developed was.

"What about your mother's dog?" she asked as Tri hopped into the truck once more.

"They get along fine. As far as I can tell she's in the 'not a threat' category for him. But I'm sure Quinta's with them tonight anyway. She's popular in town. She has perfect manners."

"Your mother seems to instill that," she said as he held the door, waiting for her to get into the truck.

"She did. Too bad the cooking skills didn't take."

"Meaning the chicken and egg thing?" she asked as she got in herself, obviously quoting Lucas's description. "What is it?"

Chance lifted a brow at her. "Worth the trip and the time," he promised, then shut the passenger door and walked around to the driver's side.

When they got there, he tried to ignore that she'd gone over to study the painting on the wall again. Tried not to wonder what she was thinking. Tried not to think himself, about how he never, ever spent this much time trying to figure someone out, beyond whether or not they were a good match for the dog they were here for.

On that question, he was already half-convinced. Not just that she might be a good match for Tri, but that she might be the only match. But he couldn't and wouldn't commit to that until he was certain, for Tri's sake. No matter how much he might want her to take her unsettling self on out of here. No matter how strange it felt to be here alone with her, about to sit down to a dinner together. Because no matter how he tried to convince himself this was no different than the meals he'd had with kindly Mrs. Yates, he knew better.

"This," Ariel said at her first bite of his mom's concoction, "wasn't just worth the trip from your place, it was worth the trip from San Diego."

He couldn't help smiling at that. "I'll tell Mom. She'll be pleased."

"What is it called, really?"

"I don't know. It's got some fancy name, maybe Italian, but Dad always called it 'that chicken and egg thing,' so that's what it is."

She took another bite, clearly savoring. "It doesn't need a fancy name," she said. "It's simply wonderful."

That was pretty much the universal opinion of anyone who tried it, but somehow coming from her it seemed…more meaningful. He really would tell Mom, first chance he got. Of course, maybe it was just him it seemed more meaningful to. And wouldn't Mom just love to have that idea to run with? So maybe not.

He'd found a pitcher of cocoa in the fridge as well, with a sticky note on it saying, in Sydney's distinctive hand, "Help yourself!" So after they'd eaten, he heated up enough for a couple of mugs, handed one to Ariel, and watched as she took her first sip.

Her eyes widened. "Wow."

"Yeah. Sydney's brew."

"Cinnamon I get, and something else spicy?"

"No idea. She learned it somewhere in her many travels."

"I looked up her company's website after I met her. What a life she's had," Ariel said after another long sip. "It's amazing—"

She stopped at a muffled sound, and he was so unused to it that it startled him in the instant before he realized it was his cell phone.

"Keep forgetting they get a good signal here," he muttered as he pulled it out. He glanced at the screen, frowned, said a quick "excuse me" to Ariel, and answered.

"Mom?"

"Oh, good. I hoped you had your phone on you, since you didn't answer at your place."

She'd tried both? That implied some urgency. "You okay?"

"I'm fine. But my car's not."

He frowned again. "What's wrong with it?"

"The battery, probably. We came back to get something, and the interior lights didn't come on, so I tried to start it and not even a click."

"No trouble before this?"

"Maybe. Anyway, Keller and Sydney and Ry headed for the saloon before the lighting. And Cody's off with Sean Highwater somewhere, probably rewiring the entire town for higher speed internet or something."

"So you and Lucas are stuck?"

"Of course we're not. Because you're going to come get us."

He sighed. "I am, am I?"

"No sense in interrupting someone else's holiday enjoyment when I have a son who refuses to enjoy it at all, and thus won't be interrupted."

It made a Mom kind of sense. "All right. I'll dig out the jumper cables. But I'm not coming until it's over."

"You're so stubborn." That, he thought, was a given. "It wouldn't kill you." He said nothing, and she eventually gave in. "All right, nine o'clock then. Lucas should be wound down by then."

"All right."

"Is your lady still there?"

And there it was again. *Your lady.* And denying it would only show his mother she'd hit a nerve. So he went for diversion. "We just finished eating. She says the chicken and egg thing was worth the whole trip from San Diego."

"Ah!" He could almost hear the smile in his mother's voice. "I suspected she had good taste." If there was a hidden meaning in that, he chose not to think about it. "Bring her along."

He ignored that. "Where are you parked?"

"I got a spot behind city hall."

"All right. I'll see you there later."

For a moment after the call ended, he just stood there. Without looking at her, he told Ariel what the call had been.

Then, quietly, she said, "So, you're going to get to suffer the joy after all, huh?"

"Lucky me," he muttered.

"So you don't want to go and run into everyone you know?"

He shrugged. "Won't matter. Nobody misses having me around."

Well that sounded a bit whiny.

"I doubt that. But I'm sorry if you don't want to go."

"My own fault. Mechanical stuff is sort of my responsibility around here, and I'm a little behind. I should have done a check on her car by now." Tri had seen to that—he was behind on a lot of things because of how much attention he'd had to give to getting the dog even slightly settled. He grimaced. "At least I don't have to go through the count-down."

"Countdown?"

"Ten, nine, eight, they do the whole thing. Then the tree lights up, everybody cheers, then heads out for a glass or mug of whatever Christmas cheer convinces them this means something."

For a moment she just looked at him. Then, quietly, she said, "You're even more of a Grinch than me. I don't participate, but I don't begrudge it to those who do."

He realized before she'd said it that he sounded particu-larly barbed. He let out a long breath. "I don't. Not really. Sometimes I even—" He stopped himself, looked away, determined to put an end to this uncharacteristic habit he'd developed of just blurting things out to her.

"Wish you could feel that way?" she asked softly. His gaze shot back to her face. And whatever she read in his made her add, "So do I, sometimes. Sometimes I wish I could recapture some of that Christmas feeling."

"Want to go, then?" So much for not blurting. "See if it's as bad as we think it is?" We? *We?* Just shut up, Rafferty.

"I thought you weren't going until after the tree lighting, to avoid it?"

"I wasn't. I hate crowds." He paused, then went ahead.

"But...as Mom said, it won't kill me. And she said to bring you along."

"I don't know," she said, sounding hesitant.

"No pressure," he said quickly.

"Just want to share the misery?"

"At least you understand it," he said. "They don't. My family, I mean. Ry's the next oldest, and he says they pretended to like all the celebration for Mom's sake. Because she was trying so hard. But gradually, it wasn't pretending anymore."

"But you weren't here for that."

He nodded. "I made sure I wasn't. Not that that stopped Mom from sending stuff to wherever I was."

"Edible stuff? Dean always said he was the most popular guy in the unit because of my cookies."

Chance's breath caught. He'd forgotten. "The Hawaiian cookies. I had a couple once. They were incredible."

"He called them that because of the macadamia nuts. He loved those things."

"He loved you. They could have been sawdust and he would have said he loved them." *Well that was a stupid thing to say.* "But they really were great."

She was staring at him. Looking, not hurt but...surprised? She shouldn't be surprised that he was a conversational idiot. He'd shown her more than once since she'd arrived.

"Let's go," she said suddenly.

He blinked. Incredulity made him stammer. "You want to go? Into town? On tree lighting night? While it's all going on?"

"No reason you should have to face all that joy and cheer alone," she said. "At least, if we can take Tri. I don't want to leave him alone."

That distracted him enough to where he could at least think. "It might be a good experience for him, seeing all those people and having none of them bother him. But I don't think we can risk letting him out of the truck. I wouldn't want to learn how he deals with both you and a crowd that size without preparation."

"We can do that later," she said, nodding in understanding.

And the next thing Chance knew he was loading Tri back into the truck. He put the harness with the grab handle on him, as a precaution, all the while wondering what had possessed him to even suggest this, when he'd been so eager to see that rental car's taillights leaving.

Wondering why she'd suddenly said yes.

Wondering how, after all his own warnings, he'd slipped back into saying "we."

And wondering why she said it so easily.

Chapter Nineteen

ARIEL CONCENTRATED ON petting Tri, who was clearly aware something different was going on. She tried to narrow down her focus to just that, to avoid thinking about the stunning realization that had gotten her into this.

Pain. Or rather the lack of it.

When Chance had said that about those silly cookies, *they could have been sawdust and he would have said he loved them*, she'd expected the usual agonizing stab of pain, what she always felt at things like that, when someone would voice a memory of something Dean had done or said. But it hadn't come. She'd still felt all the love she'd had for him, and all the sadness at his absence, but that sharp, debilitating pain had faded. It might return the next time it happened—if there was anything she'd learned about this, it was that it was utterly unpredictable—but this time, it had indeed faded. Not away, but to where she could keep breathing.

And that was probably what had brought on her impulsive answer to his unexpected invitation. That, and the fact that he'd looked as surprised to have made it as she'd been to hear it. Chance Rafferty was, by his own admission, not a sociable guy. Of course, he also apparently thought he was not lovable, even by his family, which she found both ridiculous and wrenching. How could he not know his own appeal? Not know how his family loved him? How his friends, like the Buckleys at the inn, missed him? And if that wasn't enough, she could name a half-dozen women she knew who could probably fall for him in a rush.

Her hand froze in its stroking of Tri's fur. A split second later alarm shot through her. Alarm at her stomach's churning reaction to the very thought of any of those friends of hers falling for Chance. Not that it would happen, given none of them would be trekking to Texas, but that didn't seem to matter to her suddenly alarmed system.

He drove the quiet Hill Country roads with easy familiarity. They crossed a small bridge, and she saw the glint of water beneath. A little farther on, the road dropped into a gully, and she glimpsed a vertical sign like others she'd noticed, warning of flash floods and potential water depths in storms. Not something she was used to in San Diego.

And in a shorter time than she expected, she thought she saw a glow in the sky. She remembered the copious Christmas decorations she'd tried to ignore as she'd driven through Last Stand on her way to the inn.

"When is this tree lighting?"

"Eight o'clock, first Friday of December."

"Always?"

"Always. At least, the last century or so."

"Wow."

"I think they missed a couple of years here and there. Depression, World War II, that kind of thing."

"And a lot of people turn out?"

"If by that you mean most of the population, then yes." He gave her a quick glance. "Not many Grinches like me in Last Stand."

"Another benefit of small-town living?"

"Or curse," he muttered. Then, almost sheepishly, he added, "I don't really mean that. Most of the time Last Stand is great. It's me who's out of whack this time of year."

She found the loyalty to his hometown sweet, although she doubted he'd want to hear that. But she was still fascinated by this, having grown up in a place where, while incorporated communities might be small, they simply blended into the next and the next, into the sprawl known as Southern California. Were it not for the stronghold of the Marine Corps at Camp Pendleton it would probably run uninterrupted from the Mexican border to well north of Los Angeles. She found the idea of a place where most of the residents probably knew each other, by sight if not by name, unusual.

And maybe, just a bit appealing.

Maybe that was what shifted her perception a little, enough at least to not cringe when she saw the town lights—and the added decorations—up ahead. They were already in traffic, and she saw he hadn't been kidding when he'd said most of the population.

But the sparkle was undeniable, the smiles unmissable, and the cheerful waves and greetings frequent. She even thought she heard… She rolled down the window a little, and the orchestral sound of a Christmas carol rolled in.

"Meant to warn you about that," Chance said. "It's piped all over town. I think there are speakers at least every ten feet."

"So no escape?" she asked, although with less sourness than she usually would have felt.

"Exactly."

"Let me just hunt down that ignore button," she said.

He gave a short but undeniable chuckle, and she felt as if she'd been given a gift to match the season flowing all around them.

"I always have trouble with that because the lettering's worn off," he replied.

A nearly matching chuckle escaped her, and he glanced at her as if he felt the same way she had.

"Okay, all sorts of science fiction-y explanations are floating through my mind now," she said. "Like the music is really secret, mind-affecting sound waves that alter your thoughts."

"It would explain the group think," he said, his expression utterly serious…except for that little twitch at the right corner of his mouth. Right below where that dimple would be, if she could get him to grin the way Lucas had.

Don't even think about that. Stop letting that image pop into your head. Besides, it's not your concern, making this man grin.

But oh, it was a killer grin.

As distraction, she looked around, amazed anew at the scope of the décor. "I'm surprised they don't have an ordinance requiring everybody decorate everything," she said in a wry tone.

"I wouldn't doubt they've tried." He grimaced. "Right after I got home my mother and brothers snuck down and decorated my place. I didn't speak to them for a week."

"Did they notice?"

It was out before she could stop it. His head snapped around, and she raised her brows at him. And slowly, he lowered his gaze, gave a slow shake of his head as he smiled ruefully.

"Probably not."

Tri let out a slight whine. She'd noticed he'd begun going from side to side in the small back seat of the truck, peering out the window on each end.

"Has he ever been here when it's this crowded before?"

"A couple of times. I bring him with me whenever it's cool enough for him to stay in the truck, which around here usually means the dead of winter or the crack of dawn, and sometimes that's questionable."

"Fewer people around then too, I suppose."

"Than this?" he said, glancing around at the masses of

people on the sidewalks and clustered wherever there was enough space. "Yes. But that's true most of the time. Except maybe rodeo week."

"Rodeo week?"

"Fourth of July."

"You have an actual rodeo here?"

"Yeah." He grimaced, making her curious. But then, everything about this guy made her curious.

"You don't like rodeo? I thought all Texans liked rodeo."

He gave her a rather pointed glance, although only a glance as they continued to try to make their way through streets crowded with vehicles and people. "*All* Texans don't like any one thing. We're not monolithic. And I do like and appreciate rodeo."

"My apologies," she said, although she'd meant it more teasingly than seriously. She must be truly out of practice with the teasing part, if he couldn't tell. "I don't know much about it, except it looks like it's hard on the animals. But why the look?"

"Just…family stuff," he muttered as he turned onto a side street.

"Uh-oh." There, she got that out lightly enough it was obviously teasing. But then she remembered what he'd told her. "Your brother. Keller."

He let out a long breath but didn't look at her since he'd found a place to park behind a Western store happily labeled Yippee Ki Yay. She wondered if anybody saw that and didn't think of the famous—or infamous—line in what had been Dean's favorite Christmas movie. Wondered, not for the first time, what he would think of what she was doing.

Once Chance had the truck in park, he spoke, but still didn't look at her. "Yeah. My brother gave up his dream of pro rodeo, and vet school, to stay home and hold the family together."

"While you, like Dean, took the easy way out and joined the military to risk your life protecting your country," she said quietly. He twisted in the driver's seat to stare at her then. She shrugged, as he so often did. "When you belittle your own service, you belittle everyone's."

He was still staring at her. But now she could see that her words had registered. More than registered, they'd hit hard. "I…never thought about it like that."

"Obviously. Someone told me once—" she didn't say it was a grief counselor, because she didn't know how that would go over "—that no one is harder on us than we are on ourselves. No one expects as much from us as we do ourselves."

"And you believe that?"

"Even if I didn't, I would now. Having just met the textbook example."

He didn't seem to have an answer to that. She let the silence spin out, noting the furrow in his forehead; he was, at least, thinking about it. Then Tri, as if sensing something, stuck his nose out and nudged Chance behind the right ear.

He didn't quite jump, but he went very rigidly still for an instant. As if it were a sneak attack. But almost before she could put a name to it, he relaxed, reached up and patted the dog.

"I'm okay, buddy. Thanks for worrying."

And for a moment all she could think was that they were two battle-weary warriors, bonded in a way only a pair who had been there could be.

Chapter Twenty

"YOUR BROTHER DIDN'T do that, did he?"

Now that Tri was settled again Chance looked at her, to see she was gesturing at the back of the store where they were parked. He was so used to it he barely noticed anymore, but he could see where the big sign would be an attention-getter to someone new. It showed a saddle bronc rider aboard a wildly bucking horse, the man's head snapped back as the horse's heels aimed for the sky. The sign always made him think of Keller's friend, Chase Walker.

"No. He was a roper," he answered.

"Oh. That seems better. That looks kind of cruel."

"Worse if you get thrown. Or stomped."

"I meant the horse."

"I know."

She blinked. It was nearly dark now, but he could feel her staring at him. He didn't say any more, because an idea had occurred to him when he'd thought of Chase Walker. But he shoved it aside for now; he had enough to worry about, just getting through tonight. And wondering why he'd let himself—hell, it had been his idea!—get into this.

"It's okay if we park here?" she asked as he reached to open his door. "I wouldn't want your truck to get towed, especially with Tri inside."

"The stores don't care where you park this time of year. They know people appreciate the courtesy and will remember it when it comes time to shop."

"People here, maybe," she said dryly. "Where I come from, they figure they're putting one over on someone."

He gave a slow shake of his head. "Not much of an advertisement for where you come from."

"Maybe it's more an advertisement for where we are."

It was his turn to blink. That had sounded like she was actually impressed. And he wasn't sure what to think about that. He got out of the truck and walked around to her side, using the action to cover that he had no idea what to say. He pulled the door open for her. She had leaned back to push her small purse out of sight between the seat and the center console. She turned around and started to slide out of the truck in the same motion. He stepped forward in case she needed help; he knew she wasn't used to high-off-the-ground trucks. He'd thought she would use the running board, but instead she slipped right past it to the ground.

And ended up pressed against him shoulder to thigh.

He heard her tiny gasp. He would have made a similar sound himself if he'd had enough breath, but it had all blasted out of him at the feel of her. This wasn't like when she'd been overwhelmed with painful emotion and he'd held her because he hadn't known what else to do.

For a few seconds that seemed to spin out forever neither of them moved. The sane part of his brain was yelling at him to say "Excuse me" and back away. Every other cell in his body was screaming for more. More of being this close. More of being closer yet. More of her. He wanted more than anything to hold on to her. Tighter. He wanted to touch her, stroke that smooth skin, nuzzle that slender neck. Damn, he wanted to get her back in the truck and hightail it to the closest bed. Or maybe forget the bed and just—

The music blanketing the town shifted to a rather rocking version of "The Twelve Days of Christmas," and it shattered the mood. Whatever the hell the mood had been. His mood, at least. He had no idea what hers was. Probably wondering what was wrong with him, thinking he could take such liberties with her.

"Sorry," he muttered, and stepped back.

"Mmm." He had no idea what the noncommittal sound meant. She turned away, but leaned in to pet Tri, so he didn't know if that was the reason or getting distance from him was.

"Now what?" she asked briskly, after giving a last pat to Tri and assuring him they'd be back.

That dispelled the last of the cloud of confusion that had enveloped him. "I need to go find Mom's car, make sure that's all that's wrong."

"If it is, can you go get a new battery and put it in now?"

He shook his head. "Every store in town will be closed, because everybody's here. That'll have to wait until morning. Right now I just want to either get it started, or get her and Lucas home safe."

"Oh." She frowned. He could see it in the light from the fixture over the back door of Yippie Ki Yay. "Maybe I shouldn't have come, in case everybody has to get into the truck."

"We'll fit."

And that quickly it was there again. A flash of all the different ways he and this woman could fit slammed into him. He couldn't remember the last time he'd been hit with such fierce waves of need. Wasn't sure he had ever been. And it was wrong in so many ways he couldn't begin to count them all.

Before he could say anything to make it worse, he turned and started toward Bluebonnet Lane, intent on avoiding the crowd on Main Street, and trusting she'd follow. She did, saying nothing, as if she'd heard nothing in his words but the simple reference to the seating space in his truck. He supposed he should be glad. At least she hadn't slapped him.

You're kind of pretty yourself.

The words she'd said went through his mind, not for the first time. He was sure she hadn't really meant it, they'd just been joking about Cody, but...it had still knocked the breath out of him.

Pretty. Him. Not hardly. That was definitely Cody's

bailiwick. Well, and Dorado's. He'd never—

"Chance? Chance Rafferty, where the hell have you been hiding!"

He snapped back to reality. Saw Gary Klausen, who worked there at the hardware store, turning after apparently locking the back door of the business.

"Gary," he said. The older man looked at Ariel curiously, and Chance made a quick, first-name introduction.

"Haven't seen you in town for the tree lighting in years," Klausen said.

"Not here for it now. My mother's car died on her."

The man frowned. "Maggie? You need anything from us? I'll open back up."

"No, thanks. Go...enjoy."

Ariel watched the man go. "He really would have reopened, wouldn't he?"

"Yes, if I'd needed it." He gave her a sideways look. "Let me guess, never happen where you're from?"

"Depends on the store. Or rather, the owner."

They walked on. Bluebonnet was still busy with people, but not as crowded as he knew Main Street would be, so he kept going toward the back side of the city center square that housed the library, courthouse, police department and city hall, where his mother had said she'd scored a parking spot. That would put her just fifty yards or so away from the tree lighting in front of the library.

But that also meant the crowd was even thicker, and it

took them as long as if they'd been on Main, at least it seemed so to him. He hated crowds, in large part because he hated being surrounded. Having unknowns at his back made him nervous. But tonight the problem wasn't unknowns. Because, to his shock, he was stopped every few feet by someone greeting him, in surprise and some in shock, but by all appearances delighted to see him. He hadn't had to come up with so many hellos and stiff smiles in one go since he'd come home.

And then he was struck almost speechless when they nearly collided with the redoubtable Mrs. Valencia, the former history teacher at Creekbend High School, the woman who struck both fear and admiration into every student she'd ever taught, including him. Reports were she'd mellowed since her daughter, Elena, had married Sean Highwater early this year, but Mrs. Valencia mellowed was still a tougher nut than most. Which was why her words so surprised him.

"It is good to see you, Chance Rafferty. Welcome back."

"Mrs. Valencia," he said, touching the brim of his cap. "I…haven't been gone," he added awkwardly.

"Yes, you have," she countered quietly. Then to his shock, the stern, uncompromising woman reached up and patted his cheek almost maternally. Sean Highwater, he thought, feeling more than a little stunned, wasn't just Cody's friend, he was a freaking miracle worker.

"Obviously you were badly mistaken when you said no-

body missed you," Ariel said in the next gap between surprised greetings.

"They're just being nice," he said, not looking at her. By
the time they had reached the city hall parking lot, he was
almost numb with the weight of it all. All this interaction, on
top of spending all this time with Ariel—

*All this time? It's been barely over twenty-four hours. And
only half of it actually with her, not counting all the time you've
wasted thinking about her. So less than a day with the woman,
and you're a basket case?*

"Just Christmas spirit, huh?" she asked.

"Holdover from childhood and not making Santa's nice
list."

"Cynic much?"

"Not nearly enough."

He finally looked at her. She was grinning at him. Or
laughing, he wasn't sure which. The memory of the moment
when she'd broken down flashed through his mind, and he
suddenly didn't care if he had to put up with all this, not for
that expression on her face now.

Then he spotted his mother's compact SUV parked in
the end slot of the row of parking behind city hall.

"I don't see her, or Lucas," Ariel said, scanning the area.

"They're probably holding their good spot in front of the
library. Doesn't matter, I've got a key," he said.

He activated the door lock from the key, and reached for
the door handle. It swung open, and he stopped dead. The
interior light was on. And it got no dimmer as he stood

there, staring at what his mother had told him wasn't happening. He slid into the driver's seat, having to adjust the seat position back significantly from where it was for his mother's petite stature. He put the key into the ignition and turned it one notch. Everything that should light up on the dash did. And nothing that shouldn't, did. He turned the key.

The engine turned over instantly. Not in the draggy, hesitating way of a car with a weak battery, or the barely-did-it way of a battery that had rested just long enough to regain enough power to start. No, it started quickly, easily.

He sat there, listening to the smoothly running motor, staring at the spot where the red battery warning light would be if it was on. Which it wasn't.

"It started right up," Ariel said, puzzlement in her voice.

"Yes," Chance said, staring at the gauges.

"But she told you—"

"Yes," he repeated.

For a moment he just sat, but his focus on the task at hand faded. Since it clearly wasn't a task at all. The sounds coming through the still-open door began to penetrate again, the sound of people chattering happily, and Christmas carols echoing off the walls of every building around, it seemed. He wondered vaguely if Cody and Sean Highwater had wired that, too.

He was in the middle of where he'd never wanted to be, a Last Stand Christmas. And it was only beginning. There were three more weeks of this to come. And it would get only crazier and crazier.

"I don't understand," Ariel finally said.

"I think I do," Chance said grimly. And then he swung out of the seat, left it pushed back for his longer legs, closed the door and locked it. He looked at Ariel. "You may want to head back to the truck and Tri. This might not be pleasant."

She drew back slightly. "What might not?"

"Me confronting my mother."

"Confronting? Why?"

"Because," he said flatly, "I'm pretty sure she set me up."

Chapter Twenty-One

A RIEL COULDN'T HELP it, she laughed. She had a split second to marvel at the still unaccustomed feel and sound of it before his head snapped around and he stared— or was it a glare?—at her.

"I'm sorry," she said quickly. "But that is so something my own mother would do. In fact, did, a couple of times. Trying to get me to be…more sociable."

"Sociable." There was no missing the derision in his tone.

"I get it. I really do. Personally, most times I'd rather just stay home with a good book." He looked doubtful. "I know, crazy. Dean was such a gregarious, outgoing sort. He always wanted to be out and about. What tension there was in our marriage stemmed from that."

"He thought your marriage was perfect." His tone had changed completely, softened but still with a rough edge.

"It was close to perfect, but every marriage has its mo-ments. Two different people, individuals, no matter how much they love each other, are going to have those. Usually I let him tease me into going out with him. And eventually he understood I needed…down time."

"He was always…"

"On? Yes, he was." And that was enough of talking about her. "I'm sure your mom is just worried about you. It's part of her job, you know."

"The mother job?"

"Yes. Besides…" she began, then halted, not sure what she'd been about to say was the wisest thing right now.

"Don't stop now," he said dryly.

"She was right. It didn't kill you. In fact, judging by all the greetings, it probably did you good."

"Mmm."

She smiled now, although it held a tinge of sadness. Dean had often sounded like that, given that noncommittal, nonverbal, open-to-interpretation response when they occasionally strayed into things he didn't want to talk about. It was a useful habit she resorted to herself sometimes. But this, and the whole warrior thing, were the only things she'd seen so far that both men shared. And with Dean, she'd sometimes wondered if all the cheer and bonhomie hadn't been cover, so no one would probe too deeply and find the uglier memories. The kind that Chance and all those who'd served in combat zones likely carried. He'd kept that apart from her, rarely speaking of it, instead always distracting her with his teasing good cheer.

These were things she'd never thought much about, until it was too late. Until he was gone.

"So don't be too hard on your mother," she said, doing a little avoidance herself.

"Did you go easy on yours?"

"Once I realized it was done out of love, yes."

He let out a long breath, gave a twisted sort of smile, and she could feel the tension fade out of him. "Let's go find her," she suggested. "You can let her know you saw through her ploy and aren't happy about it, without chewing on her too hard. Or ruining her enjoyment of the festivities."

"Don't participate, but don't begrudge it to those who do?"

She nearly gaped at him as he quoted her exact words back at her. Scrambling for something to say, all she could come up with was, "Yes. So if you start singing along with—" the familiar tune had registered the moment it had begun "—'Deck the Halls' I'm out of here."

To her surprise he let out a full-on burst of laughter. And that dimple she'd wanted to see flashed. "Not something you want to hear, trust me."

Recovered now, she smiled. "So no fa-la-la-ing?"

"Not a trill," he promised.

They started toward the city buildings, where what appeared to be a huge, packed crowd was gathered. Everybody seemed to be heading that direction, and their progress got slower and trickier, as people jockeyed—albeit politely—for position. And then a group of half a dozen kids barreled through the crowd, singing along with the next song, "Jingle

Bells," at the top of their lungs. They managed to cut between her and Chance, separating them by a few feet.

And suddenly she was surrounded by people, all strangers, and while her common sense told her she was in no danger, she did feel a bit lost, since she didn't know where anything was, let alone anyone. Would she even be able to find a cab or an Uber around here, to get back to the inn? But wait, they'd passed the police station on their way here, hadn't they? Surely they'd have someone who wasn't out here among the throng who could help? She could—

Chance looked back, as if he'd sensed she was no longer close. She saw his gaze narrow until he spotted her, and his expression cleared. For some reason that simple action struck a place deep within her that hadn't stirred for a long time. And then he came back toward her, shouldering aside people and covering the distance in two long strides. "Being in a crowd isn't your favorite thing either?"

"Good guess," she said.

"We should stay together, then," he said.

She was nodding and about to say she'd been trying to, but the kids—

Chance reached out and took her hand.

Her breath jammed up in her throat. Her pulse leapt. And she thought she'd never felt anything warmer, anything stronger than his hand wrapped around hers.

They rounded the side of a large, stone, two-story building, and she got a glimpse of the true size of the gathering and assumed the street she could barely see through the throng was Main Street. She could also see why he'd avoided it; it was even more solidly packed with people.

She felt the moment when he quit just trying to get through the crowd but instead was arrowing on a course. He must have spotted his mother, or at least one of his family. She moved slightly to one side—making absolutely no effort to free her hand—and looked in the direction they were heading now. It took her only a moment to spot the diminutive figure of Maggie Rafferty, mainly because she was a foot taller than usual. And she had her arms around the also suddenly taller boy in front of her. Lucas, who had his hands on her forearms as if he didn't mind at all.

"She grew," Ariel said with a laugh. "They both did."

Chance looked back at her. "They put crates out for shorter people and kids to stand on, so they can see. And knowing my mom, she told Lucas she needed him to help her not fall off."

"Which makes it all right for her to hold him like that in front of everyone," Ariel said with an understanding smile.

"Exactly."

He'd let go of her hand, and she spent a silent moment regretting that before saying, "You know, I quite like your mother. She reminds me of mine. And she obviously loves you a great deal. So keep that in mind before you bite her head off for the car thing."

He gave her a look she couldn't quite interpret before

saying, "I won't. You defused that bomb pretty nicely."

And he didn't. When they reached the pair atop the sturdy wooden crate, Maggie gave him a slightly guilty look, but it was also defiant. "You came early."

"You set me up," Chance said, his voice almost surprisingly mild.

"A mother's prerogative," Maggie said in a voice that matched her expression.

"Not playing fair. And not the first time," Chance retorted.

The woman met her son's gaze steadily, but her expression softened. "I just wanted you to see it really wouldn't kill you. Christmas, or being out with people."

"It didn't." The same mild tone.

Maggie's head tilted in puzzlement. "I thought you'd be mad."

"I was," Chance said.

And then Ariel's breath caught in her throat as he looked at her, as if publicly giving her the credit for the change in his mood, for quelling his anger. As they stared at each other, the music stopped. There was a hum of low voices around them as people politely hushed others, and people began to turn toward the front of the building they'd gathered around. This must be the library, she realized belatedly.

A man, some city official she supposed, stepped up to the microphone that was next to a box with a large lever, both up on a small platform. He said a few words of welcome, something about his pride in serving the town of Last Stand, then seemed to be about to start to list the things he'd done when a voice from the crowd called out "It's not a campaign stop, Mayor. Just get on with it!"

The laughter that rose around them made Ariel smile. The man seemed to take it good-naturedly, and said, "All right, all right. Merry Christmas, everyone, and here's the real star of the night, the indomitable, undefeatable Minna Herdmann!"

"She made it," Maggie said with delight. "Another year." What she'd said made sense when Ariel saw the slim, silver-haired woman make her way toward the stage on the arm of a tall, powerful-looking man in a dark gray cowboy hat. Maggie saw her notice. "That's Minna Herdmann, the town matriarch. A hundred and three now, and still running the show."

The man with the diminutive woman let go of her as he took the two steps ahead of her, and Ariel realized that it wasn't a failure of those Texas manners when he turned back, bent and actually lifted her carefully to the stage.

"The chief is really strong, isn't he?" Lucas said.

"He is." Maggie grinned at the boy before adding, "But Minna only insists he always escort her because she has a crush on him."

"The chief?" Ariel asked Chance quietly. "The police chief?"

Chance nodded. "Shane Highwater."

The man she'd read about. The pure, unadulterated hero. Now that she saw him in person, it was utterly believable.

"He's a good friend of Keller's," Chance went on. "Brother to Sean, Cody's friend. Other brother, Slater, runs the Last Stand Saloon." He gave her a sideways look. "You may have met the youngest brother, Kane, he works out at the inn."

"The guy with the voice."

"That's him."

A connection she'd missed hit her. The article on the inn, the name of the writer, hadn't it also been…? "Is there a writer in the family, too?"

"Lily? She's married to Shane."

Married to a hero. Silently wishing the woman she didn't even know luck, she refocused on the stage as the apparent guest of honor stepped up to the microphone, which the chief carefully lowered for her.

"All right, everyone, listen up!" Ariel almost laughed at the way everyone did just that, but she was in awe at the unexpected volume and snap of command coming out of the woman who—despite her age, or maybe because of it—had the attention of the entire crowd instantly. "I haven't forgotten what it was like to have to listen to people bloviate up here when all I wanted was to see the tree light up. So we're going to cut to the chase here."

The crowd cheered in obvious appreciation. The chief was smiling. The mayor was laughing. She stole a glance at

Chance, and even he was smiling, shaking his head as if he, too, was amazed at the level of her energy and her snappy dialogue.

"Merry Christmas to our beloved Last Stand!" Minna announced, then reached out and tugged the lever toward her.

The big tree she'd only seen as a dark shadow in front of the building before exploded into a sparkling tower of colored lights. In the same moment, the stirring chords of "Joy to the World" poured out of the sound system. Ariel was startled by the sudden tightness in her throat. She hadn't expected that, at all.

She glanced at Chance again. His eyes were closed, as if the sight of all that colorful light had been too much. His head was tilted downward, but he hadn't turned away. Then she saw him swallow visibly, as if his throat was as tight as hers. Driven by an urge she didn't quite understand she reached out and took his hand, needing the warmth of it again. His eyes snapped open and he went very still. He didn't look at her. But he didn't pull his hand away.

And after a long moment—or at least it seemed an eternity—his fingers curled around hers in welcome.

Chapter Twenty-Two

*Y*OUR FATHER LOVED *Christmas.*

His mother's words as they'd turned to go echoed in Chance's head as they worked their way back through the crowd. He was certain only his explanation that Tri was in the truck, waiting, had made her leave it at that and not try and persuade him to stay for the post-lighting celebration.

"Dean loved it, too."

Ariel spoke quietly, so quietly he wasn't certain he was supposed to have heard her. And he only did because the music over the speakers at that moment had segued to a chipper version of "Oh Christmas Tree."

"If you want to stay, stay," he said. "Mom'll see you get to the inn." He grimaced. "It'd be the least she could do, after tricking me into this."

"No. Thanks, but this was…enough." She sounded a bit on edge, but not a wreck. And even as he thought it, she added, "But it wasn't as bad as I expected. I mean, it was actually lovely. I just didn't hate being here as much as I thought I would."

To his surprise, he had to admit he hadn't either. "Minna helped. She's a dynamo.'"

"Is she really a hundred and three?"

"She is. Town started throwing birthday parties for her when she turned ninety-five, figuring…you know. Now her birthdays are probably the biggest deal in Last Stand, after—" he jerked a thumb over his shoulder back toward the still-mingling crowd "—this, and maybe the rodeo."

"It was very calm, too, for a crowd that big. No scuffles, even."

He gave her a glance. "Shane sees to that. Anyplace near the ceremony, you were probably within ten feet of a cop."

She blinked. "I didn't see any."

"Plainclothes. They'd likely be here anyway, so they just come prepared. And the locals all know, so most people behave. If there is any trouble, it's over quick and it's usually tourists."

"Quite the peaceful little town you've got here."

"Shane sees to that," he said again.

"Does he also decide when the party's over?"

To his own surprise he smiled. "Nah. The music does."

"What?"

"'Silent Night.' It's the cue that it's time to clear the square. It'll be late tonight, though, because it's a Friday."

By then they were back to the truck, where Tri was on alert, but the dog seemed only a little wound up as they got back in. And he calmed as soon as he was able to greet Ariel with a canine kiss.

Lucky dog.

Chance froze with his hands on the steering wheel, although he hadn't even started the engine yet. Lucky dog? That brave, traumatized animal that, until thirty-six hours ago, he'd doubted would ever be able to function out in the world? How the hell had things gotten so upside down so fast? His fingers tightened around the wheel. But all he could think about was how her hand had felt in his, warm, soft yet strong, and so very alive.

"You said this wasn't the first time your mom had…not played fair," she said as she fastened her seat belt.

"No, it wasn't." Considering his inner turmoil, that had come out fairly evenly.

"So, she does this a lot?"

"No. Only when…" He stopped before he could vomit out things she didn't need or want to hear, and he didn't want to say.

"Only when she's worried about her sons?"

I'm worried about you.

Don't.

How can I not? Don't think I don't know the stats because I do.

I'm fine.

No, you're not. But you remember one thing, Chance Rafferty. We vowed to keep this family together in your father's memory, but another loss will end us. Do you really want to die knowing you'll be destroying that, and all of us?

That's not playing fair, Mother.

When it comes to my boys, that's as fair as I get.

"I do what it takes." He barely whispered it into the darkness of the truck. Was barely aware he'd spoken his mother's fierce words aloud.

"Sounds like a good mother's mantra," Ariel said quietly, as if she'd somehow realized who he was quoting. And maybe she had. Dean had always said his Red was ace at reading people. "What was she worried about then?"

He turned to look at her then. The light from the fixture over the back door of the building lit only one side of her face, since she was already looking at him. It didn't make her any less beautiful. In fact, it made his gaze linger on the soft shape of her mouth, the delicate angle of her jaw, her cheekbone, and the sheen of the eye he could see. She waited quietly, patiently, not pushing, not prodding, but letting the silence spin out and do it for her.

She had to know, must have thought about it. This was Dean's wife.

His precious Red.

And he had no business having the kind of feelings he'd been having around her. It was time to put an end to this.

"That I'd become one of the twenty-two."

She didn't even blink. So she knew perfectly well about the average twenty-two veterans a day who had been committing suicide at the time. She had worried about it all the time Dean had been deployed, when thinking about their life after he came home. She'd never gotten that life, but at least she hadn't lost him that way. Things had improved since then, thanks to an overhaul of the VA, but at the time, just a few years ago, things had been ugly.

"Were you thinking about it?" she asked, so matter-of-factly that he answered her.

"No. I wasn't in great shape, but...I already knew what she'd told me. That one more blow would destroy my family."

"I'm glad."

She left it at that, throwing out none of the platitudes that were half the reason he stayed away from people.

He started the truck, and its headlights came on, lighting up the back of Yippee Ki Yay. Her head turned toward the image on the sign, of the bucking horse, and it reminded him of the thought he'd had earlier.

"You taking the weekend off?" he asked.

She looked back at him, brows arched. "Test question?"

"Just checking."

"Do you take it off?"

His mouth quirked. "Half the time I don't know when it is."

That made her smile. Which in turn made him feel...he wasn't sure he recognized the feeling.

"I was planning on spending it with this boy here," she said, reaching back to pet the dog who seemed to never take his eyes off her.

Chance had already developed a surprising amount of

certainty that the dog would never turn on her. It wasn't yet ninety-nine percent—as high as it ever got, because there would always be the chance that something would trigger a fight reflex in the dog—not yet, but it was amazingly close.

"Good." Then, despite wondering if he should, he plunged ahead with his idea. "I want to see if the difference in him holds around other people and in other places."

"Tomorrow?"

"If you're up for it."

Without hesitation she answered, "Absolutely. What time should I be there?"

"Do you need anything out of your car?" Looking puzzled, she shook her head. "The inn is almost on the way. Why don't I drop you off. I'll bring Tri over in the morning, and we can head out to…a place I thought of taking him. Then you can pick up your car when we get back to the ranch."

"Sounds logistically feasible," she said.

The words, spoken so often by Dean while contemplating an upcoming mission, and usually leavened with the implication that everything was logistically feasible for the person who didn't have to carry it out, slammed hard into Chance's mind. For a moment he couldn't think. And it was a longer moment before he could speak.

"Did you pick that up from him, or did he get it from you?"

"I got it from him. But I didn't mean it like he usually

did, sarcastically."

"Yeah. He did."

They were out on the road, having left before most of the crowd even thought about it, and headed for the Hickory Creek Spur before he realized his left hand was curled into a fist as it bounced on his left thigh. A painfully tight fist, his nails digging into his palm. Tight enough it could cramp if he didn't let up soon.

He didn't let up. He kept the hand clenched.

The hand that had held hers, when he had no right.

Chapter Twenty-Three

ARIEL WASN'T BLIND. She knew the moment things had changed, the moment he'd gone cold, withdrawn. It had been the moment when she'd tossed off that phrase Dean had used to use.

And yet when they arrived at the inn, with its own Christmas lights glittering, the manners held. Stiffly, and without speaking, he opened her door for her. He stood patiently while she said a crooning good night to the suddenly anxious Tri, who only settled at a fairly sharp command from Chance. And then he escorted her—there was no other word for it—up to the doors of the inn.

They stood on the expansive front porch, which was more of a veranda she supposed, and she was wondering if he was actually going to walk her to the door of her room—a scenario that was both sweet and disquieting—when Frank Buckley stepped out of the inn. She'd only met the former Texas Ranger briefly, but he'd been charming, insisting with a warm smile that she call him Frank. If she hadn't seen the official portrait of him hanging near the doors out onto the deck overlooking the creek and seen the scars on his hand

and the way it didn't work quite right, she never would have believed he'd been one of the legendary agency.

The older man smiled and greeted her, but then focused on Chance.

"Been a while," he said quietly.

"Yes, sir." Chance said it flatly, but still respectfully.

"Good to see you." Then, as if he could sense Chance's tension, he asked, "Here under duress?"

She heard Chance let out a breath. "Not my best time of year."

"Understood." It was spoken in the manner of one who meant it deeply. Then Frank looked back at her, and she dug down for an effort at normalcy.

"Are you already back, or did you not go with the rest of the town to the tree ceremony?" she asked.

"Someone needed to man the ship," he said with a smile. "Kane offered to stay, but it's his first Christmas home and Karina wouldn't hear of it."

She wondered where the handyman with the incredible voice had been, but it was not something she wanted to ask now, when Chance was strung more tightly than those Christmas lights over their heads.

"I'll see her in, if you like," Frank offered. "So you can get that antsy dog I see in your truck home and settled."

Chance hesitated, but then nodded. Ariel wondered if, despite his neutral expression, he was grateful.

"We'll be here about nine," he said to her, rather formally.

"Will you be back for the parade tomorrow night?" Frank asked.

Chance looked startled, and he looked quickly back at Ariel. "I didn't think...sorry, I assumed you wouldn't want—"

"And you assumed correctly," she said. "Being maneuvered into watching a tree lighting is one thing, Santa rolling down Main Street is something else again."

"Maneuvered?" Frank asked.

"My mother," Chance answered dryly.

"Ah. Maggie Rafferty, a Last Stand force of nature."

"Pretty much."

Frank looked at him a moment longer, then said, "We should go fishing again. I could use the company."

"I've been told I'm not much. Company, I mean."

"Exactly," Frank said. "You won't bend my ear off."

Ariel only realized how concerned she'd been by Chance's sudden coolness when he let out a low chuckle at Frank's wry observation.

After watching the truck pull away, she glanced up at Frank. He turned and reopened the front door of the inn and held it for her. "You've been fishing with him before?" she asked.

"Not lately," Frank said. "Not since he's been home, anyway. I'll be rectifying that. I promised his father I'd look out for his boys."

"You knew him? His father?"

"He was a good friend. As were our fathers, grandfathers, and probably back even longer."

Ariel let out a small, compressed breath. "This seems so strange to me. At home we're lucky if we know our next-door neighbor's name."

She was still thinking about the wonder of that later as she climbed into the comfortable bed in her room. And then Chance's words crept into her mind. *I've been told I'm not much. Company, I mean.*

He'd been plenty of company for her. A challenge, yes, but if she was honest about it, she'd…enjoyed it? It had been so long since she'd enjoyed anything, it took her a moment to name the emotion.

She thought about it some more and had herself almost convinced her reaction was simply because she'd isolated herself for so long. Maybe too long. But those thoughts soon gave way to the memory of the way he'd looked back for her in concern when they'd become separated in the crowd. The way her pulse had leapt when he'd taken her hand.

And in the morning she muttered to her image in the bathroom mirror that, after allowing those memories to grip her, she had only herself to blame for her crazy dreams. Crazy dreams that they'd done more than just hold hands. A lot more.

Since she'd awakened early, she took her time. She did what she could to camouflage the dark circles under her eyes, hoped her bangs would distract from the weary look, and decided a simple ponytail would do for the rest of her hair. She wasn't, after all, out to impress anyone. When she'd done all she could and was looking forward to a cup of Karina Buckley's wonderful coffee, she picked up her small purse and walked over to the window to glance outside and see if her lightweight jacket would be enough.

He was already here. She saw the truck, unoccupied unless Tri was hunkered down in the back seat, parked where he'd parked last night. She glanced at the time to be sure she wasn't late, but it was twenty to nine.

She headed downstairs, and met Karina just coming in from outside. "Chance is down at the creek overlook," the woman said, pointing. "With the dog."

"Thank you."

Karina looked at her consideringly. "It's really good to see that boy out and about again. Thank you for that."

"It's not me," Ariel said honestly. "I think he'd do anything for a dog in need. Even rejoin the world for a while."

"Whatever the cause, it's a good thing. Although I think you underrate yourself," Karina said, and with a wide smile and a wave left her to it.

Ariel headed out in the direction Karina had pointed. That was sweet of her to say. But then, almost everyone she'd met here was unfailingly polite. Even Chance at his gruffest had been that.

It was cooler than she'd expected, and as she crossed the

parking area she pulled on her jacket. She had been meaning to take this walk anyway, following the signs pointing the way to both the creek overlook and a walking path through the trees that grew along the banks of Hickory Creek. It was a lovely setting, really. Especially here, where the creek took a slight turn around a limestone ledge that jutted out into the creek bed, the ledge that had been weathered into what looked like a nearly comfortable place to sit.

Tri was there, but was hock-deep in an almost quiet pool of water that had formed in the angle of the ledge. He wasn't playing, exactly, not as a normal dog would, but he was nosing the water with interest. She also noticed the leash today was attached to the harness with the handle on the back. She'd seen it before, and knew they served to both assist the dog with a lift or pull, and to extricate him from situations.

Today she was guessing it was insurance, in case this didn't go well, and Chance had to pull him off someone or something. The thought not only spoke to his caution and thoroughness, but also pounded home to her the risks of what she was doing, of what she wanted to do. Even as she thought it the dog's head came up sharply, and he lost interest in the water. He was looking her direction, nose and tail up now. And she took heart from the fact that that tail was starting to wag.

She kept walking. And as the path curved, the ledge itself came into view. She'd already known Chance was there, so it was silly the way her nerves kicked up as if it were a surprise to see his tall, lean, broad-shouldered self. He was wearing a long-sleeved, gray knit shirt tucked into jeans today, not the baggier camo pants with the extra pockets. And that alone about stopped the breath in her throat, since his back was to her and she found herself staring at—and admiring—his backside. And his trim waist, and those shoulders.

"Come on down," he said, clearly aware she was there even though he'd never looked around. She suspected that he would have known even if Tri hadn't signaled her approach; she doubted anyone could really sneak up on this man.

"That water must feel a little chilly this morning," she said as she stepped off the path onto the limestone ledge.

He still didn't look at her, keeping his gaze on Tri, who was scrambling up over the stone bank as fast as he could, although slipping a bit as he struggled to get traction with only one front leg to pull with. But he answered.

"I think it probably feels good, when you've been in a place that hits a hundred and fifteen degrees by this hour."

"Then I'm surprised you're not in there with him."

"Thought about it."

The images that shot through her mind then, of him peeling off that snug shirt and those butt-cupping jeans, made her very glad he was watching Tri and not her. Desperate for something sane to say, she asked, "Is there a point at which you help him?"

He shot her a glance then, although it was barely a flicker

before he went back to the dog. "Thinking I should be?"

She knew he was still gauging her, judging whether she was up to handling Tri. "No," she said, "he needs to handle what he can. It was an honest question."

"When do you think, then?"

More judging. "When he's too tired or in genuine danger of being hurt."

He nodded, still focused on Tri, who had finally gotten himself up onto the ledge, instinctively shaken off what water he could, and headed for her with that rolling, lopsided gait. She dropped down to her knees to greet him, hoping it wasn't wishful thinking that had her seeing a change in the animal, a lighter sort of feeling about him.

She didn't care that his head was wet as he nosed at her, not when he was greeting her with that welcoming, happy little whine. Not when that slight wag of the tail had become a full, sweeping arc. Most of all not when he looked like an ordinary, glad-to-see-you, happy dog who just happened to be on three paws instead of four.

But she was happiest of all when she raised her head and saw Chance looking down at them both. And he was smiling. Widely enough that that dimple was showing in his cheek.

Ariel had the thought that she could use a dip in that cool water herself.

Chapter Twenty-Four

C HANCE WAS STILL having a little trouble believing they were already at this point with Tri. Even as amazing as the dog's response to her had been. As they headed out on US 290, he found himself second-guessing, questioning his judgment. Or more accurately, questioning whether she had adversely affected his judgment. He knew she'd affected it; he just wasn't sure which way.

She'd affected a lot of things.

"Where are we going?"

"A ranch outside of Whiskey River. Town a few miles from here."

"Why?"

"They're friends. They have dogs I want to try him with." He didn't mention the other reason he'd chosen the Walker Ranch for this experiment.

"And he's all right with strange dogs?"

"So far." He grimaced. "Haven't dealt with a pack this size though. They've got ten or so. Maybe more by now."

"Wow."

"They're incapable of not taking in the strays that get

184

dumped near them."

She let out a long sigh. "Sometimes I really don't like people. But then I meet someone like you, or your friends, and realize most people are better than that."

Warmth blossomed in him at that "someone like you," but he said only, "I don't know about most, but the Walkers definitely are."

He made the turn at the sign for "Walker Ranch Paints," onto a long gravel road that made its way over the rolling hills. Just as at home, most of the numerous trees were leafless now in December.

"Paints?"

"They breed them." He glanced at her, saw her brow furrowed, realized she'd made the mistake many non-horse folks did. "Paint horses, not paintbrushes. Pintos."

Her brow cleared. "Oh. Sorry."

"Not your life," he said with a half-shrug.

They drove through a thick stand of trees, although they were leafless now.

"I'll bet it's pretty around here in the fall," she said.

"The leaves put on a show," he agreed.

They reached a spot where the trees cleared out and they could see the house. A big ranch-style that had a log cabin sort of feel to it. There was a big wraparound porch with chairs and flowerpots, and a porch swing near one corner of the house. And while there were a few tributes to the season—a wreath on the door, a Christmas tree visible through the window—it wasn't overwhelming.

"That's lovely," Ariel said.

"It's what made Mom decided she wanted a porch swing."

He drove slowly past the house toward the large barn. Beyond the round pen next to the barn several fields spread out, many with horses grazing. As they neared a man came out of the barn, a tall guy with dark hair wearing faded jeans, battered boots, and a well-worn Stetson. He waved and was smiling as he walked toward them while Chance pulled to a stop. He had a few of the pack of dogs at his heels.

"He looks like a working cowboy," Ariel said.

"That," Chance said, "is two-time world champion saddle bronc rider Chase Walker."

Her eyes widened. "You mean…like in that picture, at the store?"

He nodded. And got out of the truck before she could ask any questions. By the time he got around to open her door Chase was there, and he made a quick introduction.

"This your problem boy?" Chase asked, nodding at Tri, who was peering out the window with great interest as the dogs gathered around him, including two more who darted out of the barn to join the others.

"Yeah. But he's changed a lot in just a couple of days." He nodded at Ariel. "Ever since she arrived."

And he's not the only one.

She was bending now to greet the dogs who were clustered around them. Tri gave a little woof but left it at that.

"That one," Chase said, gesturing at the black Lab-looking dog Ariel was petting, "is Johnny Cash. The dynamic duo there are Waylon and Willie. The blonde there is Dolly Parton. Hank and Loretta are off with my brother Marshall somewhere."

Ariel smiled. "I'm noticing a theme there."

Chase smiled back. Chance felt a jab of…something, until he remembered that Keller had said the guy was flat-out crazy about his lady, Ella.

"Blame my sister, Damaris," he said. "She's the namer-in-chief."

"How's the newest arrival doing?" Chance asked.

"Good, settling in. Come on, I'll introduce you, then we'll see how your boy does with this gang of troublemakers."

They followed him into the barn and down to a stall where a white horse's head stuck out as the animal watched them come. Chase reached into his pocket, took out a couple of sugar cubes, and handed them to Ariel. "Just hold them out on your palm when you meet her."

"Okay," Ariel said, with just enough nervousness in her voice to make Chance remember what she'd said about always liking horses but never having the chance to be around them.

"Hey, you ol' nag," Chase said affectionately when they got to the stall, "meet some new friends. Pretty one first.

Ariel, this is our new addition to the Walker Ranch, Sugar Lips. Sugar, be nice."

"Sugar Lips?" Ariel said, relaxing into a smile again as she held her hand with the cubes out as instructed.

"For obvious reasons," Chase said with a grin as the white horse gently swiped the cubes from her palm with nothing but lip, not a trace of teeth.

"That tickled!" Ariel was grinning back now.

"And that's her thank you," Chase said when the horse gently nudged Ariel's hand. "You can pat her now."

"Hello there, you sweet thing," she said, reaching out to pat the horse's neck. The animal nickered softly.

"Try rubbing under her jaw," Chase suggested. "She loves that."

Ariel did so, and after a moment the horse's eyes started to drift closed blissfully. "She's so sweet!"

"She is," Chance said. "Very...docile."

"She's pretty mellow," Chase agreed, glancing at Chance. Chance nodded at him to go ahead, as they'd discussed when he'd arranged this yesterday. "You'd never guess she stomped me hard enough to put an end to my rodeo days."

Ariel went still. Looked from Chase to the horse and back. "What?"

"Bucked me off in a couple of seconds, like a rank beginner. Broke my shoulder, then stepped on me and cracked a couple of ribs. My final wake-up call."

She stared at him. "You're saying she threw you, stepped

on you, and you…bought her?"

"Pretty much."

Chase patted the horse's head, and the mare nuzzled his hand affectionately. And Chance saw Ariel, belatedly, realize.

"Wait a minute… She's a bucking horse? A rodeo bucking horse?"

"She was. She'll be focusing on motherhood now. Plan on getting some good bucking stock out of this girl."

"Doesn't seem too abused, does she," Chance observed neutrally.

Ariel shifted her gaze to him. "You learned well at your mother's knee, apparently. Nice setup."

He couldn't read her expression, but he risked a slight smile.

"Is she mad?" Chase asked.

"I can't tell," Chance answered, not looking at her. "I hope she's not."

"She might be if you keep talking about her in the third person when she's right here," Ariel said. But she still didn't sound genuinely angry.

"Sorry," Chase said, "but for some reason Chance here wanted you to have the truth. She's a sweetheart, and bucking is her job just like pulling a wagon or plow is for some horses, jumping over fences is for others. It's her job, and she knows it well. And when she's not working—" he gestured at the mare who had nudged Ariel's hand when she stopped rubbing her "—she's this."

She shifted her gaze to Chance. Chase coughed and excused himself hastily, saying something about rounding up the rest of the pack. Chance braced himself as he said, "You laughed when my mother did it."

"So you thought I'd laugh when you did it to me?"

"No. Just hoped you wouldn't take my head off." He made himself meet those blue eyes. "I know about your temper, but you said you didn't get mad anymore."

She let out an audible breath. "No. No, I don't." Then, in a slightly different voice she added, "Especially at the man who decides if I get Tri or not."

He felt as if she'd punched him in the gut. Was that what was behind all of this...whatever it was? The conversations? The getting him to talk? Going with him last night? Was it all an effort to get on his good side, to influence his decision about Tri?

"If you think anything but his welfare would change that decision, you're wrong," he said, his tone cooler than he'd even meant it to be.

For a long, silent moment she just looked at him. Then, the corners of her mouth—that damned, luscious mouth— twitching, she said softly, "Gotcha."

He blinked. "What?"

"Payback's a bitch, ain't it?"

He stared at her. Memories raced through his mind, of tales told, of laughs shared as Dean talked about the folly of ever trying to best his Red, who wasn't just gorgeous, and had a temper like an IED, she had a mind like a steel trap except more devious. And he'd just stepped into it.

"I've been set up twice in twenty-four hours, is that it?"

"Something like that."

"So, are we even?"

"For now," she agreed, rather blithely.

And as she turned to greet the new canine arrivals, Chance was left to ponder why what he was feeling was pure relief. Because that was crazy. She was Dean's widow. Yet this relief made it seem like he wanted everything he was feeling, had felt since she'd arrived, to be real. And possible.

And it couldn't be.

Chapter Twenty-Five

ARIEL WATCHED CHANCE go to get Tri out of the truck apprehensively. If something went wrong here, with these clearly normal ranch dogs, it could affect everything. The trepidation pushed aside her relief that he'd taken her jab as it had been meant, a little payback for this scenario he'd engineered. Which she had to admit worked; when she'd seen that image of a strenuously bucking horse on the back of that store, the last thing she'd pictured was a pampered, sweet animal that loved sugar cubes and could practically fall asleep under a human caress.

And human caresses shouldn't be in her mind at all right now.

She felt a bump at her knee and looked down to see the dog Chase had called Dolly Parton, a lovely animal who looked mostly like a golden retriever. She patted the dog's head, then looked at Chase. "I think it's wonderful, that you take them all in like this. Not many people would."

Chase shrugged—did all men resort to that?—but gave her a steady look with bright blue eyes when he said, "Seems to me the Raffertys do the same, only they took on an orphaned kid."

"Lucas," she said.

"Keller found him pretty much the same way I found her," he said, nodding at the golden dog. "On the run, trying to steal food. And ended up taking him in." He nodded toward Chance, who had the truck door open now. "And he was the strongest vote for it. Well, after his mother," Chase finished with a grin.

She didn't doubt that, especially after seeing Maggie with Lucas last night.

Tri's anxious yip drew her attention. He was looking at her rather than the cluster of dogs below. She felt the urge to go to him, but stayed where she was, knowing Chance wanted to see as pure a reaction to the other dogs as he could get. She watched as Tri jumped down from the truck, maintaining his balance even without the help of that missing leg. He looked at her again, and she couldn't stop herself from whispering, "It's okay."

He reacted as if he'd heard and turned his attention to the approaching pack. Chance took a strong grip on the harness as the other dogs gathered around for a mutual sniff and greet. She noticed two newcomers to the group that she guessed were the Hank and Loretta that Chase had mentioned, but she kept her gaze on Tri.

He seemed a bit edgy to her, and she wondered if his hackles were up, beneath the heavy harness. But there was no snarling, no sign of teeth at all, just that hyper alertness.

Which, she realized, she'd be feeling herself if she found herself dropped into a crowd of half a dozen strangers. And eventually, Tri relaxed enough to almost play, although he never got far away from her. And Chance.

She wondered if Tri realized what a defender he had in Chance, that the man who held him in check would make sure he would not be hurt again.

If you think anything but his welfare would change that decision, you're wrong.

She hadn't meant her jab to hit quite that hard, but she knew the cool answer he'd given her was pure truth. Nothing, but nothing would make him decide in anything except Tri's best interest. And while he may have meant the words and tone to be chilling, they had instead steadied her, made her even more determined for him to see her as that best interest.

Of course, she also felt that what happened had to be in that best interest. And that niggling little worry rose up again, the worry that had come to her when Tri had reached out to Chance as they'd neared the place he'd never wanted to be, the middle of the obviously big-deal Last Stand Christmas tree lighting. The worry about whether Tri could ever bond with her the way he did with a fellow warrior.

Because Chance Rafferty was that, there was no doubt.

At least he's out now. So I'll never find out one day that an IED or enemy sniper took him out.

She broke off her own rampaging train of thought, wishing she could someday stop this relating everything to potential death.

…one of the twenty-two.

Somehow that seemed worse than Dean's fate of being KIA. For a vet to come home so mentally wounded, whether there were physical scars or not, that suicide seemed the only way out was heart-wrenching in an entirely different way.

You should do something. Something to help.

She was still tangled up in her thoughts a couple of hours later as they left the Walker place after Tri's lengthy interaction with the pack. Only a nudge from a cold, wet doggie nose now shook her out of it. She reached back and stroked Tri's head, scratched behind his ears.

"You did so good, sweetheart," she crooned to him. "I think you even had a little fun after a while." She looked over at the man behind the wheel and added, "Don't you think? Or did I miss something?"

He kept his focus on the road ahead as if it were a crowded freeway. "No. He did fine. Wary around Chase, but I expected that. Overall, he did better than I anticipated."

"He even kept up with them most of the time."

"Yes."

"Too bad they don't make prosthetics for dogs."

He glanced at her. "They do. He didn't have enough leg left to make it work."

"Oh. I didn't know they did."

Another glance. "Had one come in a year or so ago, missing a hind foot. They'd tried to get him to adapt to a prosthetic, but he kept gnawing at it. So Cody watched him for a while, then designed a different kind for him. It took a while to get him to leave it alone, but once he did it made all the difference. His entire mentality changed. Enough that a retired vet's family, one with kids old enough to understand, was able to adopt him."

She'd already guessed the pretty boy had useful skills, besides clever ones, so the thought that registered with her now was that Chance had said more in that explanation than he'd said in one go the entire first day she'd spent with them.

The first day that was all of two days ago.

Two days, and it seemed like everything had changed. She felt as if the center of her world, her life, had somehow shifted. Home, or at least the place she'd always thought of as home, seemed not just distant in miles, but in time. She didn't feel much of a pull at all, especially since her parents had moved to Florida. Right now the most powerful pull she felt was right here in this truck. And no matter how much she told herself it was from the dog in the back seat, she knew deep down it was more than that.

When they got back to Last Stand and made the turn onto the Hickory Creek Spur she was sure, from her two trips out there, it should have been a right turn. Which meant they were now going in the opposite direction from the Rafferty ranch.

"We're headed somewhere else?"

He nodded.

"Too much to ask where?" she asked, even as she wondered if he'd run through his allotment of daily words with that explanation about the prosthetic.

"Lock and load," he said.

She blinked. "Is that a place or an order?"

His head snapped around, as if he were startled. Then as he looked back at the road, she thought she saw a rather sheepish smile tugging at the corners of his mouth. "Sorry. *Lock and Load* is a place. Shooting range. It's run by a vet, and another one works there. They'll be used to MWDs."

She looked at Tri, then back at Chance. "And you want to see how he does with strangers without the distraction of a pack of friendly dogs?"

He nodded. "And they'll be able to handle it if he goes haywire."

"Do you think he will?"

"I'm hoping he'll be too tired, from all that pack interaction."

"As long as he's not tired and cranky," she said, then turned back to Tri, who was indeed lying on the back seat rather than sitting up as he usually had so far. "But you're not, are you, m'boy? That normal dog inside is fighting to get out, isn't he?"

She reached out to stroke his head, and tired or not, Tri swiped his tongue over her wrist. Chance glanced over, and Ariel caught an odd expression on his face before he turned back to the road ahead. She studied him for a moment, thinking that even in profile this was a man you'd notice, with that masculine jaw, strong, corded neck, and quiet air of competence and determination.

As they drove, she was distracted by the signage for what was obviously the town's cemetery. She wondered if his father was there but given he didn't even look, she thought not. He was probably in a military resting place, as Dean was. She bit the inside of her lip, as she always did to fight down the other, worse pain. But although the ache was there, as always, it wasn't as swamping as it usually was.

As if he'd sensed it, Tri nudged her. He must be the reason it was less. It must be that she had something else to focus on now, someone hurting just as she was.

And—she glanced again at Chance—a man who had been there, who understood. A man who had known Dean, had liked and respected him. That mattered, made his approval more important to her. That had to be all this was, this strange feeling she had around him. Surely that's all it was. Well, that and maybe she wasn't quite as numb inside as she'd been.

Or he was man enough and attractive enough to wake her up a little.

It wasn't until they pulled in at the *Lock and Load* sign that the juxtaposition with the cemetery next door registered. "I guess they don't get many noise complaints from the neighbors," she said.

"Nope. But they're closed for the day anyway, with most

people focused on the parade tonight."

He'd chosen this day for this for just that reason, she realized.

"They're closed?" she said, looking at the two men approaching. One was a wiry, tanned older man with salt-and-pepper hair in a buzz cut. The other was taller, and younger, late twenties she guessed, with sandy-brown hair. He moved with an easy grace that reminded her of Chance.

"They agreed to meet up here for this."

"Good of them."

"They respect the dogs," he said simply. She suspected some respect for him and what he was doing played into that, although she also suspected he would never admit—or expect—that.

And she wondered why on earth that mattered so much to her, about a man she'd met two days ago.

Chapter Twenty-Six

"MIKE FLEMING'S THE range master," Chance said as the two men approached the truck but stopped several feet away as he'd asked. He and Ariel and Tri stood next to the vehicle, as Tri watched the men intently. "The younger guy is Scott Parrish. Just out of the Marines early this year. He's engaged to the Highwater sister, Sage."

He had no idea why he'd felt compelled to add that. People's social and romantic connections didn't generally mean anything to him. Not enough to talk about to strangers, anyway. And that's still what she was. Wasn't it?

The crazy thought joined the long string of crazy thoughts he'd been having since she showed up.

The two men were in civilian clothes, but they were standing as if at ease, in a posture Tri would recognize. And while the dog let out a low growl, it wasn't a threatening one, more a signal of awareness of the strangers, an alert anyone who'd worked with these dogs would know meant a stranger was around.

"Easy, they're friendlies," he said quietly. "Sit."

The dog sat, and the growl subsided, although alert, dark

eyes still fastened on the two. Chance kept a firm grip on the leash.

On a sudden impulse he said to Ariel, "Go talk to them. They know who you are." He'd told them on the phone that she was the widow of Tri's handler. "I want to see if he responds to you going to them first."

She only hesitated for a moment, but then crossed the dozen feet between them to Mike and Scott. Tri didn't like her leaving. He was trembling with the urge to go after her. The sit command held, but he kept looking up at Chance anxiously, clearly hoping to be released.

Chance waited until Tri was no longer vibrating with that urge. Then, with a quiet "Heel," he started forward, ready at the first sign of trouble to grab the harness and pull the dog back. But Tri obeyed, even though Chance could sense his eagerness to get to her through the taut leash.

When they got there, Ariel used that high, cheery tone she always used when soothing the dog, and introduced him to both men as if it were some royal reception line. Chance noticed she put a hand on Mike's arm as Tri watched.

"Tri, this is Mike. He's one of us," she said, and the older man crouched down despite some obvious stiffness in his back. He held out a hand, palm down, and let the dog sniff. Tri did so, and Chance felt a tension through the leash, but the dog's body language read alert, not frightened or ready to attack.

After a moment the dog looked back at Ariel, who nodded at Mike. Mike spoke softly. "Back ain't what it used to be, Rafferty, so if it's okay with you, I'm going to take her arm to help me up. Let's see how he reacts."

Chance hesitated.

"I'll take the flank," Scott said, edging sideways to where he could help grab either the dog or Mike if necessary. Tri was aware of him moving, Chance saw his ears swivel, but he didn't take his eyes off Ariel.

"All right," Chance said.

Ariel held out her arm, still talking to the dog in that voice he seemed to love. Mike reached up and put a hand on her forearm and slowly levered himself upward. Tri made a little sound, but Ariel kept talking to him and he held as Mike got himself upright.

"And this is Scott," she said, not giving the dog time to think about it, just walking over to stand next to the younger man. "He's served with your canine buddies, so he's a friend. Come over and meet him, nicely, all right?"

Chance gave the dog just enough slack in the leash to see what he would do. He hopped over to the pair, but not in a rush. Scott greeted him the same slow, easy way, although after crouching down for a couple of minutes he got up under his own power.

Whether it was that he really was tired after the encounter with the Walker dogs, or Ariel's going to the unknowns first, or simply that he somehow sensed these were men like the one he'd tried to save and had nearly died for, Chance didn't know. And it didn't really matter. What mattered was that this entire day had gone so much better than he'd dared hope, and Tri himself had come so far so fast.

All because of the beautiful redhead who was now talking quietly to Mike and Scott, Tri sitting at her side, watchful but not on the alert.

They spent an hour or so walking around the range, with Ariel asking questions that made it clear she knew a little about weaponry, probably about the amount any military wife would pick up. Tri followed along, and once given the "at ease" command and some slack in the leash, inspected the premises much as any dog would. Chance had wondered if the familiar scents of gunpowder and gun oil would unsettle him, bring back unnerving memories, but the opposite seemed to happen—the dog seemed to relax.

"They're good guys," Ariel said when they were back on the road, this time definitely headed for the ranch.

"Yes."

"And a lot of respect between them."

"Yes."

"And for you."

He stopped himself from looking at her and merely shrugged.

"Men," she muttered. Before he could react to that she went on. "Mike said if you and Scott had a medals competition, it would be close."

He lost the fight then and glanced at her. "What? The

guy's a freaking trophy-winning sniper."

"And you single-handedly saved the lives of an entire platoon that was pinned down by the enemy."

Damn, he didn't know Mike even knew about that. "I just got lucky," he said.

"Uh-huh. Pure luck that you skylined yourself on that ridge to fire that rocket launcher into the middle of the enemy. Twice."

"I was the first one who saw them. I had the shot."

"And they shot back."

"And missed. Mostly."

He had, in fact, taken a round through his side, but he'd been lucky. It had missed anything vital, and the rest of his men were there by then, including the medic, who patched him up well enough it held until they took out the rest of the bad guys and got the trapped guys out of there.

"So he said. Mostly."

He hadn't thought about that day in a long time. It had gone well, yes—aside from the hole below his ribs—but there were other days when it hadn't gone so well, and it seemed all he could think about was the guys who hadn't made it. He tried to focus on something else. Anything else.

She'd gotten along with them well. If Scott wasn't so obviously head over heels about Sage Highwater, he might have been...

Damn, he'd almost thought jealous.

Now that's a woman.

Mike had said it in that approving way a man did when stating the obvious. And Chance hadn't argued with the obvious. He could have done without the crusty old guy's next not-so-casual observation, which was that a woman like that got a young man thinking about a cozy house, nights at home, and kids someday.

Kids.

We were going to. Start a family, I mean…when he got back…

He needed to remember what she'd said. She'd loved Dean enough to want his children. To raise a family with him. That was not something a woman like her thought or did lightly. Maybe that would accomplish what he seemed unable to do himself: quit thinking about her as the woman who stirred him as none ever had and remember she was the widow of a man who would count on him to treat her with the respect she was due.

"—also said you're a hero, no matter how you deny it."

He tuned back in abruptly. "I'm no hero."

"You are by his standards." She paused, then added softly, "And mine, too."

Mike's parting words rang in his head. *If it was me in your boots, at your age, I surely wouldn't let that one slip away.*

He had to stop this. Stop thinking this way. Stop her thinking this way. And there was only one way he could see to do it. He had to tell her. Tell her what he hadn't—that would change the way she saw him. He'd been a coward long enough.

"I'm not," he said, his voice as cold as the chill that had risen in him, because he knew what would happen when he finished saying it. "There's something you should know. About what happened to Dean."

Her brow furrowed. "I know what happened. They sent them after that terrorist enclave and—"

"No. I mean why. Why it happened."

"Why?"

"It happened because I..."

He had to stop. Realized he shouldn't be driving, if he was going to do this. He pulled to the side, off the road. He clenched his jaw until he regained control. And then, resolute now, he turned to look at her—she deserved that—and finished it.

"It happened because I couldn't talk the brass out of it. I knew it was impossible, what they were asking. I'd been there. That was the mission where the platoon got pinned down, my last one. That mountain stronghold wasn't just a difficult target, it was impossible. It was huge and dug into dozens of caves in the mountains in that canyon. There was no way to maintain stealth. They had equipment and weapons we'd had no idea they had, including drones and surveillance, and there were three times as many fighters there as we'd been told."

She was staring at him now. He went on doggedly.

"You could maybe have taken it out with a tactical nuke,

but nothing less. But they wouldn't listen. Not to me. I couldn't convince them. And so they sent them out, including Dean. On a…"

He couldn't get the words out after all. But he saw in her face, in those huge eyes, that he didn't have to. "A suicide mission," she whispered.

"Because I couldn't get through to them." His fist slammed into the steering wheel. He shifted his gaze to it. Hit it again as he went on harshly. "I couldn't get them to listen. They all died, because I couldn't get them to listen."

He sat there, staring unseeingly at the wheel, the dash, the gauges. The silence spun out. He was surprised he couldn't feel waves of the anger or hate or whatever she must be feeling toward him now coming off her. He didn't know how much time had passed before she spoke, but it felt like forever.

"You see that power pole there?"

He blinked at the total non sequitur. He looked at her, but she wasn't looking at him, she was nodding at the tall, solid pole a few feet from the front of the vehicle. He glanced at it, then went back to her. "What about it?"

"Convince it that it should move to the other side of the road."

He blinked again. Opened his mouth, couldn't think of a thing to say and shut it again.

"You can't," she said softly. "Because it doesn't have the capacity to listen."

You can't persuade someone who doesn't have the capacity to listen.

Dean's words rang in his head, words he'd completely forgotten until his beloved Red quoted them back to him. Uttered after some of that stateside brass they so often complained about had blown through on a planned media junket. The guy in the fanciest uniform—without a combat ribbon to be seen, they both had noted—had asked questions that were clearly for the media group that was the reason for the trip. Questions he didn't really want the answers to and wouldn't have cared about anyway.

"Do you feel some sort of guilt? Survivor's guilt or something?" she asked softly. "Because you couldn't convince people who wouldn't listen to scrub that mission?"

The pressure building inside him was almost unbearable. It was so fierce he couldn't have spoken even if he'd had any words left in his head. But she kept going, relentlessly, as if he had answered.

"Is that why you…shut down? Why you've isolated yourself? Why you don't talk to friends and barely to your family? You don't think you have anything worth saying because some bureaucrat officer said so?"

He had to look away from her again. It was too intense. "They died," he said hoarsely. "They all died. If I'd said it better, if I'd—"

"You couldn't have. Dean knew that. That's why he always said you can't persuade someone who doesn't have the capacity to listen." She even said it with Dean's intonation. "There was nothing more you could have done. You aren't responsible. Those deaf power poles are."

He wanted to believe it. He couldn't. Could he? The pressure became nearly unbearable. He wanted to get out of here, run...except Raffertys don't run.

"Look at me, Chance."

She said it quietly. So quietly it should have been easy to ignore. It was impossible to ignore. He looked at her.

"He wouldn't blame you." She spoke firmly and with finality. Then, much more gently, and holding his gaze steadily, she added, "I don't blame you."

He felt as if he'd somehow ruptured inside. As if the pressure had reached the critical point and he'd exploded. He didn't even try to talk. Not, this time, because he didn't see the point, but because he truly didn't know how to put what he was feeling into words. Not any that made sense, anyway. It was all almost dizzying, but he wondered what was left. If there were enough pieces left to put himself back together again. Or what he would be if and when he did.

He didn't know.

Chance drove the rest of the way to the ranch in silence, trying to process his whirling thoughts. Ariel seemed content to coo over Tri, telling him over and over what a good boy he'd been today. And the dog seemed more content than Chance had ever seen him.

By the time they reached the gate, he thought he might

be able to function. When they pulled up at the ranch house, where her car was still parked from yesterday, his mother was on the porch with Quinta, wrestling with full grocery bags and the front door. Tri whined at the sight of the other dog, but in such a normal way it almost made him smile. He said a quick "Excuse me," got out of the truck quickly and went up to help his mother, taking all the bags and carrying them inside once she got the door open.

"How did it go?" she asked.

"He did great. Better than I could have hoped."

"And Ariel?"

"She...I...she's..." he stammered, caught off guard. There was no way he was ready to talk about what had happened today, sitting by the side of the road. He wasn't sure it would make sense to anyone but him.

And Ariel.

She'd understood. Somehow she'd understood what had been eating him alive all this time, and with her simple words and the authority of being the one who would know behind her, she'd absolved him.

His mother raised a brow at him as he stood there in silence. "I meant how did she do with Tri, but I think I like your answer better."

Sometimes this woman saw too damned much. But then she smiled at him, that loving, all-forgiving smile, and everything faded away except the certainty that he'd been utterly blessed in the mom department.

"Don't leave her—and Tri—outside. Bring them in. You're staying for dinner, right?"

"I am?"

"No, you both are."

He opened his mouth to answer, then shut it again. Did she mean him and Tri, or him and…Ariel? He just stared at her, unable to come up with an answer that wouldn't betray the crazy thoughts he'd been having.

"And Tri, too, of course," she said, with that look that told him she already knew.

"Mom—"

"She's a good one, Chance. And the first woman you've felt anything for in far too long. Don't turn your back on her."

He stared at this woman who'd borne him and his brothers, who had been their rock, and who often said she knew love when she saw it because she had loved their father beyond measure. And he wondered how he'd ever thought he could hide anything from her.

"She's Dean Larson's widow," he said, at this moment not caring what he was admitting, not to this woman who would never, ever stop loving him.

"And you think he would want her to stay forever alone?"

"She only came for Tri." *And apparently to salve my guilty conscience in ways I never thought possible.*

"And found more, I think."

"She doesn't…"

"Feel like you do? How do you know? Did you ask?"

He nearly gaped at her then. It took him a moment to ask, "Does this mind reading thing come with motherhood?"

"Of course it does," she said with an impish smile. "Otherwise we'd never survive it."

He knew she loved him. But sometimes, this irrepressible woman was more than he could deal with. But she always seemed to know when he'd reached his limit, and then she pushed him a tiny bit further.

And sometimes, that's why he loved her most.

Chapter Twenty-Seven

"DINNER?"

She'd been about to get in her rental car and head back to the inn, after reluctantly saying goodbye to Tri, when Chance had come back outside. And at her first sight of him she had that old saying running continuously through her mind, about if you want to know how a man will treat his wife, watch how he treats his mother. She had no business even pondering that.

"She insists. You don't want to try to resist my mother when she insists."

"So I gather," she said, thinking of all the people she'd encountered since her arrival who had been of the same opinion, that Maggie Rafferty was a force to be reckoned with.

"Will begging work? Because I'll take the heat if you don't stay."

She stared at him. The promised clouds had arrived, and somehow the grayness of the sky seemed to make his eyes look more gray than blue. She wondered if she would ever get tired of looking at them. Then she wondered if she'd lost her mind, thinking things like that. She tried to snap herself out of it with a teasing response.

"You, beg? I think not."

The front door opened, and Maggie stuck her head out. "Please stay," she called out. "Keller and Sydney are in town, Rylan was hit with inspiration and is holed up, and Lucas is off with Cody and Sean Highwater getting ready for the parade. Which I promise I won't try to trick you into going to. But if you don't stay, I'll be stuck alone with Mr. Mono-syllabic here."

Ariel couldn't help it, she laughed at the description, even as she thought she wasn't sure it really applied anymore. He'd certainly been more than monosyllabic with her, on occasion. But she gave in. And secretly, she knew it was because she wanted to, she hadn't really wanted to leave at all. She knew something important had happened today, when she'd hit upon what had been eating at him so badly for so long. He'd looked so shell-shocked at first, but gradually, slowly, as they'd driven back here she'd seen, and thought she'd felt, a change in him. Something deep and heartfelt. And she wanted to know if she was right.

"All right," she said.

She turned to get her purse back out of the rental, while Chance went to get Tri out of the truck.

"I thought you were required to do the grocery shopping?" she asked as he bent to remove the harness, leaving the leash in place.

"Holiday exemption," he said as he tossed the harness back inside. "Mom does all the holiday food." He gave her a sideways look. "It's past the first, so any moment she'll be starting the baking."

She laughed again, and again it struck her how often that was happening. And on the heels of that thought, it struck her how much she liked his. She felt a pang, and she wasn't sure if it was missing Dean, and how they'd always laughed, or…guilt at liking Chance's rarer laugh so much. Maybe that was it. Because it was much rarer, it was more…precious.

Precious? That idea, that word, rattled her out of her thoughts and she focused on getting Tri inside.

Once they were inside Quinta immediately trotted over to greet the newcomer. Tri looked back at Chance. "At ease, buddy," he said quietly, unhooking the leash. And the dogs set off to apparently make security rounds of the house.

"Amazing," Maggie said, watching them go. "He's a different dog."

"Yes," Chance said.

Maggie shifted her gaze to Ariel. "Bless you for coming for him. Don't give up."

"I know it won't all be as easy as this seems to have been," she said. "But I have no intention of giving up." She smiled at this woman she already liked. "I'm stubborn that way."

"Good," Maggie said. "You'll need to be." And Ariel had the strangest feeling she was no longer talking about the dog.

The meal was delicious, a spread of build-your-own soft tacos that included some delicious shredded pork, beef, and unexpectedly, some fish Maggie said had just come off the truck in town and she'd sautéed up with butter and a lemony dill sauce that was the perfect counterpart. Topped with homemade guacamole and rich sour cream, they were incredible, and Ariel found herself eating more than she had in recent memory. The final touch was an unexpected but delightful peppermint tea that lightened things just enough. Even Chance, who said he wasn't a tea drinker, downed a cup of the sweet stuff.

"Wow," she said when she finally had to admit she was too full for another bite. "I quite made a pig of myself."

"Delighted to see it," Maggie said. "Except now you'd better go walk some off or that pie I picked up in town this morning will go to waste." She shot her son a sideways look. "It's Char-Pie's pecan, in case you're thinking about skipping out."

Ariel looked at him just in time to see him lower his gaze to his own empty plate, and she couldn't be sure who he'd been looking at. "I wasn't," he muttered.

They cleaned up the dishes, the three of them working together, Chance silent except for the occasional task-oriented comment or question. He politely asked if she wanted to go for that walk his mother had suggested. Too politely. Sometimes those manners were a pain, or a buffer she couldn't seem to get through. Which then inevitably gave rise to the question of why that mattered so much.

Tri was sprawled on the floor, with Quinta, obviously tired from his busy day. His head came up when they headed for the door. Chance looked back at his mother questioningly.

"Let him stay," she said. "He seems tired enough to stay calm, and if not, might as well find out."

So Chance repeated the "at ease" command and the dog's dark head went down again.

"Check on Bonnie and Two, will you? And Ariel," Maggie added, "take one of the heavier jackets by the door. It's frosty outside now that it's dark."

"Your mom is amazing," she said as they went outside, into indeed frosty-feeling air.

"She is."

"I can't imagine how hard it must have been for her."

"There were times we didn't make it easy."

"I'm sure. Four boys, by herself."

"Three." At her look, he gave her that damned shrug again. "Keller wasn't a boy from the moment our father was killed."

The sky was dark now, with no moon, so she couldn't see his expression. After a moment, in the most casual tone she could manage, she said, "So Keller took on your father's role here, while you took on your father's role for your country."

He stopped in his tracks. She didn't have to be able to

see him to know he was staring at her. She shrugged back at him, on purpose. "Where am I wrong?"

He didn't answer. She hoped it was because he realized she wasn't wrong. Just as she hoped he'd accepted that neither she nor Dean blamed him for what had happened. Because she'd meant every word.

After a moment they continued walking. She could almost feel him thinking. But he didn't speak. He just headed toward the big barn. They went through the small door in the big, sliding door and stepped inside. She could sense the life inside, smell the scent of hay and grain, hear the rustle as animals reacted to their presence. Just inside there was another door, and he reached through to flip a switch in what was obviously a room for all their gear: saddles, bridles, ropes, things she had no names for. A tack room, she thought that's what it was called.

Soft, not quite dim lights came on throughout the barn. He started down the wide aisle, and equine heads popped out as he went. She noticed the stalls were numbered by signs above each door, odd numbers down the left, even on the right.

"Do they have names? Or just numbers, like Quinta?" she asked, making sure she was smiling and her tone teasing.

He nodded toward the first stall where a gray horse stood watching them. "That's Seven. He's Mom's."

She hadn't really expected it to be true. "Oh."

"His real name is Lucky Seven, but she wanted to keep

to her theme."

She looked back at him. And now, with the lights, there was no missing the tightness of his mouth. She might have thought he was angry, but for the twitch at the corners. She played along.

"And who's this?" she asked as a sleek, black head turned to watch them approach. "Three, because of the stall number?"

"No. Three—Trey, really—Cody's bay, is in stall four."

"So three is in four." She stopped, waited, sensing there was more coming. There was.

He nodded toward the black horse. "That's Flyer. He's in number three because he belongs to Ry."

She frowned, then got it. "The third-born."

"Where's Keller's horse?"

He gestured with a thumb to the other side of aisle. "Stall two," he said.

She looked and saw the horse she'd seen Keller on earlier, the one that had looked almost blue in the sunlight. "But he's not named Two...too, is he?" she asked, thinking of the baby out in the corral the other day.

"That's where it breaks down," he said, sounding almost sorrowful. "He's just Blue. Because he's a blue roan. No number involved."

The twitch at the corners of his mouth came again, but this time it was obvious. "You're pulling my chain," she accused.

"Yep." He admitted it—surprisingly—so easily that when he finally quit fighting the smile she couldn't help smiling back. He reached out and patted the bluish horse's neck. "Cody says Keller has no imagination."

To her own surprise she felt a jab of irritation through the humor. "Maybe he's just been too busy to indulge it." He gave her a startled look. "Sorry. A bit defensive there, because I admire what your brother has done."

"Don't apologize. So do I. More than…I've ever told him," he said quietly.

"Tell him," she urged. "Don't assume he knows."

After a moment, he nodded. He looked as if there was more he was thinking about saying, but then he looked away as a soft whinny came from the far end of the barn. "I think we'd better go say hello to Two and his mom now."

She chuckled at the necessary rhyme as they headed that way. The golden head of the mare came over the bottom door of the stall, which Ariel now saw was about twice the size of the others. The pair of golden horses with black markings and mane and tail looked just as pretty to her as they had outside. The little one poked his nose at her, and under mom's watchful gaze she patted him gently.

"You said he looks just like his…?"

"Generationally, his great-grandfather. Buckshot." He seemed to hesitate, then went on. "He was my father's. He died a couple of years ago, at twenty-eight."

"That's old for a horse, isn't it?"

"Old enough, I guess."

She studied him for a moment. "But it still must have been hard. Like losing one more daily link to your dad."

His eyes widened, just slightly, but she knew she'd hit home. They shared so much, she and this family, things nobody wants to share.

Chance took in an audible breath and then said a hair too briskly, "And now Two here looks just like him. Same coloring and markings, down to the crooked part of the blaze on his nose."

The little colt apparently decided he'd exerted enough energy that he needed sustenance and turned to his mother to nurse.

"Sweet," she whispered, watching the pair.

"Yes."

Something in his voice, some low, rough note made her turn to look at him. And something about his expression, about how close he was, reminded her of that moment when she'd slid out of his truck and ended up practically pressed against him.

And when he moved, when he put his hands on her shoulders—gently enough that she could easily pull away—and bent his head, she knew what was coming. And in that moment she realized she'd been waiting for it. An idea that so stunned her she couldn't even think about stopping him.

And then she realized the most stunning thing of all.

She didn't want to.

Chapter Twenty-Eight

C HANCE ONLY FULLY acknowledged how much he'd wanted this when he did it. He'd tried to stop thinking about her mouth. He couldn't. He'd tried to stop thinking about how beautiful her eyes were. He couldn't. He'd tried to stop thinking about hair the color of fall leaves. He couldn't.

But the moment his lips touched hers, the thinking did stop. All of it. The only thing in his consciousness was the feel of her mouth, the warmth of her, the sweet taste of her, underscored by the slightest tang of the peppermint from the tea.

He deepened the kiss, and she welcomed him. As he pulled her against him every part of him that had awakened in that moment when she'd slid out of the truck against him clamored again. And that tiny voice in the back of his mind saying this was wrong faded away, because nothing could stand for long against how good this felt.

And then he felt the slightest, barest, but hottest touch of her tongue against his lower lip, and it was as if she'd started a conflagration. He tasted her more deeply, and his pulse kicked up even more when she tasted him in turn, the swipe of her tongue over the ridge of his teeth sending another burst of heat along every nerve. He groaned low and deep and pulled her even closer, wanting more, needing more.

Wanting everything. Wanting to take her down to the straw in this stall and explore every inch of her long, graceful body. Wanting to bury himself inside her and ease this ache he'd denied existed for so long. The ache he'd only been able to deny because no one had stirred him like this in longer than he could remember. No, that wasn't true. No one had stirred him like this, ever.

Liz, the one-time fiancée who had never had the kind of strength Ariel had, seemed long ago and far away. Unreal. Or maybe just the pale imitation it had been. But this…this was deep, powerful, a surging feeling he could barely fight down.

Again the little voice tried, calling out that he couldn't have picked a more unthinkable woman. Even now that he knew she didn't blame him for Dean's death, because he wasn't sure he'd entirely accepted that himself. But he knew this was real, vital. It took a high-pitched whinny from Two before he was able to fight his way out of the deluge of heat and need and pure sensation swamping him.

When he pulled back he was breathing hard—had he even taken a breath since their lips had met?—and his heart was hammering in his chest. Ariel was looking up at him as if she felt the same. There was a rather dazed look in those sky-blue eyes, as if she'd felt the same tidal wave of utterly overwhelming need. And that thought, that she'd felt the same thing he had, was somehow the most overwhelming thing of all.

Even as she stared at him, he saw color flood her cheeks. She was blushing. Embarrassed. And probably regretting, already. She opened her mouth to speak, but some sharp pain in his gut drove him to put a finger to her lips and shake his head.

"Don't say it. I know."

He didn't want to hear the word *mistake* from her lips. Not now, not when his heart seemed to have forgotten how to slow down, and he was harder than he'd ever been in his life. *Get over it. She's not yours, and she never will be.*

And it wasn't until he was a safe couple of feet from her that he realized he'd somehow gone from telling himself he didn't want or need a woman in his life to denying this one so fiercely it only proved how much he wanted—needed?— her.

ARIEL COULD BARELY focus on driving as she headed back to the inn. Her head was still reeling, her emotions pounding at her from so many sides she couldn't settle on one thought long enough to make any sense of…anything.

Maybe because none of this made any sense.

She'd been aware from the first time she saw him that

Chance Rafferty was attractive. Those changeable eyes, that lean yet powerful build, and the touch of gray in his dark hair at the temples, at odds with his young face, like a sign that this was not a naïve soul. No, that he was an eye-catching package had never been in doubt. But she'd thought that kind of attraction behind her, probably for good.

That kiss had blown that conviction into a billion or so pieces.

Back in her room she found herself pacing, unable to rest even after a busy, full day.

Because the capper of that day was a kiss that changed...everything?

She tried to stop thinking about it. But the only thing even slightly able to distract her was the memory of that moment when he'd touched a finger to her lips, shaking his head. *Don't say it. I know.*

He knew what? That that kiss had been life-altering? That he'd felt it as powerfully as she had?

Or had he meant it as an apology for doing it at all? That he knew he shouldn't have done it?

The man could give a clam lessons in keeping quiet about his feelings. And when he did talk about them, it was to deny them, it seemed.

I'm not a loving kind of guy.

Yet he had blamed himself for Dean and the others' deaths.

Yet he devoted his life to caring for the dogs that had served.

Yet he clearly accepted Lucas as part of the family.

Yet he dropped everything to go help his mother.

She slept little, and when she did her dreams ranged from guilt-laced images of Dean to guilt-inducing images of kissing Chance again. And more than kissing him.

She awoke well before sunrise, when light was just beginning to show in the sky. It was Sunday, but that made no difference. She would go to the ranch, as agreed. Whatever else happened, she couldn't and wouldn't let Tri down. She would just have to hope that when Chance had told her not to speak of it, he'd meant it and it would hold. Despite the urge that rose in her to corner him and demand they speak of it.

Unable to go back to sleep she got up, took her time showering, including washing her hair, but it was still early when she was done. She knew there would be coffee downstairs regardless of the hour, so she grabbed one of the large cookies from the guest basket that had been placed in her room, headed down and grabbed a cup of the brew, and on a final impulse headed into town.

The streets were quiet, even Main Street, with no one in sight. Given that, she was a little surprised at how many cars were parked in the area. It occurred to her that perhaps some of the townsfolk had partied a bit too hard last night after the parade, and that was the reason for the abundance of vehicles; they'd not risked driving home last night.

She finally found a place a couple of blocks down from the town center and the tree, in front of a large church building. She got out and locked the car, then started walking. She tried to orient herself and figure out where they'd been the night of the tree lighting, but she didn't remember having seen the pet bakery before. And she would definitely have remembered the name *Good Boy!* The people bakery, *Kolaches*, was conveniently next door, but sadly not yet open. But the big cookie—which come to think of it she thought had that name on the wrapping—was holding her for now. Especially after that huge meal last night, Maggie's wonderful cooking that—

She stopped that train of thought before she derailed into what she was determinedly not thinking about. Then she saw that the next shop was *Yippee Ki Yay*, and suddenly she realized where she was. They'd parked behind this row of buildings, and that was where she'd seen the image of the bucking horse, that had brought on the trip to meet Sugar Lips, and—

No! Not going there!

She kept walking, slowly, in no hurry. She passed the wine-tasting room on the corner—she remembered reading that the Hill Country was quite the developing wine-producing area—and crossed the side street to see the statue she'd noticed her first time through town. Her curiosity made her read the lower plaque first, the one next to the spot where a large chunk of the pedestal was missing. The story was short, a sad commemoration of two deaths in a fiery crash, but also of the heroics of Chief Shane Highwater, who had risked his own life to pull the one survivor out of the vehicle that had erupted into flames. That made her think of Chance, and of the two men from the shooting range; obviously Last Stand wasn't short on heroic types.

Her gaze shifted to the main plaque on the statue, the tale from the last stand that had given the town its name, and how the man commemorated here had made a desperate run for the ammunition stores, giving the tiny band a chance to hold off a contingent of Santa Anna's army. He'd suffered a fatal wound in the process, but he'd done it, and they'd held out long enough.

She wandered over by the library, where the huge tree stood. The lights weren't on at the moment, but it was still an impressive sight. As was the library building itself, nearly as big as the courthouse next door.

She walked on, and across the next street encountered the stone building labeled *Last Stand Saloon*. She found herself smiling over the proximity, with the saloon directly across the street from the courthouse and imagined the old days when someone who over-imbibed and maybe started a fight could probably be walked right across the street.

There was another plaque on the wall beside the front door, along with a more detailed story. She read it, remembering what Maggie had said, that this very building was the site of that original battle. Which explained the obvious bullet holes in the walls, she guessed.

There was, she mused as she turned to look up and down the quiet street, an awful lot of history in this little town. And some of these shops looked fun. Maybe she'd come back when they were open. Maybe she could bring Tri, and they could—

She cut off her own thought, back to what she stubbornly was not thinking about. Because that "they" would, at this point in the process, have to include Chance.

Get over it. He probably already has.

She turned on her heel and headed back the way she'd come. She looked in the front window of the western shop, trying to focus on it instead. A sign near the door caught her eye, announcing that they were sold out of Rylan Rafferty original belts. Remembering the belt Maggie had been wearing, she wasn't surprised.

She went on, managing to keep her thoughts on that other Rafferty brother until she was back to the block where she'd parked. But it wasn't as quiet or at all deserted as it had been when she'd started her walk half an hour ago. She realized why when she saw the knot of people near the church building; an early service just letting out, she guessed.

She had just reached the spot where she had parked when someone said hello to her. She looked up to see an older woman, tall, and dressed conservatively in a black dress. Her hair was dark, threaded with a little silver, and pulled up into an elegant style that looked both beautiful and time-consuming. Her eyes were dark, and brightly clear. When she smiled, Ariel suddenly placed her as the woman who had greeted Chance so poignantly last night.

"Mrs. Valencia," she said, smiling back.

"There is another service later," she said, gesturing at the church.

"No," Ariel said. "I haven't been in a church since—"

She broke off, wondering what on earth it was about this place that had her blurting out private things to people she'd just met.

"I can imagine," the woman said quietly. "As can my daughter," she added, nodding at the young woman who had come up beside her. "Elena, this is Ariel, the lady with Chance Rafferty, that I mentioned to you."

The younger woman turned a pair of equally dark and clear eyes on her. This must be the woman married to one of the Highwaters. "You're the one here for his problem boy?" she asked.

"Yes."

Elena looked at her for a moment before saying, "I've heard he was your late husband's dog."

Was nothing secret in this town? "Yes."

Again there was a moment of silence as the other woman studied her. And then, very softly, she said, "I have walked in your shoes, Ariel. It is an awful journey."

She blinked. "You…?"

"My first husband, father of our son. Also military. Some years ago."

She wasn't sure what made her ask, since she'd never cared about it before. "But you've remarried?"

The smile she got at that was warm enough to thaw even Ariel's chilly heart. "Yes. To a man who understood well enough, and had the respect, to go to his grave and speak to him, so he could tell our son he had."

Her throat went impossibly tight. She found herself blinking rapidly. She wasn't sure what any of them said in the way of farewells, but then Elena turned back, reaching out to put a gentle hand on her arm.

"If you ever wish to talk with someone who understands, do not hesitate to ask." Again the woman turned to go, but looked back once more. "And by the way, Chance Rafferty is also such a man. Likely even more so, given he sees it from both sides."

Ariel wasn't sure how she managed to make it into her car before the tears began. And the only way she managed to stop them was to wonder what had made Elena think she needed to hear that.

Chapter Twenty-Nine

IT HAD BEEN a rough three days. Chance wasn't sure he'd ever worked harder at anything—including planning tactical strikes—than he had at putting that kiss out of his mind. He'd kept a formal distance between himself and Ariel all day, each day. He'd focused utterly and completely on Tri. It was the only way he could do it.

And it seemed she was willing to do the same, pretend as if those moments had never happened. She was as business-like as he was, no more personal than if she were a polite customer and he a store clerk. And yet there were moments, moments when he caught her looking at him, studying him, as if he were a puzzle she was trying to figure out.

Don't kid yourself. The puzzle she's working on is why you'd gamble Tri's future by making such a stupid move.

But she didn't bring it up, and neither did he. Every day she'd shown up as planned, and spent the day dedicated to the reason she'd come here, the distrustful, wounded animal who became less wary every day, almost every hour. If his mother was home, she invited her to dinner, but the only time she had stayed was when others were there. Last night the whole family had been there, and apparently she'd felt like staying. Or felt safe enough to stay; he wasn't likely to grab her and plant a soul-searing kiss on her in front of all of them.

And it had turned out to be a jovial sort of night, lots of laughter and smiles…for everyone else. Sydney's stories of her life and travels kept everyone entranced, as he sat thinking he'd done some traveling himself and had never wanted anything as much as he wanted to go home. Of course, Sydney had never had a home, not like this, not like here, a place so deep in your soul it was always an ache if you were too far away.

Yet Ariel had never traveled as Sydney had, and she had never had that feeling either. That tie to a place that was like the silk of a parachute, soft and enveloping, yet strong enough to trust your life to.

On that thought he'd torn his gaze from her to check on Tri, as he should have been all along. He was plopped comfortably on the leather sofa, Quinta beside him. He was taking the chatter and noise very well, and once they had all settled at the table so had he on the sofa.

It was when—at his mother's cheerful insistence—he had walked Ariel out to her car after dinner that she'd said, "You were very quiet in there."

He shrugged. "They don't need me to carry on the conversation. Especially with Sydney there."

She opened the car door, then stood there studying him

in the faint light that spilled out from inside. He couldn't seem to stop studying her in turn, the way that bit of light caught her eyes and slid along her delicate but determined jawline, the way her hair fell, the way he didn't have to see her mouth to know the exact outline, shape, and soft warmth of her lips…

He was just starting to feel uncomfortable, wondering how long he'd be able to fight the pull he felt toward her, when she spoke, very quietly. "Need, no. But did you ever stop to think that they might want you to?"

"I answer if I'm asked."

"But only if you're asked."

"Look, I—"

"They aren't those bureaucrats who don't listen. Did you ever stop to think that maybe they're scared?"

He blinked. Drew back slightly at the unexpected words. "What?"

"They know they almost lost you, more than once. Sometimes they still feel as if they have."

He stared at her. "And just how did you deduce that?"

She shrugged. He'd never realized how annoying that could be. "My family used to look at me the same way."

He'd stood there staring at the taillights of her car until they were out of sight. Wondering how one woman had exploded his entire life in such a short time. Not even just his life, but his entire way of thinking. And just when he thought he had one part back together again, she upended another part.

They aren't those bureaucrats who don't listen. Had he really stopped dealing with people, stopped talking to them, because of…that? It had the feel of truth—he'd known it since the moment her words had released the pressure that he'd been carrying for so long.

And now the next morning he was pacing the floor waiting for her to come back and probably rattle him all over again. He'd found a balance here in Last Stand, this place that was small enough that he didn't feel surrounded. And a home in this cabin close to but not in the middle of the family he loved but could only handle in smaller doses. And something to aim what passion he had at, the dogs who needed him yet demanded only his time, and whose successful transition, while it meant them leaving, only took a little bit of his heart because it was best for them.

Then Ariel had arrived. And suddenly he was off-balance, his family was pulling at him, and he was feeling a different kind of passion for the first time in longer than he could remember.

And she was off-limits. She was Dean's Red, for God's sake.

And you think he would want her to stay alone forever?

His mother's words hammered at him, as they often had since she'd said them. He had no answer to that. It wasn't exactly something he and Dean talked about—But no, they had. He froze mid-stride, then just stood there, remembering. One of their mechanics had been killed by a hidden explosive in an abandoned vehicle he'd been trying to salvage a part they needed from.

"Wife and two kids," Dean had said glumly.

"Sucks," Chance had said, with that insulating layer of acceptance most of them had, because they lived with the possibility every day. "Better hope Red never gets that visit from the chaplain. It about killed my mom."

"She'll be okay. She's as tough as she has to be, when she has to be. And I've seen to it she'll have enough money." Then he had grinned, that silly Dean grin. "But not too much, so if some guy comes along, she'll know it's for love and not her money."

He'd left it there that day, because he didn't know what to say. And now here he was, pacing the floor waiting for that same tough as she had to be when she had to be woman to arrive.

At a sudden noise from behind him he spun on his heel, half into a crouch before he realized. But it was only Tri, up on his feet, hopping toward the door, his ears arrowed forward. It was the tail wag that gave it away; he'd heard Ariel's car coming. She'd insisted it was silly for him to have to keep coming up to get her—she could drive down to his place. He hadn't been able come up with a reason to say no, because the only reason there was, was that this meant saying good night here, alone, usually in the dark, when what he really wanted to do was ask her to stay.

"Soon enough," he muttered, wishing he'd never explained to her how this worked, that eventually she'd be staying here with him—them—to take over Tri's care and see how it went. Wishing he could think of some other way, some method of making sure they would be all right together, rather than throwing him into the mix, with this woman who stirred him up in ways he hadn't thought he was capable of any longer.

He watched Tri, who stood staring at the door, as close to happy as he'd ever seen him. As close to normal. Such a distance to have traveled in a week. Had it really been only a week since this woman had walked into their lives and shifted everything? The dog he would have least expected it with had come the furthest the fastest. He was already at the point where, were it any other dog, he'd be thinking about—

The sound of the car door closing, and Tri's excited whine stopped his thoughts. But as he watched the dog the idea came back, and he found himself wondering, "Why not?" He walked over and made the reluctant Tri sit and hold, then pulled the door open.

If he'd hoped the idea that had formed would distract him from the usual punch in the gut seeing her was, he'd been wrong. He watched her get out of the car, moving with that lithe grace. She had on jeans that hugged long legs and the low-heeled ankle boots she'd been wearing each day. Today she'd paired them with a long-sleeved knit shirt in a color that wasn't quite green or blue but somewhere in between. It was a color that made her long, red hair, today in a single thick, loose braid that fell down her back past her shoulders, pop.

He didn't even give her a chance to say hello. "You up for a trip into town?"

She blinked. "You want to go to town, voluntarily?"

She didn't say it like a jab, just with surprise. He smothered a wince at how well she understood him already. But he focused on the matter at hand. "He's progressing so well, and it's early enough it shouldn't be too crowded, even on Main Street. I think we should see how he does. I'll put the harness on him just in case, and stay within reach," he assured her.

She pondered this for a moment. "You've never walked him on Main Street before?"

He shook his head. "Never dared risk it, he was so edgy. Wouldn't now, except…he's settled so much." She deserved it—even in this week she'd proven her dedication to the animal, so he added, "Thanks to you."

"I expected it to be much worse," she admitted. "But don't think I'm assuming it will be easy. I'm sure there will be times when it's not."

Last Stand was fairly quiet when they arrived. Only a few people were around because few places were open this early, even at the Christmas season; Java Time and the bakery among them. They found a parking spot near the Carriage House, and Tri jumped out of the truck willingly, almost curiously.

"Heel," Chance cautioned the dog as he watched the animal look around. But Tri seemed simply interested and alert, maybe a bit wary, not fearful. He looked up at Ariel, and she cooed something at him, and his tail wagged in acknowledgment. He was, quite simply, amazing with her.

And why not? She's an amazing woman.

Tri did all right. He got a little wired when a stranger got close, but a quiet word from Ariel settled him. And she was clearly reading him well; she seemed to sense when he was tensing up and forestalled it with a word or touch. He never had to even start to reach for the harness as they walked down Main Street.

"At least the Christmas music isn't on," she said.

"It will be, 24/7," he said dryly. "Starting this weekend with the Christmas Market, and then the Christmas Ball the next Saturday."

"It's really a ball? Like a formal dance?"

"Black-tie type," he said with a grimace. "But it's mainly a benefit. To raise scholarship money, for the high school rodeo program."

"Wow. What's black tie like in Texas?"

He couldn't help smiling at that. "Different."

"Of course," she said, but she was smiling back at him. And suddenly he wouldn't have cared if the music system came on full blast.

"And after that, you won't be able to get away from the music until the big day."

"Funny, it's not bothering me nearly as much as I thought it would."

"Me, either."

For a frozen moment in time their gazes locked. Some formerly numbed part of his mind wanted to give her the credit for this, for him being able to tolerate the silly carols he'd avoided for so long. But that was a stop down a road he had no intention of traveling, and he went back to watching Tri.

He was a little surprised that she knew her way around Main Street, at least enough to know that the coffee shop, which they had agreed they both needed, was down past the saloon. "I came to look around the other day," she explained. "I wanted to…understand…the hold this place has on people."

Sometimes he wasn't sure he understood that himself. "And do you now?"

"I think I'm starting to. In a way it's like…the community you have with military wives. Most are kind and generous, some are snobby, some are outgoing, some are shy, but underneath it all, binding you together, is the connection, the thing you all share." She smiled. "Here, it's this town."

He stared at her, feeling a little stunned as she put into logical words the same feeling he'd always had, that the military community had always been to him, a stand-in for this place, this town, with the feeling that while not everybody always got along, let a threat come at them from outside and they would band together to fight it.

"What?" she asked. "You think it's a stupid analogy?"

He only realized then he'd been gaping at her. And he knew he wasn't going to be able to stop the words this time. "I think," he said slowly, "that however high my opinion of you was, it wasn't high enough."

Her lips—those soft, warm lips he sometimes swore he could still taste—parted, then closed again. And she blushed. Her cheeks didn't just get pink, she full-on blushed.

"Chance," she said, and it was barely above a whisper.

And it was also the most wonderful thing he'd ever heard, his name from her in that soft, suddenly breathy voice. And if they hadn't been standing in front of the Last Stand Saloon, in full view of anyone on the street, he wasn't sure what he would have done.

That was a lie. He knew exactly what he would have done. He would have kissed her again.

Chapter Thirty

A BIT OF wind had kicked up, making the morning temperature cold enough that Ariel was glad she had her jacket to button up.

"We can head back to the car now if you're cold."

Chance said it as if that electric moment between them had never happened. He was turning his back on it, denying it. And she understood. She was rattled enough for both of them, and he obviously saw that. And was gentleman enough not to take advantage. Gentleman enough to notice her buttoning the jacket and ask the polite question.

And crazily, she almost wished he wasn't. Wished those Texas manners had failed him this time. Because he'd looked as if he wanted to kiss her again. And if she dug down deep and was honest, she wanted that kiss. And that rattled her more than anything. It would seem that part of her she thought was dead and buried as her husband was...not.

"No," she said hastily when she realized he was looking at her, waiting for an answer. "I'm fine. Let's continue as planned." She tried a smile. "I need that coffee, I think."

The barista at Java Time said Tri was most certainly wel-

come to come in, and since there was only one other customer, they decided to risk it. The older man turned to
watch as they came in, and he was smiling.

"Good to see you out and about, Chance."

"Mr. Herdmann," Chance said with a nod, then introduced the man as the editor of *The Defender*, the town
newspaper. The name rang a bell, but Ariel barely had time
to wonder if he was related to the centenarian from the tree
lighting before the man spoke again.

"Is this the dog Lily wrote about? Whose handler was
killed?"

"Yes," Chance said, with a glance at her. Again she
smiled, to assure him she was, at least, beyond falling apart at
the mere mention of the subject. And registering the name,
no doubt the same writer who had written about the inn.
The Lily who was married to the police chief.

"Looks like he's doing well," Mr. Herdmann said.

"Thanks to Ariel," Chance said. "His handler…was her
husband."

The man looked at her with sympathy, but it was tinged
with curiosity. "I'm sorry for your loss, but grateful for his
service."

She liked the way he put that, so she was able to smile
again, a better one this time. "Thank you."

The man looked back at Chance. "From what Lily wrote,
and said, I'm surprised."

"So am I." He nodded at Ariel. "Her doing."

"Fascinating," he said, and Ariel belatedly realized that perhaps the newspaperman was seeing a story in the change in the dog. This was not something she was ready to share, not when she didn't know how it was going to turn out. She knew how determined she was, but the one who would truly decide was the three-footed animal sitting alertly but calmly at her feet. And the man who had saved him from a deadly needle.

Chance seemed to sense her sudden tension and got them out of there just politely enough.

"Thank you," she said when they were back outside, warm drinks in Java Time cups in hand. Chance's in his left hand, she noticed, keep his right free just in case he needed to grab Tri's harness.

"He got that same gleam in his eyes Lily Highwater had, like he was onto something that would make a good story. And it's way too early for that."

"Exactly what I was thinking," she said, agreeing both to his interpretation of Mr. Herdmann's look and the rest.

They continued their walk, crossing the street to head back on the other side. As they did, she noticed things. When they passed strangers—to her, at least; several of them greeted Chance by name, and many of those seemed as delighted as Mr. Herdmann had been to see him—they tended to stare at Tri, which made the dog tense. But as soon as they passed by, he was all right again.

When a large delivery truck went by, engine a bit noisy,

he tensed again and tried to edge away from the street, but when it stopped and parked a couple of blocks ahead, the engine turning off, he eased up. He seemed aware that the driver had gotten out and pushed up the roll-up door at the back of the truck, but it was apparently a safe distance away for that, in his canine mind.

"Keep going?" she asked, watching the truck.

"Yes. Let's see how he does now that it's stopped." He glanced at her. "Good catch, by the way. That he reacted to the truck as well as the people."

The words of praise pleased her probably more than they should have. Just as the one about his opinion of her not being high enough had practically blasted the breath out of her. Somehow, in a week, everything this man did and thought had come to matter. And not just because he held Tri's fate in his capable hands.

Because you're wondering what else those capable hands could do?

She felt the heat rush to her cheeks again and made sure she didn't look at him. Even if she'd read that sudden, fierce heat in his eyes correctly, it was clear he wasn't going to do anything about it.

For a moment she didn't understand why she suddenly thought of his mother. But then it clicked; a woman like Maggie Rafferty would make sure all of her boys knew better than to push a woman where she didn't want to go.

But...I do want to go. I never thought I ever would again, but I do.

But then thoughts of Dean rushed back into her mind. It would be disloyal to his memory, wouldn't it? A betrayal?

An image shot through her mind, from a meeting she'd been to, a gathering of the group that called themselves war widows. They'd used the initials, because it saved explaining when they said they were off to a WW meeting; most people assumed it was about weight.

The topic that night had been just what she'd been thinking about, whether moving on was a betrayal of the man they'd loved and lost. And one of the women, who had moved on so quickly it had the rest of the group buzzing, had made an observation that had struck Ariel as rather cold at the time.

Sex isn't a betrayal, it's just a physical act. Scratching an itch. It's falling in love that would be the betrayal.

She'd thought the woman in denial at the time, denial of her own pain and seeking to drown it in what Ariel had thought to be the worst way. But now, suddenly, she understood. And saw the appeal.

Reasons started tumbling through her mind. She was in a small town far removed from her home, no one would ever know. She would be leaving soon no matter what happened. There would be no strings, because it was pretty obvious he didn't want that any more than she did.

And most overpowering of all was the startling, unexpected, and fierce desire for this man. This man, over any and all she'd encountered since Dean's death. Most of those men had never gotten through her benumbed state enough for anything more than stilted conversation. Even those few who had been willing to take what she could have given, which wasn't much, had never managed to convince her it would be worth it.

This man had convinced her without even trying.

She turned all these thoughts over in her mind, trying to figure out how to let him know that she wanted that kiss his eyes had promised. And more. She wanted more. She wanted him. But she was going to run afoul of those manners again, she just knew it. Somehow that seemed—

Bang!

The loud, percussive sound shattered the silence. Things happened so quickly she didn't have time to register them before it was over. In the same instant both Tri and Chance moved. Tri hit her legs, shoving her back, nearly knocking her down. Chance grabbed her arm, kept her upright. In the same motion he pushed her into a doorway alcove. And sheltered her. With his taut body between her and the threat.

Then she heard the sound of the delivery truck starting up again. The fading sound as it drove away. A silent, heart-hammering moment passed before Chance relaxed. And when she looked up at him, he wouldn't meet her eyes.

"The door," he muttered. "It was the damned roller door. He just let it drop."

She was still so startled she felt as if she were thinking in slow motion. She realized the sound fit what he said. But then the slow realization about what both he and Tri had done got through her ebbing adrenaline. Both of them, man and dog, had acted with split-second reflexes and moved without thought for themselves.

To protect her.

Tri had knocked her out of what in his mind was a potential line of fire. And Chance, reacting out of the same history, the same instincts, had put himself in that line of fire, set himself up to take that bullet, for her. That it hadn't been a shot fired didn't really matter. Not as she stared at this man who'd just shown himself willing to possibly die for her.

Then he moved, just a little. In fact a bare fraction of an inch, and yet her tangled thoughts were vanquished in a sudden wave of heat as she jolted into awareness that he was pressed against her, almost full length. Any thought of chill or winter or even Christmas was seared out of her mind, and instinctively she arched toward his heat, longing for more.

Oh, yes, she wanted. She wanted this heat, this need, this vitalness that only he had sparked in her, jolting her out of a two-years-long deep freeze.

Yes, she wanted to feel alive again.

She'd thought she never would.

Until she'd met Chance Rafferty.

Chapter Thirty-One

H E DIDN'T WANT to move.

Chance faced the knowledge grimly. Even now that he knew he'd overreacted to a simple truck door panel slamming, he didn't want to back off. He wanted to stay right here, pressed against Ariel from knee to shoulders. He wanted to savor the feel of her, the taut warmth of her long body curved perfectly against him. And no amount of telling himself it was the pulse of racing adrenaline fueling it stopped him from wanting, wanting so much it was over-powering.

Tri pressed against the backs of his legs. Chance tried to focus on making sure the dog was all right. He reached just far enough to give the dog a reassuring pat. Tri shifted, sat, easier now.

But Chance was not feeling any easier. The movement toward the dog had felt as if he were rubbing himself against Ariel. And then he was kissing her, and as hot as the first time had been, the blaze that leapt to life this time didn't just prove that hadn't been a fluke, it proved that if fed, this inferno could consume him.

And right now he didn't care. The tiny part of his brain still functioning was aware of only two things: how incredible she tasted...and the most crucial thing of all...she was kissing him back. Fiercely, as if she wanted this as much as he did. And for just this moment he let himself believe it, didn't even care if he was kidding himself.

She reached up and threaded her fingers through his hair, then added the slightest bit of pressure to the back of his head, as if even this conflagration wasn't enough. He responded without thought, his tongue driving deep, probing, tasting, hungry for more of this. His pulse was hammering, his body firing up until he could barely stop himself from groaning aloud with need.

He heard Tri growl in the same instant he heard a voice call out, "There's no mistletoe hanging there, you two. Take it—"

The words stopped the moment Chance jerked upright and looked around. He found himself staring into the startled eyes of Samuel Diaz, owner of the feed store and perpetual member of the town council.

"Tri, stay," he said quickly. And again, beyond all expectations, the dog held.

"Well, well," Diaz said, his dark eyes alight with interest. "Didn't expect that to be you."

"Mr. Diaz," he ground out from behind clenched teeth. The groan he'd beaten back a moment ago escaped now, only now it was a sound of dread.

"I'll just leave you to it," the man said. And then, with an unexpected smile, he added, "Good to see you in town," before strolling on down Main Street.

Chance braced himself against the wall above Ariel's head as he sagged a little, the fire, for the moment, extinguished.

"Who...was that?" Ariel asked, sounding pretty much like he felt.

He sucked in a breath and let it out slowly. "That," he said with a grimace, "was the biggest gossip in all of Last Stand."

"Oh."

"Yeah. I'm guessing everyone will have heard by lunchtime."

"Oh."

He suddenly realized he couldn't tell how she was feeling about this from that single short word, even repeated. He was going to have to look at her, look into those bright blue eyes. And when he did, even then the only thing he was sure of was that she was as tangled up as he was.

Finally she sighed. "At least Tri didn't bite him."

No. But I wanted to bite you. And lick you. All over.

He swore under his breath, then wished he hadn't and muttered a quick "Sorry. Let's get out of here."

"Agreed. That's enough town for one day."

"Yes."

"He did well, though, didn't he?"

So she was going to let it go? Just like that? He reined in

his rampaging thoughts. "Yes, he did."

"Maybe longer next time? Or later, with more people?"

"You want more people, we'll do the Christmas Market this weekend. It's like the tree lighting but spread over several blocks and the whole park."

He had no idea what had possessed him to make that suggestion. He hated the market, the crowd, the incessant music...but he hadn't hated it at the tree lighting. The crowd had made him a bit hyperaware, but he doubted that would ever change; from the other vets he'd talked to, it was a frequent hangover from service days, and only faded over a very long time, if at all. But he hadn't hated that night more than any other crowd, and the music hadn't put him on edge nearly as much as he'd expected. In fact, he hadn't hated the entire night nearly as much as he'd expected to.

But maybe it was a good idea after all. Not only would it put the unexpectedly amenable Tri to a real test, but with everything going on he'd have to focus solely on the dog and his reactions.

Not on Ariel and how much he wanted to kiss her again. How he wanted much more than just a kiss. How damned guilty he felt, lusting after a fallen brother's wife.

And how the hell he was going to get through the next stage of this transition, the stage when she took over Tri's care.

And moved in with him to do it.

TEN DAYS.

Ariel had actually called up the calendar on her phone to count them because she couldn't believe it. Ten days in this town of Last Stand, Texas, and here she was walking around a jolly, cheerful marketplace with Christmas music playing all over and she was…maybe not enjoying it, but she was fine. In fact, if she was bothered by anything, it was Chance's rigid-jawed tension.

They'd come early, while the crowd was small and some stalls for the market were still setting up. There were not a lot more people than there had been when they had again walked the dog down Main Street yesterday…the day after that very public kiss. And by the looks Chance had gotten from townspeople who obviously knew him, she guessed he'd been right about how fast that particular news would spread.

And he'd been in this rigid-jawed state almost every minute since that kiss. Every minute they'd been together, anyway. And it was showing not just in the muscles of his jaw, but in Tri, who seemed to have lost some of his progress in the face of Chance's tension.

Had the gossip done this? He didn't seem to be any warier of the gathering of people than he had been at the tree lighting, and she understood the two-fold—Tri and his own combat experience—reason for that. So did that mean it was her? Was it the kiss that had him colder than the winter weather that had even Texans in jackets and scarves?

That he regretted it was clear. It was the reason for the regret that mattered to her. Was it because he didn't want her to misinterpret what might have been a one-time impulse? But it wasn't one time—he'd kissed her twice now. So was it that that kiss wasn't the inferno for him that it had been for her? But then why had the second time even happened at all?

Stop it!

The command would have been a yell if she'd voiced it. And as if he'd sensed her inner turmoil, Tri stopped dead, maneuvered himself around to look up at her. In the same instant Chance started to reach for the harness, as if he thought this was the moment the dog had lost it.

She stifled a sigh. This was doing Tri no good.

Or you.

She looked at Chance. For the first time the cheery, upbeat Christmas carol that was playing irritated her, because she wasn't feeling upbeat at the moment. "Maybe," she suggested, unable to stop the slightly too-silky tone in her voice, "if you'd relax a little, *he* would."

His head snapped around. "What?"

"You've been on edge the whole time we've been here." She didn't say anything about exactly when it had started. That was not the discussion she wanted to have here and now. Now all that mattered was Tri. "And he knows it."

"Telling me about the dog I've been living with for months now?"

"Telling you something you'd see for yourself if you weren't so…" Words failed her as memories of that hot, amazing kiss flooded her again.

"Wound up? On edge? Jumpy?" he suggested. Then he looked away from her, and he finished with a mutter. "Yeah, I'm all of those."

"More than you were even the first time I met him."

"A lot's happened since then."

"Yes. Including two kisses."

He stopped in his tracks. She hadn't meant to say it. She truly hadn't. But the words had slipped out and there was no calling them back.

"Tri, down." The dog dropped. Then Chance turned to look at her. Slowly, as if it were a tremendous effort, but one he had to make. "You want another apology for that?"

She made herself hold his gaze, looking into those eyes that matched the gray sky today. "I didn't want the first one." She hesitated, weighing the potential for more gossip-causing against the difficulty of opening this subject again, even though she hadn't meant to this time. The latter finally won. "Why did you, the first time? Kiss me, I mean, not apologize."

His brow furrowed. Not as if he couldn't remember, but as if he were trying to decide what to say. The music shifted to a slower, classic carol that had been, back when she cared, one of her favorites for the way it built and rose, seemingly carrying your heart and spirit along with it. Finally he gave her another of those infuriating shrugs, but at least added words this time.

"What you said about Keller."

Her mind raced back to that day. So much had happened, her mind was such chaos since she'd come here, it took her a moment to isolate the exchange.

Cody says Keller has no imagination.

Maybe he's just been too busy to indulge it. She remembered the startled look he'd given her then, which made her go on. *Sorry. A bit defensive there, because I admire what your brother has done.*

Don't apologize. So do I. More than...I've ever told him.

Tell him. Don't assume he knows.

"I told him, by the way," Chance said now. "The next day."

That warmed her more than she would ever have expected. She smiled and asked, "What did he say?"

"He shrugged."

Exasperation rolled through her. "You Rafferty men, what *is* it with you and the shrugs? Why can't you carry on a conversation..." Something about the way he wasn't looking at her was the clue. The way his mouth was twitching was the proof. "You set me up. Again," she said with the best manufactured glower she could come up with.

"Seems to be in the air. Along with the music and all the cheer."

"What did he really say?"

"He did shrug." He finally met her gaze. "But as he walked out, he looked back and said not to bother getting him a Christmas present this year, because I'd just given him the best one there is." And then his voice went impossibly soft for such a powerful man. "Thank you for that, Ariel. And thank you for coming for Tri."

As he said it, he reached out and cupped her cheek with a soft touch that seemed just as impossible. And there was such warmth in his eyes it made her tremble a little. But then he seemed to remember where they were, and that they had a much more sizeable audience this time. Still, when he pulled his hand away, she felt a wrench of loss and wanted to protest.

And only being where they were stopped her. Which rattled her even more than what he'd done.

Chapter Thirty-Two

"READY FOR A run?" he asked Dorado, and the horse snorted his approval.

He mounted up and settled into the saddle. The palomino danced eagerly, ready to run, and it was all Chance could do to hold him in long enough to warm up a bit. But then he let the horse loose and they were tearing across the hills toward the main ranch house. And it was for the horse's sake, he told himself, that they took the slightly longer route and swung by the overlook. Not that he would deny loving the wild, all-out run. It was one of the few times when he felt really, truly alive.

At least, it had been, before Ariel had arrived.

He reined a reluctant Dorado in for the last hundred yards to the house. He wasn't stalling. Not really. He just needed a little more time alone to put on the mental armor he needed to deal with her when she arrived today. She was such a vivid person in her own right, it was impossible for him to see her as only Dean's widow. It was getting more and more difficult to keep distance between them.

And how, he wondered as he dropped the horse's reins

over the hitching rail outside the house and headed up the porch steps, was he supposed to do that when she turned those big, sky-blue eyes on him, or when she laughed and he felt like a genius for making her do it, or when she smiled, and all he could see was her mouth, those lips, and think how they'd—

"—don't you dare, any of you."

Chance stopped in his tracks the moment he opened the door. His mother's voice held that tone they all knew; she was laying down the law and she would brook no denial.

And they all were there. Ry, Cody, Keller and Sydney, all seated at the big table, coffee mugs before them. And they all turned their heads to look at him. Keller and Sydney both took long sips from their mugs, making their expressions unreadable. Ry was giving him that assessing look he gave anything new or unexpected, as if he were wondering if it would be suitable for a project. Cody, usually the dead giveaway, quickly looked away as if he knew he would do just that, give it away, if he met Chance's gaze.

But it was Mom who truly gave it away with the flash of emotion that crossed her face when she saw him, that if he had to put a word to would be "Oops."

Which pretty much told him whatever order she'd been giving, it was about him. And he was fairly glad he didn't know what it was. But when he heard a car approaching, then saw them all exchange a look, he knew. Because he knew the car was Ariel's. So it wasn't a big jump from their pointed looks to his mother's expression when he'd unintentionally interrupted her. Her stern "Don't you dare" had definitely applied to him and Ariel.

Even thinking of them that way, paired, coupled, sent a fierce surge of heat through him. Heat so intense he couldn't even begin to blame it on the too-hot gulp of coffee he'd just taken. He couldn't even manage the brain cells to ponder what the next words would have been after that "Don't you dare."

He wondered which of his brothers he could coerce into telling him. Keller, no way; the man was an immovable object when he wanted to be. Ry? No, Rylan would just look at him in that assessing way that made Chance think his brother was planning to sketch him or something, and that made him grimace. Cody was the most likely, not so much because he was the youngest but because he'd always been a little in awe of Chance. Mom said it was because he had followed in their father's footsteps so soon after his death.

I think he looks at you as picking up your father's sword, as it were.

He hadn't laughed, it was too serious to laugh at, but the idea of him in any way filling their father's shoes was indeed a joke.

The sound of the car door slamming jolted him out of the reverie. He'd never been much for getting lost in thought, but it surely seemed to be happening lately. He headed for the door hastily; he just wasn't up to seeing her interact with his family this morning. He had enough on his plate without seeing them all welcoming and warm toward her, and she toward them. Because his plate was full of the knowledge that, based on Tri's astounding progress, were it anyone else he'd be accelerating the pace and have the prospective adopter moving in already. He didn't have a set schedule—it was pointless because every dog was an individual. But if he'd had to set one for Tri before she'd arrived, it would be a long time yet before he'd even be thinking about getting as far as they already had.

And then she'd arrived, and everything in Tri's life— and, he admitted, his own—had shifted, changed.

"Hi," she said, almost shyly, when he opened the door and stepped out onto the porch. "I saw Dorado tied up here, so I thought you must be here."

"I ride over on Sunday mornings." It was as close as he got to going to church, and for him it was close enough. "Tri's at my place."

"I assumed. But I didn't want to go to him without you there."

For a moment he just looked at her. She may have rattled him, down to the core, she may have somehow disrupted his entire life, to the point where he went to the damned Christmas market and didn't hate it, she may have had him rethinking everything he'd ever thought he'd known about male to female, but she had never questioned his knowledge or authority about Tri.

On impulse—something he admitted had gotten him into trouble with her—he said, "Want to ride down with me?"

"Ride?"

She glanced at Dorado, and he had a sudden vision of them snugged together riding double. His body roared to life, practically screaming its approval of the idea. And giving rise to ideas about other kinds of riding that he had to fight hard to quash.

"I'll saddle up Latte for you. He's the one I told you about, that we got from the Walkers. He's a sweetheart. Riding him is like sitting in a rocking chair."

"Oh." She hesitated, and he was about to say, "Never mind," when she nodded decisively. "I've always wanted to ride a horse, so yes, I'll try." He could almost see her remember one of the reasons Lucas had chosen the dog's name, and she smiled. "If he can, I can."

"I think you could do about anything you set your mind to. Just like he cleared that kennel fence to get to you."

The look she gave him then made him a bit nervous. But once she'd made up her mind, she went full bore, and after a brief crash course on what to do, she was crooning to the good-natured, biddable paint. He was a big horse, nearly sixteen hands high, but Ariel was tall, and Chance didn't quite trust himself to be close enough to her to give her a leg up. And although she managed it, he felt guilty for not helping when she had a touchy moment before getting over the top.

It was a sunny morning, although still a bit brisk. It didn't seem to bother her, but she was so obviously enjoying the ride he wasn't sure she even noticed. She was smiling almost as widely now as she did when Tri greeted her with his ears up, tail wagging like a windshield wiper gone berserk, as he likely would when they got to his place.

"You only do this on Sundays?" she asked as they crested the hill above the main house. She was looking around with obvious appreciation. "I'd be doing it every day."

"There are ranch chores we all do. I don't ride as much as usual since I've been focused on Tri. But I ride to the main house regularly on Sundays." His mouth twisted wryly. "My mother's orders."

She glanced at him. "Gee, your mother wants to see you once a week? How very demanding."

Her tone had been more teasing than sarcastic, but still he said, "A little Sunday sarcasm?"

"More like envy," she said seriously, going back to looking at the big limestone outcropping in the distance. "If my mother doesn't talk to me every day, she worries."

He hesitated, not wanting to introduce a painful subject, but eventually said it anyway. "Was she always like that?"

She looked back at him. "No."

He only nodded and left it there. He didn't have to ask—he knew perfectly well the change had come two years ago, when she'd joined the far too numerous ranks of military widows.

And that was something he needed to remember. She had loved Dean, and by all he'd seen and heard they'd had the kind of marriage most could only envy. The kind of marriage his parents had had. The kind he fully expected Keller and Sydney to have.

The kind he would never have. Not with Ariel.

He nearly pulled Dorado up short as shock blasted through him.

Why was he thinking of marriage with Ariel at all, even in a negative sense? Hell, why was he thinking about marriage at all, when he'd long ago taken it off his list of future possibilities? He'd kissed the woman twice and he was thinking about marriage?

"Chance?"

He snapped out of it to find her staring at him. Realized she'd asked him something. "What?"

"I said I'm not pushing, just asking how you think things are going with Tri."

"I…fine. Great, in fact," he said, reining in his wandering mind much more fiercely than he would ever rein in a horse.

He wouldn't sign off unless he was certain Tri was ready, but belatedly it occurred to him that if he escalated the process, as it seemed now Tri would accept—he'd assumed it would take at least twice as long if not more to be sure in this case—she would be gone sooner. And he wasn't at all sure how he felt about that. It should be a relief, shouldn't it?

Then again, a speeding up of the process also meant she'd be moving in sooner. If he went by Tri's response compared to the standard he used with prior dogs, that would be now.

How was he going to survive this woman being under his roof 24/7?

Tri. He had to do what was best for Tri.

And if it was hell for him, so be it.

Chapter Thirty-Three

ARIEL LOOKED ONCE more around the small bedroom. With bare walls and utilitarian furnishings—a double-sized bed that took up most of the room and one nightstand—it was a stark change from her lovely room at the Hickory Creek Inn. But it was enough, because it was a step closer to achieving her goal.

All she had to do was survive this.

She realized one of the reasons for this was to show how far she was willing to go to get this done. She'd never lived this far out from a town, in fact, out from a big city, in her life, so thinking about things like groceries for meals—"Use whatever you want in the kitchen, but you're on your own for cooking"—and having to drive a few miles just for toothpaste if you ran out was new to her.

But so was the quiet. Because it was very, very quiet out here.

She sat down on the edge of the bed and listened to that quiet. Crazily, she thought she could almost feel herself slowing down, not relaxing—how was she supposed to relax with Chance in the next room?—but…easing up a little. A release of pressure she hadn't even been aware of carrying.

Of course, the minute she walked out of this room and saw him again, that whole new kind of pressure would start building again.

When he'd first mentioned this part of the process, she'd barely paused at the idea, because the reasoning made sense. But he'd been a stranger then. And now? He'd kissed her— no, they'd kissed, because she'd been a more-than-willing participant—twice. And it had awakened parts of her she thought she would never hear from again.

She turned to look at Tri, who was on the bed. He was watching her alertly, ears forward, clearly intrigued by this new action.

"You're mine to take care of now, my boy. We just need to find a routine that suits us both. And we—"

She stopped suddenly at the sound of running water.

Water heater's not very big. No twenty-minute showers. I take mine at night, so it's all yours in the morning.

She would not think about him in there, water sluicing over his tough, fit, powerful body. His naked body.

No, she would not think about that. He was just being…thoughtful. As he generally was. Or maybe this was just his routine. Maybe after a day dealing with dogs and ranch work, he usually needed the shower before going to bed.

To bed. In the not much bigger room just down the very short hallway. Just a few feet away. And thinking about that was even worse than thinking about him in the shower.

Desperate for distraction, she decided to go to the kitchen and put away the leftover two slices of the pizza they'd picked up after today's excursion into town. Downtown Last Stand, where she'd found the rampant Christmas music and cheer less annoying than she would have thought possible. Tri had done perfectly, save for a slightly snarling encounter in the park with a shaggy little brown dog, that Chance said he wasn't worried about because the other dog was notoriously cantankerous and did that to every other dog and a few people as well.

"Like owner, like dog?" she had asked when the woman who had frowned at them all pulled her cranky dog on up Oak Avenue toward Main.

"Pretty much," Chance had said, stifling a smile until the woman was well away.

Ariel had praised Tri for his forbearance. The dog wagged his tail.

"Helps that he knows he could bite him in half if he wanted to," Chance said.

"You'd think the other dog would know that, too."

"He does. That's why he's so in your face."

She remembered thinking then that that was an interesting bit of observation and understanding.

She put the leftovers—a slice each for breakfast, Chance had said, watching her as if he expected her to protest at the idea; "If I leave you one," she'd said right back at him—into the fridge, then spent a few minutes hand feeding Tri a couple of treats Chance had told her had been donated by the pet bakery in town, *Good Boy!* He took them almost delicately from her, with a care she was certain many of the enemy would find hard to believe.

She heard the shower stop. For an instant she stopped breathing. What if he, living alone, was used to heading back to his room, or worse, wandering the house undressed? What if he forgot she was here, and strolled out of the bathroom naked?

What if he remembered you were here and strolled out naked?

She whirled, turning her back to the hallway as the ridiculousness of the thought made her cheeks heat. This was happening far too often around this man. She needed to think of him as the means to an end, the end being Tri. Tri, who had followed her out here as if it were his job. Which Chance had told her it would be, in the dog's mind.

What do you know about Mals?

What I heard from Dean. And a lot of research before I got here.

Then you should know they aren't simple house pets. They need a job. And if you don't give them something to do, regularly, they will find something. And chances are you won't like whatever it is.

Maybe we need a Paralympics for amputee dogs.

He'd given her a startled look then. But at that moment they'd encountered a knot of people on the street who had wanted to know if it was all right to pet Tri, and all their focus had turned to that. Which thankfully, had gone well, although the dog had been tense throughout, he'd never made an aggressive move.

She heard the bathroom door open. Caught herself holding her breath as she stared at the photograph on the wall. She'd noticed it before but hadn't gone over for a closer look, because even from across the room she could see that it was a man in camouflage with a dog, and she had enough of those images in her head. But as she heard steps approaching, she focused on it out of near desperation.

It was Chance. There was no mistaking him, even without the touch of gray at his temples. He was crouched next to a sitting dog who was clearly the same breed as Tri but had a darker head and shoulders. Man and dog were nose to nose, Chance's hands were on the sides of the dog's head, and he was smiling widely. The dog's mouth was lolling open as if he were smiling back. The pink tip of the dog's tongue was curled upward slightly, as if he was about to or just had licked Chance's face. There was so much love in that photograph, the duo were so clearly, utterly bonded, that her throat tightened and her vision blurred a little. And she had to turn away, no matter what was coming up behind her.

As it turned out, he was in sweatpants and a T-shirt. But the shirt was snug, and clung to damp skin, emphasizing the angle from broad shoulders to trim waist. And suddenly this small house seemed even smaller, as if the size of it were pushing them together.

"You smell good," she said, rather inanely. "But then you always do." Well, that hadn't been much of a recovery.

He lifted a brow at her. "Half the time I smell like dog fur or horse manure."

"I love the first, and don't mind the second at all. Not nearly as much as I imagined I might, anyway."

"Careful," he said, and his voice took on that slightly rough tone that always made a slight shiver ripple through her, "you're starting to sound as if you like it here."

"I do," she admitted, before she realized that neither of them had been specific about exactly where "here" was. Last Stand? Or here, in this small, cozy place, with him?

When she realized both were true, the real scope of the change that had overcome her since she'd arrived here finally registered. All the clutter and bustle of her day-to-day life back home seemed to have fallen away. All the lingering pain had receded into an ever-present but bearable ache.

She'd been telling herself it was because she was focused on Tri, but she knew it was more than that. This place, this man, had worked some kind of magic on her. And in this moment, nothing else mattered except what she was feeling. And not feeling; that ripping agony that had made her certain she would never heal, never feel whole again.

For a moment she saw exactly what she was feeling mirrored in those gray-blue eyes. Saw the need, the wanting. Heard it in his quickened breathing. Saw it again in the way his lips parted, as if he were going to speak. No words came, but she didn't need them because she saw his expression change, sensed his body tense, knew somehow he was going to step back.

It was the regret that did it. She could see it in his face. He was going to back away, but he didn't want to. And she didn't want to let him.

"Don't," she whispered. He instantly held up his hands, started to take that step back. She reached out and grabbed his forearms, more aware than ever of the taut muscle beneath her touch. "I meant don't go. And don't stop."

"Ariel," he began, his tone a warning now.

She held on. "I haven't felt this way in so long. I didn't think I could, anymore."

"Don't start this," he said, his voice rougher than ever.

"Are you saying you don't want this? What...happens between us?"

He let out a short, sharp bark of laughter. "I think it's pretty obvious I do."

She knew what he meant; she'd have to be blind not to see the jut of his arousal beneath the sweats. "Then why are you stopping?"

"Because you don't want this. Not really."

"So you read human minds as well as dog minds?"

"Ariel, you don't know—"

"What I know is that a part of me I thought dead forever is suddenly awake. This is the first time I've felt anything since..."

She didn't want to bring Dean into this, not here and now, between them. But one look at Chance's face told her he was already here. And his next words proved it. "Since Dean? Don't you see that's why this is wrong? You're his wife, and—"

"His widow. But don't *you* see? That's part of it, that you...understand. That I still love him. That I always will."

"So this is...what?"

"All I know is you make me feel things I didn't think I could anymore. I'm not asking for forever, Chance. I know that's not in the cards." He'd made that clear enough. *I'm not...a loving kind of guy.* No, he understood what this was, and wasn't. He didn't need what she couldn't give. He'd been honest from the get, even before this had sparked to life between them. And it wasn't like she was looking for forever, either. The opposite in fact.

Sex isn't a betrayal, it's just a physical act. Scratching an itch. It's falling in love that would be the betrayal.

The words from that long-ago meeting shot through her mind again, and for the first time she truly understood the meaning and the truth of them. This wasn't love, this was just an unexpected itch.

"So this is just sex, and just for now?" he asked bluntly. "And you're all right with that?"

"It's all I have to give," she said quietly. "Are you all right with that?"

"I guess I'll have to be," he growled out. "Because woman, you are driving me crazy."

And only when he kissed her again now did she realize just how much he'd been holding back. His mouth on hers was no longer tentative, no longer patient. It was fierce, demanding, enflaming. And catch fire she did; she was kissing him back the same way so fast it made her a little light-headed. Or maybe it was just him. She didn't know anymore. She didn't know anything except the exhilarating feeling of being alive, truly alive again.

When his hand slid down to her breast, she was arching into the caress before she even realized what she was doing. She was pressed so close to him now she could feel his erection prodding at her. And she was stunned at how much she wanted to feel that ready male flesh sliding into her.

"Ariel—"

"Yes. The answer is still yes."

"My room's pretty plain," he said, as if warning her.

"Any Christmas baubles?"

"Not a one."

"Sold."

She was nearly dizzy with wanting and wasn't sure if he'd swept her up into his strong arms as a romantic gesture, or because she'd gotten wobbly. She didn't really care.

"You need to eat more," he muttered.

She nearly laughed. What woman didn't want to hear that?

His room was plain. Tidy. Functional. But the bed he set

her down beside was a nice size, and right now that was all she cared about. Well, that and getting his clothes off.

A little to her surprise he let her do just that, pulling the shirt over his head. She paused for a moment, running her fingertips over the puckered scar on his left side, between his ribs and hip bone. "Is that the 'mostly'?" she asked, remembering what he'd said about that rescue action where the enemy had "missed, mostly."

"Yeah."

She bent and pressed her lips to the scar, loving the way it made him suck in a rapid, audible breath.

Things happened fast then. Clothes hit the floor, and she barely had time to appreciate the solid, strong beauty of him before he'd taken them both down to the bed. She couldn't touch enough, stroke enough, and then she could barely breathe as he did just that, touched, stroked...and tasted. The feel of his mouth on her breasts, his tongue flicking her nipples sent fire pouring through her to someplace low and deep that ached with its emptiness. And in that moment it didn't matter what this was, or more importantly what it wasn't. The only thing that mattered was this man, and how he made her feel alive.

He reached out to the small nightstand and pulled a condom out of the drawer. "Cody, months ago," he said with a grimace. "As a joke, ragging on me."

When she realized he meant it to say he hadn't planned this, it warmed her heart almost as much as her body.

The first probing touch of his fierce, silk-over-iron erection told her just how alive she was; he slid easily into slick, ready flesh. She gasped at the lovely stretching sensation and shuddered when he was fully inside her and the emptiness vanished. She heard him swear, a single oath, low and harsh and heartfelt. Then he began to move, as if unable to hold back any longer.

And as if they'd both been too hungry for too long, the peak hit them both in a matter of moments. Her body clenched violently, and he went rigid. She cried out from the fierceness of it, and he echoed it, their names blending in the same instant.

Shuddering, he collapsed on top of her. And she cradled him, feeling whole again for the first time. And she knew deep down that no matter what happened from here, she could never, ever regret this.

Chapter Thirty-Four

C HANCE COULDN'T REMEMBER a time when he'd slept so little yet felt so...relaxed? Maybe he was just drained. Because the woman in his arms had drained him all right. Just as the living fire that matched her hair had seared him.

He'd never had anyone devour him like she had last night. She'd made it so blisteringly clear that she'd wanted him, all of him, that he'd slipped the leash entirely and gone a little crazy. But she'd met him, touch for touch, kiss for kiss, stroke for stroke. And every time he slid into her slick, hot, welcoming body it was a coming home like he'd never known before.

And he'd had to immediately shove that out of what small part of his mind was still functioning at that moment. Because she didn't want what this felt like to him. Hell, he didn't want it. Did he? At that moment, lying in the quiet warmth with his body curled around hers, feeling her sleek, smooth skin and the soft, sweet weight of one breast in his hand, the curve of her hips against flesh he'd thought must be too exhausted to respond yet was coming to life yet again, he wasn't sure of anything except he didn't want anything to break this moment.

In the end it was Tri who broke it, needing to go outside. The dog had accepted the new sleeping arrangement with an equanimity he'd been a little surprised by. Although why, he wasn't sure, since the dog had morphed completely from the skittish, edgy, almost dangerous animal Chance had brought here into a calmer, well-trained creature who seemed…happy. Since the moment Ariel had arrived, he'd changed, until he was almost unrecognizable. In the space of two weeks, she'd worked a miracle.

And last night had been another miracle.

A Christmas miracle?

He grimaced even as he thought the corny words. He eased out of bed, trying not to wake her. He shivered a little as he searched around for his sweatpants, not from cold but at the memory of how she'd peeled them off of him, and moments later curled those long, lovely fingers around his achingly hard cock.

He pulled on the sweats and headed for the back door. It was still dark, so maybe when Tri was done he could slide back into bed with her…and in a while slide back into her.

It looked like there might be a chance for that, because she appeared to still be asleep when he came back. But before he could shed the sweats she stirred, rolling over to look up at him sleepily.

"You're up."

Most of the night. He stifled the stupid grin that wanted to break out and said instead, "Tri needed out."

"Oh." Then, suddenly, her eyes widened and she sat up. "Oh! No, that's my job now. You should have woken me up."

For a moment Chance couldn't think. The covers had slid down to her waist and all he could do was stare at her. Not just the luscious, full curves of her breast, the pink tips that were still—or again—taut and tempting. He'd…marked her. There were reddened spots here and there that were clearly from his hands and mouth. He hadn't meant to do that.

"I…hurt you," he said, a little shakily.

It took her a moment to realize what he meant. Then, to his shock, she laughed. "Ditto," she said. His brow furrowed. "You should see your back. I'm afraid my nails dug in a bit."

Only then did he become aware that there was indeed a bit of stinging. "Want to try for more?" he asked, more than a little stunned at how fast the need rose in him again.

"Hard to do when you're over there," she said softly, and held her arms out to him.

He could no more have resisted her than he could have predicted the miracle—miracles—she'd brought with her.

Maybe there really was something to this Christmas thing.

FROM THEN ON, she took Tri over completely. She got up with him in the mornings, took him out for the last time at night, and spent the time in between making sure he was busy enough and tired enough not to get into trouble. After three days of this, Chance found himself noticing that his face was oddly sore. When he realized it was from smiling so much, he nearly laughed out loud. Yes, she'd done that, too. The daylight hours were Tri's—well, except for the times when the dog had clearly had enough and retreated to his bed to rest, times that she got a lot more of than he ever had—but the nights were his. And she didn't stint there, either. It was a sparkling time, as silver and gold as the decorations in town, the ones that somehow didn't annoy him anymore. Not as much, anyway.

They were doing so well he started to push, throwing things at them as a pair, things that had always put Tri on the edge of breaking discipline. Sudden moves, unexpected loud noises, all the things that had set him off before. The dog moved closer to Ariel but showed no sign of breaking protocol.

Then Chance made a call to Asher Chapman, over in Whiskey River. The man worked matching up service dogs with veterans who needed them, through his organization called *We've Got Your Back*, and so he was quite knowledge-able about dogs. Although their goals were different, they had worked together before, each helping the other where he could. And Asher was more than willing to help put Tri through his paces, since he was also a stranger to the animal. Suiting up in appropriate protective gear and trying to provoke Tri into an attack, with only Ariel to hold the dog back.

She never had to even reach for the harness; a simple soothing word from her and the dog settled.

"Want me to go at her, see if he'll hold then?" Asher asked.

"Hell no," Chance muttered. "Somebody goes at her, I don't want him holding back."

Asher raised a brow at him, his blue eyes curious beneath slightly shaggy dark blond hair. "Like that, is it? About time, buddy."

Chance blinked. Was it that obvious? "It's not…" He couldn't bring himself to say it was nothing, because it wasn't. He wasn't sure what it was, except something he'd never meant to happen. "She's going back to San Diego as soon as all the markers are met."

And that, he thought as they drove back to Last Stand, was going to happen much sooner than he'd ever expected.

And much, much sooner than he wanted.

But for Tri's sake he had to deal. The dog was blossoming, handling everything under Ariel's gentle but firm command. He supposed in the dog's mind, it was like having Dean back, as if time had somehow rolled back and the only thing he had to deal with was the annoying loss of that leg, not the gutting loss of the man he'd nearly sacrificed himself for. Chance couldn't think of any other explanation.

And at the same time, he watched the dog's amazing progress, saw how fast it was going, how each marker he'd established for that progress was met, in the back of his mind was a small voice urging him to slow it down. Or to change the markers, so it wouldn't happen so fast.

Because the faster it went, the sooner Ariel would be gone.

And that might be the biggest shock of all. He'd gone from wanting that—the sooner the better—to dreading it. Because he didn't want the nights to end. The nights spent with her were sweeter than anything he'd ever known. And no matter how often he told himself that it wouldn't stay that way, that maybe if the end date didn't exist it wouldn't be so sweet, he couldn't convince himself of either.

And then Keller, while he was helping him with a hinge on a stall door, blasted him out of all thought by asking if he was going to take her to the Christmas Ball.

"What? No, I... She isn't... Why would I?"

"Because you just gave me the same look you used to have when you got caught raiding Mom's jar of jelly beans."

"If you want to liken her to popcorn-flavored jelly beans, you'd best take it up with her," he said dryly, hoping he'd covered the lapse. He should have known better.

"But then," Keller went on as if he hadn't spoken at all, "you're looking like that a lot lately, bro. Glad to see it."

He thought he'd gotten himself back in hand by the time

he got back to his place, where Ariel and Tri had been happily playing find the toy since he'd left. He got there just as the dog found his beloved and worse-for-wear knotted tug-of-war rope she'd hidden behind a couple of hay bales, and for a moment he just watched her coo over the delighted dog. The dog who hadn't been capable of anything close to that before she'd arrived.

And neither were you.

She looked at him then, smiled, then frowned. "What's wrong?"

He gave a weary shake of his head. "Keller. He wanted to know if we were going to the Christmas Ball."

She blinked. Looked utterly taken aback. "Did you tell him—"

"I didn't tell him anything. He just asked. I only mentioned it now…in case you actually wanted to go."

"No." She didn't shudder but looked as if she were close.

And there's your answer, Rafferty. She doesn't want this to be anything more than it is, a nice interlude between two consenting adults.

He did shudder, inwardly, at the word "nice." That was hardly the word for it. So focus on the interlude part. Because that's all it was. A break, a pause in the day-to-day routine that had become his life. The life-by-rote routine that he'd striven for and achieved, and would go back to as soon as she was gone.

After a moment she added, "I'm doing much better about Christmas, but not quite that good."

He only nodded. And the day continued as before, and the next, and the next. The nights only got sweeter, including the night when she'd made him simply lie there and let her trace every inch of him, first with her hands, then with her mouth, until he utterly lost it and couldn't hold back a shout of her name. It wasn't until hours after that that it occurred to him she'd acted as if she wanted to memorize him.

Like he wanted to memorize her, to have these moments to hold close in the darkness of the endless nights to come without her.

Chapter Thirty-Five

ARIEL MADE HERSELF stay calm as the group of four approached. They paused, the couple and two children, girls, who looked pre-teen. The girls immediately wanted to go to Tri and pet him, and while she readied herself to grab for the handle on the harness if need be, she merely told them it was okay. The duo cooed over him, told him how brave he was, and the dog tolerated it all. In fact, she saw the tip of his tail wag slightly, as if he didn't mind this at all.

She knew Chance was around, somewhere, as he had been each day they'd done this. He'd told her he would always be in sight, but would probably stay in the truck so that Tri would be less likely to pick up his scent. So in essence she and Tri were alone, walking the Main Street of this town that had so unexpectedly captivated her, thinking with no small amount of shock, that she would miss it. Decorations and all.

He wanted to know if we were going to the Christmas Ball...

Even thinking the words reminded her of how hard she'd had to fight to suppress the longing that had leapt in her at the very idea. But that's not what this was. They'd made that clear at the beginning, and she'd answered the only way she could, to show him she hadn't forgotten that.

A Christmas Ball. With Chance.

It had taken some time for her to beat back the images that wanted to form in her mind, of Chance in formal wear. He would be...breathtaking.

And you'd have had to go in jeans and a T-shirt.

But it didn't matter now. It was over, and they'd spent last night in their own kind of dance. And it was enough.

It had to be enough.

Last night she had dreamed about that incident just a block from here, when the delivery driver had let the roll-up door of his truck fall and slam with a crack that had echoed off every building. And how Chance had reacted, his first, instinctive thought to put himself between her and possible danger. She'd awakened with a start, more certain than ever she had to keep this a casual, no-strings fling. Because she knew herself. Knew what her values were. She'd proven who she was long ago when she'd fallen in love with a hero the first time. This was the kind of man she could too easily lose her heart to. And she couldn't afford that. Not again.

She just wished she could convince herself she hadn't already done it.

She made herself focus on what she was doing. Tri was progressing perfectly, but she didn't want to slip up. They walked on, and while the objective was Tri's interaction with people, she couldn't help noticing how nice they all were. And they were sweet to the dog, one woman even asking if he could have a piece of her pastry as a treat. She'd regretfully said no, but thanked the woman.

"We're all proud of what Chance Rafferty is doing," she'd said. *So am I.* "You're adopting this one?"

"Yes," she said firmly.

"Good for you. Always makes Christmas better to have a dog in your home."

Christmas. In her home. Ariel kept on walking but could no longer deny what was so rapidly approaching. Tri had taken to her so quickly and settled so fast. She knew it had to be Dean, that somehow Tri knew she was connected to him, and guessed she had somehow taken his place in the dog's mind and instincts.

He's acting like he has Dean back, and all's well in his world.

She knew she hadn't really been meant to hear those words, spoken to Lucas. Or the rest of the conversation.

You're going to let her take him?

It's best for Tri.

That's what counts. Your mom says you'll miss her.

I...will.

Something in his voice on that last word sent a shiver through her. Because she would miss him, too. A lot. And it wasn't just the nights, and the glorious heights he drove her body to, it was the mornings when she woke next to him and felt so content it was almost surreal. It was the first cup of coffee as they planned the day's agenda. It was the way they'd ended up both preparing meals in the compact kitchen, even though he'd told her she was on her own. It was the way he played with Tri, ever careful of how much the dog could handle. The way he pushed to test the extent of her control of the dog. It was the leisurely dinners with Tri sprawled in pleasant weariness on his bed a few feet away.

It was all of that she would miss.

It was life with Chance Rafferty that she would miss.

HE COULDN'T DENY it any longer.

Chance sat in his truck watching Ariel and Tri deal with the group of kids who had just come barreling out of the barbecue place down the street. The dog was on his feet, and had immediately edged closer to her, but there was never a moment when he thought the dog might turn aggressive. He endured several pats on the head with equanimity, and when the kids had moved on so had they, as calm as before.

Four days of soloing with the dog, here in Last Stand and at random other places, and it was clear they were ready. All the markers had been met. In fact, he'd known it in his gut after the first day he watched them alone, he'd just had trouble accepting that it could have happened so fast. If it had been any other dog, he wouldn't be having qualms at all.

Or any other person.

But it wasn't. It was Ariel, who had worked her own Christmas miracle in twenty days. Ariel, who by rights he should clear to adopt right now, so she could take Tri to his new, and no doubt happier home by Christmas.

Leaving him without a dog to work with, probably until next year.

Leaving his house empty, hollow, echoing.

As they arrived back at that house, Ariel following him with Tri in her back seat, he could see in the rearview mirror that she was talking to the dog, no doubt praising him unstintingly. And when he pulled the truck to a stop next to the corral, his house looked exactly that. Hollow and empty.

He felt a jab, sharp and deep. The next twelve days yawned out before him, stark and chilly. Christmas, New Year's, holidays celebrated by so many. Holidays he'd always dreaded, a feeling exacerbated by the music, the decorations, the seemingly unending cheer of others.

But this year it hadn't bothered him. And no amount of telling himself it was because there was a chance to save Tri had worked. It was Ariel, and her sweet, giving presence that had wrought that particular miracle. And not just with a dog he'd thought traumatized beyond redemption.

And now she would leave. Go back to her life. Tri would live out his days with her, getting all the love and attention he deserved. And he would go back to his quiet life without her. The life he'd been content with a mere three weeks ago. Content, not happy.

Happy had been the last three weeks.

Suddenly he had to get away from her, as if he could no longer breathe around her. He grasped at the first thing that occurred to him and told her he needed to write a follow-up report to the guys at Lackland, the base that handled most MWD repatriations, and where he got his "hard cases" as they called them. They weren't going to believe it, especially with Atlas as they remembered him, but he was going to send it anyway.

He made up an excuse about needing to go to the house to do it, although he'd sent them from his pitifully slow dial-up before; it just took a while. But Cody, of course, had broadband that left his connection in the dust.

"Does this mean you've decided?" she asked as she got Tri out of her car.

"Yes," he said gruffly, before he could change his mind and tell her it would be at least another six months, maybe a year, maybe more before he could be sure, and she'd just have to stay.

"Chance?" she asked, a little breathlessly, when he didn't go on.

"You're clear. He's yours."

Her gleeful crooning to the dog was still echoing in his ears when he got to the house. He wrote his report, and somehow putting it down in words made it seem even more impossible. He felt the urge to finish it off with "Then magic happened," but knew it wouldn't go over well. But it didn't feel like anything less, to him.

Report sent, he sat in the desk chair he'd borrowed, staring at the screen. He didn't know how long had passed before a soft voice jolted him out of that damned recurrent reverie.

"It's official?" his mother asked. "Tri is cleared for the adoption?"

"Yes."

"Amazing. A Christmas miracle, in fact."

He couldn't snort, since he'd had the thought himself.

"So now what?" she asked when he didn't say anything.

"She'll take him home. She's leaving in the morning." And *I'll let her go. No choice. That was the deal.*

He knew he was in for it when she pulled up a chair and sat, looking at him seriously. "And you go back to life as before?"

He went still. "What else would I do?"

"Do you think I'm blind, my dear, precious son? Do you think I don't see the change in you, since she's been here?"

He snapped his gaze back to the screen, where Cody's chosen screen saver, of the sweep of the Milky Way across a Texas night sky, had come on. How different did it look in San Diego? Could you even see it there, with all the glow from the endless swaths of lights from San Diego to Los Angeles?

"She's been so good for you, Chance," she said softly. "Don't let that go."

"No choice," he said, his chest tight and his voice thick, and not even caring that he was confirming her guess.

No choice but to say goodbye to the woman who'd turned his life upside down and his heart inside out.

The minute he thought the last words the knot in his chest exploded.

Damn.

Damn it all, he loved her.

He loved her, and he was going to let her go. Because he'd promised. Because of Dean.

Because she didn't love him.

Chapter Thirty-Six

S HE SHOULD BE overjoyed.

Ariel knew she should be, yet she was having trouble convincing herself. She had done what she'd set out to do—brave, beloved Tri was hers now, and she would care for him for the rest of his life.

She paced the room in the small, old, but spotlessly clean Arizona motel she'd stopped at simply because she was suddenly exhausted. More exhausted than she should be. She'd planned on stopping overnight, for Tri's sake, but she'd hoped to be closer to home when she did.

Closer to home. That didn't even sound right in her head.

She should be…exhilarated, shouldn't she? Mission accomplished? But she felt only weary. Yet as tired as she was she couldn't seem to settle. And so she paced. And paced. With Tri—who had been welcomed by the veteran who managed the place—watching her alertly, clearly sensing her restless mood.

Leaving Last Stand, leaving the Rafferty ranch—face it, leaving Chance—had felt so wrong. And she'd felt hollow inside from the moment she'd cleared the gate.

"You're braver than I," she told the dog as she paced past him. "I lost Dean, but you lost both him and a leg. Yet you never gave up trying."

So how can you do any less?

She shoved away the thought. She shouldn't be restless like this. She should be glad. Sure, she'd gotten used to being with Chance. How could she not when she'd lived with him all those days, and made glorious, sweet love with him all those long Texas winter nights?

The memory of their goodbye ran through her mind again. The moment she'd snapped at him as she was loading Tri into the car, when he'd been giving her the long list of behaviors to look out for. Again.

"I've got it, Rafferty! Just back off."

He'd given her a startled look, but backed off, hands up. She'd glared at him, and it hadn't been until she'd negotiated her way out of Last Stand that it had hit her, she'd actually yelled at him. Because she'd been angry at him for not realizing she had his damned list memorized.

She'd been angry at him.

I don't care about anything enough to get mad anymore...

Her own words had echoed in her head as she passed the green sign telling her how far she was from Interstate 10. And she'd known then she'd done it—she'd fallen for Chance Rafferty. She hadn't admitted it until then, even to herself, but she knew it was true. She who had thought herself done with love, had gone and fallen for the closed-off guy who hid the biggest of hearts behind that silent, gruff façade.

But they had been temporary—they'd agreed to that from the beginning. She'd get over it. She'd survived losing Dean, she could get over losing Chance.

Except you didn't lose him. You walked away from him.

Because that was what they'd agreed to. He didn't want any more than what they'd had. He'd said so. And it wasn't his fault that she'd fallen for him.

But he didn't want...love. He'd said so.

He also said he wasn't a loving kind of guy, and you know that's not true.

Now, in that lonely motel room, she was still pacing when she glanced at her phone to check the time. It belatedly struck her that there was something she needed to do. She did the time zone math and, knowing his habits, decided it wasn't too late to call.

"Hey, Pop," she said when he answered.

"Good to hear your voice," Dean's father said.

"I know it's been a few days. But...I have him, Pop. I'm on my way home with him."

"Mission accomplished, then."

"Yes."

"So...why don't you sound happy?"

"I just...I guess I'm tired. Drove for twelve hours."

"Nice try," he said. She'd never been able to get anything

past him any more than Dean had. "What's really wrong?"

It took her a moment to get it out, but in the end she couldn't stop herself. "I…didn't want to leave."

"Because?"

She took a deep breath. "The guy who runs the program…he's pretty special, Pop. And he knew Dean."

"He did? What's his name?"

"Chance Rafferty."

He sounded startled when he exclaimed, "Boots is running that operation?"

"Boots?"

"You remember, don't you? Dean used to talk about him all the time. More as Hondo's handler, though." Ariel felt a sudden shiver. Boots. Hondo. Names she knew. "I'm not surprised. Those two boys were all about the dogs. They—"

"Pop, wait. Are you saying Chance Rafferty…is Boots? Hondo's handler?"

"Well, yeah. You didn't know?"

"No. I didn't." She sank down to sit on the edge of the bed. Tri hopped up beside her, giving a tiny whine of concern as he put his head in her lap. She stroked his fur, and it steadied her a little as Pop went on. "I never knew his real name."

"I met him a couple of times when I went to see Dean. He's a good man, and what he's doing now proves it."

There was a stretch of silence because Ariel couldn't think of anything to say. She couldn't think of anything except the conversation she and Dean had had before he'd gone, that last time.

Looks like Atlas and Hondo'll get to say hello before we go. Hondo's guy is going to hang tight for another day to see us off.

That's nice of him.

Boots is pretty bummed he has to hand Hondo off, though. At least, as bummed as a guy who's going home for good can be. She remembered the look he'd given her then, suddenly intent. *He's a good guy, Red. The best. If anything ever happens, you could go to him.*

She knew what he'd meant by "if anything ever happens." He'd meant the worst. Him being killed. She hadn't even wanted to think about the possibility, and so had shoved that right out of her mind.

Until now.

Go to him.

She wasn't really sure what she said to Dean's dad Walt after that, before ending the call. She sat for a long time, petting Tri, thinking, remembering.

Go to him.

The look in Dean's eyes when he'd said it, it hadn't been joking, it hadn't been casual, it had been serious.

Deadly serious.

Go to him.

Dean had never mentioned his real name. Just Boots, hung on him by some smart-alec who was jealous of the whole cowboy vibe. She'd thought it cute at the time. But now…in that box she'd stowed away and never wanted to look at, the box that held the will, legal death certificate, and all the other detritus of a life ended, did the never read just-in-case letter hold the name Chance Rafferty?

Go to him.

When Tri nudged her with his nose, hard, she took it as a sign. A moment later, she was on her feet and moving.

CHANCE HEARD THE car pull up as he was just putting on his jacket—the heaviest one he had, given it had dropped to near-freezing after Ariel had left, as if she had taken all the warmth with her—and figured it was Mom coming to make sure he was doing as he'd promised. Even if it meant him once more missing Christmas Eve. She usually would be here pushing for him to join the family. She never gave up on that. They were all probably gathered up at the house right now. But this year, she'd made an exception.

Mom would have just belted in the door though, not knocked first. He glanced at his watch, knowing he needed to leave in the next few minutes if he was going to make it. He was announcing that before he even got the door fully open.

"I've got to get going—"

He stopped. Knew he was gaping. Didn't care, because standing on his small front porch was the reason for it all.

Ariel.

For a moment neither of them moved or spoke. But then she found her voice, and words started to pour out.

"I know it's crazy, I was on my way home, I just kept feeling worse and worse every mile, and when I stopped in Arizona to rest I couldn't, I couldn't even begin to sleep and Tri was so restless and worried about me because I kept pacing the floor of this little, old motel room and all I could think was I didn't want to be there, I didn't even want to be home, I wanted to be here."

He stared at her. He managed only one, hoarse, rough syllable. "Why?"

The flood started again. "I haven't felt anything for so long, I didn't think I ever would or could again, but I felt it with you, felt alive again, like there was still some good in my life, some hope, and I don't want to give that up, not if there's the slightest possibility you—" she took a breath, the barest fraction of a pause, then barreled on "—felt the same way I did, even though you were clear you don't want anything long-term, I'm…I'm okay with that, I just want as long as it can last, but if you don't want that then just tell me—"

He couldn't take it anymore. He reached out and touched a finger to her lips, hushing the flow of pent-up words. She stopped, staring at him, and he saw hope begin to fade from those sky-blue eyes. He bent to the duffel bag on the floor by the door, and pulled his phone out of the side pocket. At a press and a swipe it came on to the app he already had open. He held it out to her.

Ariel stared at the screen. He saw her realize what it was. The virtual record of his plane ticket to San Diego.

Her gaze shot back to his face. The moment was so intense he wanted to look away but knew he couldn't. But he had no words. He could only look at her. Silence spun out between them, wire-taut.

"You were…coming to me?"

"I have—had an hour and a half to get to the airport in Austin." An almost-smile pulled at the corners of his mouth. "I thought you'd be home by the time I got there."

"I would have been, except…" She lowered her eyes before finishing ruefully, "I wasted a lot of time pacing the floor."

He realized they were still standing in his doorway, but he was almost afraid to move, to shift, to change anything. "Was the decision…so hard?"

This time when she met his gaze she held it. And he could practically feel the way she steeled herself to do it. "Only because I wasn't sure you would want this. Want me."

"I know the feeling," he said, his voice rough again. "I was afraid when I showed up at your door you'd think I was crazy, to even imagine…" He couldn't find the words for what he'd been imagining. "I thought I could say I was just going to see how Tri was doing, that I'd have been checking later anyway, I'd just moved it up a little, but…it would have been a lie. An hour after you were gone I was doing my own pacing. This place was so empty. I was so empty. I didn't realize until you were gone how much of me you filled up."

It sounded lame to his ears. He sucked at this, and always had. But Ariel was looking at him as if he were beautifully reciting Shakespeare or something.

"Yes," she whispered. "Yes, exactly that."

He swallowed hard, his throat tight. "I know this isn't…easy for you. You can have all the time you want, all you need. It's all your call, Ariel. I'll never…assume."

She smiled, and it was balm to his uncertain heart. "I know."

"Does that mean…you want to try? Us, I mean?"

The light that came into her eyes then made them a brighter blue than a Texas summer sky. "Yes. Yes, yes, yes."

His pulse kicked up even higher than it had when he'd opened the door to see her standing there. "I know I'm not Dean," he began, but stopped when she shook her head.

"I talked to his father last night. I didn't put it together until then you were…Boots. And Hondo's handler."

He blinked. The jab of pain at the dog's name still came, but it wasn't quite as sharp as it had always been. "I…does it matter?"

"Yes. Because…" She took a deep breath and told him about a conversation she'd had with Dean, before that final deployment. He stared at her, not sure what to say. "So you see, it's like…he would approve. Of us."

He was surprised at the relief that flooded him. And in a

way honored, that Dean had thought well enough of him to say that to the woman he loved more than his own life.

The woman Chance now loved.

It was a tremendous effort, one of the biggest of his life, to hold back and address the one remaining question.

"I don't think I could live in California or move this—" he gestured vaguely toward the kennels "—there."

"Whereas I think I could easily get used to living here, in a town where people actually know each other, help each other, stand for each other."

"But…your work?"

She smiled then, and it seemed to hold his entire future. "Are you saying Last Stand doesn't ever hold any events that need organizing? Like maybe a fundraiser for *They Also Serve*? Or for veterans? Oh, and those Paralympics for injured dogs. And I seem to remember hearing about one of the biggest Bluebonnet Festivals in the state, the Fourth of July rodeo, an Oktoberfest, and…Christmas. I hear Christmas is a big deal here."

"It is," he said, and his voice nearly cracked as if he were a kid again. That seemed significant somehow.

"You gave me that back, too," she said softly. "It's no longer only a time of grief and pain and sadness. It's also a time of…hope. I don't hate it anymore."

He had to move then. He reached out, gently grasped her shoulders. She felt so warm and vibrant and alive under his hands, and a rush of memories of these last weeks when she'd given him herself, and so much more, flooded him.

"I don't either," he said, his voice still rough. "Not when it's brought me the first gift that's really mattered to me in years."

And then he was kissing her, and the fire they ignited together felt as if it would warm his entire world. No longer would this time of year be simply the marker of the end of a way of life. It could be—no, would be, he vowed—the start of a new way.

It was some time later, after they had retrieved the puzzled but clearly delighted Tri from her car and he had kissed her thoroughly again, that he asked, "Do you feel up to heading to the big house?"

"With the tree and all the lights and music and Christmas spirit?" She'd clearly noticed that as she'd driven by. On her way here. On her way to him.

"Yes. I need to…give my mom that present she's been hoping for. You."

She gave him a smile that held more promise than any he'd ever seen. "Do I need to wear a bow?"

"Later," he said, his voice rough again. "When that's all you're wearing."

This time she kissed him, fiercely, with all the answering promise he could have wished for. "I can't wait."

They stepped outside. Stopped in shock. Chance stared at the impossible sight. It was snowing. In Texas. On Christmas Eve. And as they headed to the main house, Tri in tow, Chance was smiling, a smile that he was certain went clear down to his soul.

Snow. Christmas Eve. With his family, the family who had stuck by him no matter what. With the woman who had pulled him back into the world, the woman he loved with a fierceness that stunned him.

And soon there would be a Christmas morning he had a feeling he'd never forget.

Maybe Christmas really was a time for miracles after all.

The End

Want more? Check out Keller and Sydney's story in *Nothing But Cowboy*!

Join Tule Publishing's newsletter for more great reads and weekly deals!

If you enjoyed *A Texas Christmas Miracle,*
you'll love the next book in....

The Raffertys of Last Stand series

Book 1: *Nothing But Cowboy*

Book 2: *A Texas Christmas Miracle*

Book 3: *Once a Cowboy*
Coming January 2022

Available now at your favorite online retailer!

More books by Justine Davis

The Texas Justice series

Book 1: *Lone Star Lawman*

Book 2: *Lone Star Nights*

Book 3: *A Lone Star Christmas*

Book 4: *Lone Star Reunion*

Book 5: *Lone Star Homecoming*

The Whiskey River series

Book 1: *Whiskey River Rescue*

Book 2: *Whiskey River Runaway*

Book 3: *Whiskey River Rockstar*

Available now at your favorite online retailer!

About the Author

USA Today bestselling author of more than 70 books, (she sold her first ten in less than two years) Justine Davis is a five time winner of the coveted RWA RITA Award, including for being inducted into the RWA Hall of Fame. A fifteen time nominee for RT Book Review awards, she has won four times, received three of their lifetime achievement awards, and had four titles on the magazine's 200 Best of all Time list. Her books have appeared on national best seller lists, including USA Today. She has been featured on CNN, taught at several national and international conferences, and at the UCLA writer's program.

After years of working in law enforcement, and more years doing both, Justine now writes full time. She lives near beautiful Puget Sound in Washington State, peacefully coexisting with deer, bears, a pair of bald eagles, a tailless raccoon, and her beloved '67 Corvette roadster. When she's not writing, taking photographs, or driving said roadster (and yes, it goes very fast) she tends to her knitting. Literally.

Thank you for reading

A Texas Christmas Miracle

If you enjoyed this book, you can find more from all our great authors at TulePublishing.com, or from your favorite online retailer.

TULE
PUBLISHING

27220698R00185